The Soul Cavern Series

Jivaja

Blue-Edged Soul

Visci

Want updates on the series? Free stuff?

To get all the news on books,
appearances, and more, drop me a line:

https://www.venessagiunta.com/sc-signup/

Visci

Venessa Giunta

https://www.VenessaGiunta.com/

Visci
Copyright © 2020 by Venessa Giunta

E-book ISBN: 978-1-7326860-3-8
Print ISBN: 978-1-7326860-4-5

Cover Artist: The Book Brander
Proofreader: Melissa McArthur
Published in the United States of America by Fictionvale Publishing, LLC.

https://www.VenessaGiunta.com

Dedication

For Shirley Mae, who always supported me, even
when I made really stupid decisions.
I hope I've made you proud, Gram.

Chapter One: Jenny

A bitter breeze whipped Jenny's scarf in front of her. The frigid air sneaked into the sleeves and collar of her coat and chilled her skin. But it was fine. It matched the chill in her heart. It matched the chill of the procession to her father's grave.

Surrounded by people—some she recognized, but most she didn't—Jenny felt more alone than she ever had. Even more than when she'd gone to London for her first study abroad semester. That had been nothing compared to this.

Sounds came through muted, like the adults in a Charlie Brown movie, and everything around her had a weird, fishbowl quality to it. The coffin balanced over the grave. Green fabric meant to give the illusion of grass lay over the surrounding dirt. As if that made putting someone into the ground easier. Fake green grass.

The cherry wood of her dad's coffin gleamed in the sunlight. It was closed.

The mortician hadn't been able to…make his neck presentable, presumably.

Did these sorts of random thoughts go through everyone's brain when they buried their dad?

The man speaking—a pastor that Jenny had never seen before—talked about her dad's great accomplishments in life and how much he'd be missed.

This stranger. She'd bet her last dollar he hadn't even known her dad. Hadn't even had a single *conversation* with her dad.

A scream built in the back of her throat.

Icy fingers wrapped around her fist and squeezed. Jenny glanced at her mom. Green eyes, surrounded by puffy red skin, gazed back at her. Jenny realized that the smile her mom gave was meant to be reassuring, to give her strength.

But Jenny didn't want reassuring.

I want my dad.

Most of the people surrounding them had shown up to pay their respects to the city councilman everyone loved. They weren't true friends. Jenny only recognized a few faces.

Mrs. Taylor, her dad's assistant from work who'd been with him since he'd practiced law, was a kind, matronly woman who always gave soft peppermints to Jenny when she'd visited his office as a kid. After the service, Mrs. Taylor had come over, her eyes only a little red and puffy, and given Jenny a gentle hug and her grandmotherly smile. She hadn't spoken a word. Jenny had been glad of that.

A few neighbors were scattered among the folks gathered. She wondered if any of the anonymous faces were part of the council that her mom told her about, the Visci Council that ruled the southeastern part of the US.

She hoped not. That would be gruesome. Jenny was positive someone on that council had killed her dad. She studied the unfamiliar faces as the preacher droned on.

And there. Mecca's dad. David Trenow.

He stood far away, as far as he could possibly stand from them and still be considered at the grave site. He stared at them from his spot on the small rise.

If Mecca had been there, would she have stood with her dad? Or would she have insisted on staying here, by Jenny?

Jenny wanted to believe her best friend would have stood with her.

But Mecca was in the hospital, recovering from a compound leg break. And Jenny hadn't visited her yet. For reasons.

Things were more complicated now than they'd been before Jenny had gone to London. Complicated, because she knew Mecca was something called Jivaja. But Mecca didn't know she knew. How awkward was that?

Add to it that Jenny never shared with her best friend that she was Visci. How do you bring that up to your best friend?

Hey, so I drink blood to survive and can't really be killed. Oh, also, I'm faster and stronger than you. Cool? Great. Let's get pizza.

But she'd have to talk to Mecca about it soon. The knowledge was too heavy for Jenny to carry alone.

Maybe tomorrow, when she planned to finally stop by the hospital.

Jenny should have seen Mecca right away. She felt pretty shitty about that. But with Dad's funeral and the insurance guys and the cops... Apparently, a person being murdered left a lot of things on the to-do list.

She welcomed the numbness that stole over her. It was easier to deal with than the pain. The anger. The grief.

David met her gaze, and she was pleased to see that he seemed sad. She wasn't sure whether he would. Ever since Jenny and her mom had learned that David had Jivaja powers—he could kill them easily, if he wanted to—Jenny wondered if his friendship with her dad had ever been real.

He dipped his head in a tiny nod.

Did he want her forgiveness?

He'd been the one who'd found her dad. Maybe if he'd tried to help more...

Jenny ground her teeth together.

Numbness. Stick with the numbness.

More than fifty people had come to the cemetery. The funeral had had three times that many, easily.

Everyone stood clustered about the grave—the pastor guy was still talking—so Jenny couldn't help but notice the three individuals who'd gathered much farther away, even beyond David.

They all seemed to be around her age, maybe a few more years, mid-twenties, one guy and two women. The guy, short and stocky with broad shoulders, stared at her with dark eyes. He looked Latino, and his black hair fell around his ears in shiny curls.

On his left, the woman was more interested in Jenny's mom. She looked older than a college student, but not much. Her brown skin contrasted with the brightly colored, over-sized knit hat she wore. Dark braids stuck out of the edges, hanging down about her body. She held her wool coat tight around her curvy frame.

The third woman, if she was old enough to be called a woman, was thin, pale, and waif-like, sort of like Jenny's mom. She wore black, round sunglasses which hid her eyes, but she seemed not to be looking at the grave site at all, but rather anywhere else, like she didn't want to be there.

Jenny brought her gaze again to the dude, and *his* gaze shifted to her mom. She didn't know why they were here. Who were they?

She—the taller woman—met Jenny's gaze, and the intensity in those eyes almost made her gasp. The pastor had wound down and was saying what sounded like his final blessings. The man said something to the shorter woman, who frowned at him.

Jenny released her mother's hand. People began milling about, moving toward them in a wave, but she ignored them. Had to ignore them. The trio across the cemetery spoke amongst themselves, the taller woman pointing at the grave site. The man shook his head.

Jenny's mom began greeting the attendees, shaking hands, inviting people to the house.

I can't do this.

With a pang of guilt, Jenny took two steps backward and left her mom to be surrounded by the throng of bodies. She worked her way along the fringe of the group, giving nods to those who expressed their sorrow, but not letting them stop her. She kept her gaze on the three in the distance.

The man noticed her movements with wide eyes and a look of alarm. He spoke to his companions, and they all began moving away, winding through the headstones.

When Jenny cleared the mass of funeral-goers, she broke into a sprint, glad that she'd worn flats, against her mom's advice. Someone called after her, but Jenny ignored them. Her breath puffed out in a white haze before of her.

The three rounded the corner of a mausoleum near the trees and disappeared from Jenny's sight. When she got there herself, the cold air icing her lungs, she realized they'd ducked into the woods.

She stepped inside the shaded canopy of the tree line. The temperature dropped a good ten degrees from what it had been in the sunshine. She shivered as she peered into the surrounding haze, searching for movement, but found none. The scents of evergreen and molding leaves mingled in her nose. Straining her ears, she focused, hoping to hear a twig snap or the crunch of leaves underfoot.

But again, nothing.

They'd vanished.

-->>><<--

Jenny climbed into the limousine behind her mom. The warmth of the space off-putting and strange after the briskness of the grave site and her run through the cemetery.

Why did these stupid thoughts keep coming to her?

Dark circles had settled beneath Carolyn Barron's eyes, and her skin looked pallid and drawn. Jenny hadn't realized how exhausted her mother looked until now.

"Are you okay?" Jenny asked.

Her mom nodded but remained silent.

It would be a long drive to the funeral home for their car, thirty minutes, but at least they weren't in a procession anymore. That had taken forever.

The driver asked if they needed anything, but her mom just waved at him, and he got behind the wheel. As they pulled away from the curb, Jenny considered the three people she'd chased.

Why had they run? Were they Visci?

And why had they been spying on her dad's burial?

So many questions.

In London, her mom had finally told her that there were others of their kind in Atlanta and that she'd kept Jenny from them on purpose. She still wasn't past her anger at her mom over that.

Their kind. Were those three "their kind"?

When Jenny hit puberty, she'd gotten a weird talk. Nothing the health classes at school covered. Her mom explained their need to drink blood, which freaked Jenny the hell out.

It would have—should have—freaked *anyone* out. Vampires, for fuck's sake.

Her mom hadn't named them then, only told Jenny of their weird needs and began feeding Jenny every week or two from her own wrist. When Jenny asked how her mom got her…food, she said that Jenny's dad allowed it so that her mom didn't have to take from others.

And all Jenny's life her mom emphasized that they *weren't* vampires. That it wasn't necessary to kill people. That they should always take blood from people willing to give it.

It suddenly hit Jenny—even more than his funeral and putting him into the ground just now—that her dad was gone.

No. Not gone. Dead.

Despair hit her hard. Her whole body ached. And behind it…grief, anger, fear. How would they get blood now? How did that even work?

She stewed in her emotions until her mom spoke.

"You're very quiet."

"How do you expect me to be? My dad is dead," she snapped. A tightness formed in her chest. "There's an entire group of people out there like me that you kept a secret from me. And there's a whole other group of people who seem pretty hell bent on killing us. And apparently my best friend is one of them. So what is it you think I should be saying, Mom?"

Her mother cringed but finally nodded. "That's fair. But you're not the only one affected by your dad being gone."

"Dead, Mom. Not 'gone.' Dead."

"Yes." The pain in her eyes made Jenny seethe more. How could she just agree without screaming? Jenny wanted to scream all the damned time.

It wasn't rational, and she knew it. Yet she had to handle the rage that boiled in her, that tightness that wouldn't loosen. But she didn't want to discuss her dad being dead anymore. She couldn't. "Why didn't you tell me about these people like us?"

"Because I left them when I met your father."

"Why?"

Her mom remained silent for a long, long moment. A police car went by, its sirens screaming. The sound bored into Jenny's head like an icepick.

She looked over to her mom and realized her anger had lessened. Only a little. But she couldn't have said why.

She was a hot mess.

Her mom stared back at her. She had always been the most beautiful woman in the world. Every little kid thought that about their mom, really, but Jenny believed it even through her teen years, when she and her mom fought as if they'd hated each other. That was mostly Jenny's fault, in truth.

But now, her mom looked tired, worn. Each wrinkle on her face stood pronounced. Wrinkles Jenny had never seen before. Or maybe never noticed. Her mom's green eyes dulled by grief, she looked...defeated.

"I didn't want the politics, the back-biting, the manipulations to be a part of our lives. I'd endured that for centuries. May even have enjoyed it for part of the time."

The furrow to her mom's brow told Jenny that she *had* enjoyed it at some point. That was the expression she pulled when she was forced to acknowledge something she didn't want to be true. The last time Jenny had seen it was when she'd found Jenny's stash of condoms.

She waited for her mom to continue. The anger still bubbled below the surface, and she wanted to yell at her mom for getting her dad killed. But she needed information on these people, these Visci.

Her emotions were all over the place. Fractured.

"When I met your dad, and we eventually talked about a future together, I realized that I wanted something simple. Much more simple than any life I'd ever led. I only wanted to take care of him, have a family, take care of you."

"Didn't do a great job this week, did you?" She couldn't help it. She hadn't meant to say it. It just came out.

Her mom's wounded gaze lowered.

"I'm sorry," Jenny said. She was, and she wasn't. But it didn't matter. Everything felt disjointed. Bungled. Erratic.

Her mom shook her head and looked up again. "So I disengaged from society. I told my father, my family. They were not happy at all, but they ultimately accepted it. There was no other option for them. And I told the new ruling group. They were glad to see me gone."

A ruling group. The Visci were big enough, organized enough to require a government, for fuck's sake. Heat gathered in the base of her skull and the rage rose again. *How could she keep me away from these people like* me?

She wondered why the rulers would care whether her mom was there. "I don't understand why they were glad to see you go?"

Her mother sighed and peered out the window. The day had gone gloomy. "That's because you also don't understand how dangerous they can be."

"Don't you think keeping me ignorant is worse than me knowing what the hell is going on?"

Her mom nodded, but her reluctance was clear. "You're likely right," she said. "It doesn't mean I'm glad to have to tell you."

"Oh my God, just *say* it already."

The limo pulled onto the highway and picked up speed. The ride smoothed out.

"For millennia," her mom began, "royal families ruled the Visci. The most ancient of the lines. It was hereditary and had all the same problems that every hereditary ruling system has. People who are ruthless. People who are crazy. People who don't care. And none could be removed, because…"

When she didn't finish, Jenny did it for her. "Because the lines were hereditary." She was rewarded with another nod.

"A generation ago—our generation, not a human generation—the non-royals came together and decided they wanted a more...accountable system of governance. And so the royals were set aside and councils formed for each region of the world, which were composed of individual Visci who ruled a city or area."

It annoyed Jenny to find herself interested in her mom's details. "So the royal families walked away?"

Her mother shrugged. "Some did. Some even became involved in the governance change, believing that having a royal system led to corruption rather than effective governing." Her tone had become strong and matter-of-fact. "Others...did not want such a change. However, Visci are neither easy to get rid of, nor easy to kill."

Jenny nodded. Her mother had given her the talk about their kind's strengths and weaknesses when Jenny was fifteen. Being hard to kill had been a "skill" Jenny thought was cool as a kid. Her mom never elaborated on what "hard to kill" meant or how they *could* be killed. Jenny wondered why she'd never noticed that omission.

"And while there was fighting and some bloodshed—mostly human anculi, unfortunately—the governance of our kind shifted to one a bit more like a democracy than a monarchy."

Jenny thought back to how her mom had started this explanation. "Hang on. They were glad to see you go because...because you were part of the hierarchy?" She couldn't imagine that was right. Her mom lived a normal, suburban life. A princess? Really?

Jenny watched with a strange surreal detachment when her mother said, "Yes. I am—and you are—of Visci royal blood."

Jenny sat there for a moment. It felt like the strangest concept she'd ever heard. "So you're what? A princess? A queen?"

The subtle coloring of her mother's cheeks told Jenny that she wasn't used to talking about her status among the Visci. "The equivalent of a princess in human terms, yes. My father ruled a large part of the European continent for several centuries."

"Wait. You mean Gramps? Gramps is a king?"

Her mom gave her a smile. "Yes. Though he doesn't rule anything anymore."

Jenny watched through the window as they passed the Atlanta King and Queen—office buildings that resembled chess pieces. *Weirdly fitting.*

The vastness of what she didn't understand grated on Jenny's nerves. How could she navigate such a foreign, alien world not knowing a thing about it? From her experience in London, she had more knowledge of Jivaja than her own people.

"Who called?" Jenny finally asked.

Her mom didn't answer. It was like she hadn't heard.

"Mom?"

"Sorry. Sorry. What did you say?"

"In London. Who called? Who gave us the jet we came home in?"

"Ah. Claude." She looked thoughtful and then continued. "I've known him since I was about your age. He was only a child, as most full-blood Visci are. You might say we grew up together."

"Why would he send someone to call you? Why not just…" Jenny held up her phone. In London, a man had approached them with a telephone, and her mom spoke to Claude on the man's phone rather than her own. It felt very *Mission Impossible*.

Her mom smiled. "Because he doesn't have my phone number. I imagine he would be able to find the house number, but he doesn't have my cell. When I said I cut ties, I meant it."

Jenny nodded and ran her finger over the phone's dark screen. "Why did he call you? Because of Dad?"

"Yes. He wanted me to know…"

When she didn't finish, Jenny said, "Know what?"

She frowned and shook her head. "Nothing."

"Tell me."

It was clear that her mom didn't want to.

"No secrets. Remember?"

"Yes, I remember."

Jenny waited. After what seemed an hour but was most likely just minutes, her mom spoke.

"He said he took care of who killed your father."

"What?" The words did a double-tap to her heart. The first tap was that Claude knew who'd killed Dad. The second was that this stranger had already "taken care of" them. "You mean you know who killed him? Why he died?" She sat up straighter.

"I don't know why." She spoke slowly, as if each word were a Herculean task to get past her lips. "But, yes, I know who. At least, who Claude told me it was, though I don't doubt him in that."

"Who?" Jenny slid to the edge of her seat, staring at her mom. *Why didn't she tell me this sooner?*

"Her name was Emilia Laos. She led the Atlanta Visci and the Southeastern Council."

Her heart thumped. *How can that...?* Why would the Visci kill her dad? She slid back in the seat. Had her mom done something to piss them off? How did this work? Had they declared war on the royals?

"I am going to the council once this is settled," her mom said, waving her hand around the limo. "I need to find out if she acted alone."

Jenny's mind turned fuzzy. Her own people may have killed her dad. Anger, frustration, and disappointment whirled inside her. "Who...who do you think helped her?"

"I don't know."

"But you have some idea?"

"No. Not really. But I need to work out who is doing what. I haven't been involved in..." She sighed and leaned back on the headrest, closing her eyes. "So long."

"I want to come with you."

She didn't move. "No."

"I deserve answers too."

"And I'll get them. I can't... Do we have to talk about this right now?" Strain sounded in her voice.

Jenny took a good look at her. Her mom, always thin, looked almost gaunt now, with hallows in her cheeks and those dark circles beneath her green eyes. People always commented on how young her mom looked. But now, her mom seemed...ancient.

Jenny's anger had all but dissipated. But nothing replaced it.

It should have been unnerving how fast her moods shifted. But she couldn't bring herself to care.

She was glad for the numbness again.

⟶⟫⟪⟵

The next thirty-six hours had been a great big blur of people visiting the house, offering condolences and casseroles. Apparently, they go together like peanut butter and chocolate. Only Jenny hated peanut butter.

She was still jet-lagged, even though they'd been home several days now, and her patience had worn thin more than once. Her mom had intercepted her several times, but there had been an unfortunate incident with one of the conservative politicians Jenny's dad had been forced to rub elbows with.

Jenny was pretty sure she'd be getting a bill having to do with removing melty cheese from Armani fabric.

Today hadn't started much better, with the biohazard cleaning company in at eight in the morning to "take care of the office," as her mother put it.

Or…cleaning Dad's blood off of everything in the room, to put it more plainly.

Crime shows never showed this sort of thing. Cleaning up the gross.

The office had still been sealed off with bright yellow tape, which proclaimed only "Police Crime Scene." Jenny expected it to also order them to "Stay Back" or "Do Not Cross," but no. Just a label about a crime.

Her mom had told her clearly and adamantly that she wasn't to go into her dad's office, even going so far as to lock the door.

She hadn't needed to bother. Jenny found herself too terrified to even touch the door, much less go inside. So when the cleaning company started to make all sorts of crazy noises early, Jenny had curled up more tightly under her comforter and waited.

Mecca's dad was coming this afternoon. When her mom had told her that, Jenny was all set to jump in with a bunch of questions she wanted to ask him. But, instead, her mom asked her to stay in her room—as if she were ten years old and unable to handle adult conversations.

Jenny agreed, but even as she'd said it, she'd known she was lying.

When he arrived not long after lunchtime, her mom brought him through the house. Jenny trotted quietly down the back stairs, which led to the kitchen, and settled on a step about halfway up. Her mom offered David coffee, but he declined.

"When I was young," her mom said, "I used to be very spoiled and drank this with so much sugar, it would have made a cow diabetic. But that was a long time ago, when sugar was harder to come by. I reveled in it when we had it."

At the base of the stairs, in a framed photo collage's reflection, Jenny was able to see her mom's head—well, the back, anyway. David's face was unclear and ghostly, but it was obvious that he stared at her mom.

"I don't want this to be antagonistic," David said.

"Is there a reason it would be?"

Jenny waited for his reply, staring hard at his face's fuzzy image in the glass, willing herself to see more detail that wasn't there.

"Ken told me about London," he said.

"So we both appreciate each other's secrets."

After a long, uncomfortable moment, he said, "I have to ask you something. I need you to tell me the truth." When her mom didn't answer, he continued. "Did you know anything of Mecca's kidnapping?"

How can he even ask that?

"No." Her mom didn't even hesitate. "I would never do anything to endanger her. And if I had known of some sort of plot, I would have stopped it."

Jenny smiled a little. Her mom sounded so much stronger than she had in the car when they'd come home from London. So matter-of-fact. Regal. Jenny couldn't help feeling proud. And she knew that her mom spoke the truth. Even if her mom had kept things from her own daughter, no *way* she would have let anything happen to Mecca. Not if she could have prevented it.

"How would you have stopped it?" he asked.

"In truth, I am unsure whether I could have done anything. If I had had any idea that Mecca was in danger, I would have gladly broken my promise to myself and re-entered that…culture."

"So you're not involved in their whatever it is? Their society?"

Her mom paused for a second and then said, "I didn't realize this was going to be an interrogation."

"I have to know that I can trust you."

Now came that sound that her mom made every time she'd caught Jenny in a lie as a kid. That unbelieving snort. It was the most unladylike sound her mom had ever made. Jenny couldn't help her grin.

"Trust *me*?" her mom said. "You've been lying all these years." The wavering image in the glass that was her mom's reflection leaned forward. "Tell me, David Trenow, is that even your name? Your brother's name is Fontenot. Why is yours different?"

Jenny hadn't even thought of that. In London, Uncle Ken had approached them by introducing himself with his full name, but she didn't pay attention to what he said. She'd known him most of her life, and he was just Uncle Ken. The fact that his last name was different from Mecca's hadn't crossed her mind. She'd never really noticed.

David let out a sigh. "Ken and I grew up in the swamps of Louisiana." He leaned back in his seat and looked at the ceiling, his eyebrows lowering and pinching together. "Ramshackle houses, kids with dirty feet, dirty clothes. Eating hot dogs every night because they were cheap. I hated it. I wanted to be better than that." His gaze dropped back to her mom. "When I left, I got rid of my accent and changed my name."

She remained quiet for a moment, before she said, "All right. And the rest?"

"And the rest." When he repeated it, it was a statement, not a question. He knew what she was talking about.

"Jivaja. Your powers."

"I don't know how to answer that. I'm only familiar with the word because Ken told me about it and about the woman he met—you both met, I guess. We never called ourselves anything. We're just people with a Gift."

"Tell me more."

Her butt began slipping, and Jenny realized she was literally sitting on the edge of the step. This was the bit she'd wanted to hear.

In the reflection, David shook his head. "It's your turn. Tell me about the Visci. You say you had nothing to do with Mecca's disappearance. I think I believe you."

There was a long pause, and Jenny wished again that she could see more clearly.

He continued. "But I also wonder how you can *not* be aware. I was at that property. We're not talking a conspiracy of two or three people. It looks like an entire *society*. A very organized and large group. How could you not know?"

Her mom's voice tightened. "Do you know everything that goes on in your human society? I left the Visci when I married Jim."

Sorrow wedged into Jenny's heart as she thought of her dad. Sorrow, followed by anger. She'd forgotten for a moment. In her excitement...she'd forgotten. She raged against his murder, and she raged at herself for having forgotten.

She bit her lip. Hard. The familiar, spicy taste of blood tickled her tongue. She bit a little harder, and the sharp prick of perfect pain brought her back to the moment.

Her mom's voice broke in. "I decided I'd had enough of the scheming and the politics and the manipulation." She shifted in her seat and revealed her profile. "I only wanted to love him," she said. "And then love Jenny."

Tears filled Jenny's eyes, along with a rush of sadness mixed with pride and awe. Even with all their talking in the limo, it never hit home that her mom had given up her life—her *entire* life—to make them a family. Jenny tried to imagine what it would feel like to give up her mom and her dad and couldn't envision it. She was having trouble with her dad being gone, let alone if she'd had to leave him.

When David didn't respond, her mom kept going, her tone hard as steel now. "And I'd stayed out for more than two decades. Right up until she murdered him."

"Emilia Laos," David said.

"Yes." Her mom's voice cracked just a little bit, and Jenny's heart broke. Again.

"She's the one who kidnapped Mecca."

"Yes."

In the glass, David lowered his gaze, saying nothing for a little while. When he raised his head again, he said, "I'm sorry that he got caught up in everything, Carolyn. I truly am. I tried to save him, but he was too far gone. His life simply leaked out. I struggled to stop it, but…" His voice had gotten higher toward the end and thick with emotion.

She knew her dad was dead. Of course. She'd seen him in the casket before the funeral, grey, with his throat… Yes, dead. Definitely.

But this vision, this one that David brought up…

In her mind's eye, her father lay between dead and alive, but skidding toward death with every second.

She envisioned David crouching over her dad, trying to feed him life and all of it draining away like water down a sink. She didn't even really have an idea of what that might look like, but it made a lump form in her throat like a softball.

"His life leaked out."

That was the sentence.

Jenny bit back a sob and slung her head from side to side, trying to dislodge the image.

"Whether Emilia was the only one involved, I can't be sure," her mom said. "It's been a hard decision, but I am stepping back into society. I will reconnect with the Southern Council, and I will discover the truth."

"Really?" David said. "They'll let you back in, just like that?"

"I have the credentials."

Yes. She was a princess, after all. Of course they would let her back in. Jenny didn't dive very deeply into why she felt that bitter. Her emotions gave her whiplash.

Instead, as she thought about her mom's words, Jenny realized that her voice had taken on a much more formal tone than she usually used. Jenny wasn't sure what to make of that.

"What will you do?" David asked.

The laugh that came from her mom was soft but sardonic. "I don't exactly know as yet. I will need to work out the lay of the land first. But I plan to use whatever advantage I can to find out what really happened to Jim. Who really killed him."

Watching the filmy image in the glass wasn't enough anymore. Jenny remained low and crept down two more steps. Now she could look through the banister struts and barely see both David's face and her mom's back. She tried to remain still so he wouldn't catch sight of her.

"I'll do what I can to get information on his death, as well," David said. "I am positive Emilia was behind it. I'm unsure whether anyone else was involved in the planning. Certainly, she wasn't the one who carried it out."

"I don't care about her little men. They do whatever a stronger will tells them to do."

David nodded. He seemed to be thinking hard about something, an intensity in his eyes. The silence drew out.

Jenny held her breath.

"Do you know someone named Claude?" David asked. "A Visc—" He leaned back. "Clearly, you do."

Apparently her mom's face told that story. "Yes," she said. "Though I'm surprised that *you* recognize him."

He didn't look directly at her. "I made a deal with the devil." Now he raised his gaze. "I haven't decided whether I can trust you enough to tell you about it."

Her mom nodded. "I understand."

Why didn't she say anything? Jenny wanted her to reassure Mecca's dad that yes, he *could* trust her! What was the deal? Who was the devil? It was all she could do to keep herself quiet and stay on that step.

"Will you tell me what you know of Claude?" he asked.

Jenny thought about what *she* knew of him. Claude had sent a plane for them in London. A really nice plane. Jenny had never experienced that level of luxury. Leather swivel seats, tables, even a sofa that laid out into a bed. They'd had their own flight attendant. The flight crew outnumbered the passengers, because they'd been the only passengers.

Jenny only knew that Claude and her mom had known each other as kids. They'd sort of grown up together. And he was obviously crazy rich.

She listened to her mom tell David about knowing Claude when she was young.

"He wanted us to marry. And I liked him well enough." Pensiveness infused her voice in a way Jenny hadn't heard before. And the bit about almost getting married! She'd hadn't heard *that* before either. "But sometimes you get a feeling."

"Which feeling?"

"Claude is...ambitious."

"He wanted to marry you because...he would go further with you as his wife?"

"Exactly."

David grinned at her, though it wasn't amused. But Jenny saw Mecca in that grin, and it made her miss her best friend.

"So you're a big-shot Visci, then?" he said. There was no accusation in it.

Her mom lifted one shoulder in a shrug. "I was."

David nodded.

"Did you ever find out why Emilia took Mecca?" her mom asked.

"Ken said that you saw what that woman... Noor? What she did to the Visci guy at the hotel."

"I did."

Jenny had seen too. Noor basically sucked the guy's life out. He'd been a shriveled husk on the ground when Noor had finished with him. Jenny shuddered.

"Emilia wanted to use Mecca as a weapon."

Jenny gasped softly and slapped her hand over her mouth. *Dammit.*

David looked up, and her mom turned in her seat.

"Jennifer Aileen."

She stood. It wasn't like she could hide that she was there anymore. They'd both seen her now. So she came down the stairs and stepped into the kitchen. Their stares burned into her the entire way. She tried to come up with some excuse but decided she didn't need one. She sat in the chair opposite David.

"How long were you there?" her mom asked.

"The entire time."

"Jenny, I told you I wanted you to stay upstairs."

"I know. But I'm a grown adult, and I'm already part of this. So keeping me in the dark is not helping."

"Keeping you out of things will keep you safe."

Jenny looked at David. "It didn't keep Mecca safe, did it?"

A moment went by as he looked at her with pain in his eyes. She tried not to flinch against it. Finally, he shook his head. "That isn't the same. I agree with your mom."

"That's too bad. I'm involved. Period."

"What do you think you're going to do?" Her mom's tone was harsh, but her eyes were…frightened?

"I don't know." She really *didn't*. "Maybe I can help in whatever is going on. But at the very least, if something happens, I don't want to be flailing around like an idiot."

"What is it you think is going on?" David asked.

"I don't know that either. And there's the problem. You're all keeping it from me. Whatever it is, it got Mecca kidnapped and my dad killed."

David exchanged a glance with her mom. They both sighed, almost in unison.

Her mom's jaw was set. "I'm not willing to risk you."

"It's not your decision."

"Whether I share information with you? Yes, that's absolutely my decision."

"Sure. Leave me to the wolves with no protection."

Her mom raised a brow. "Don't you think you're being melodramatic?"

"Am I?" Jenny asked. "It's hard to be sure, because *you're keeping me in the dark*. I don't know about these people, but I'm going to end up dealing with them. You're leaving me ignorant, which means they will always have the upper hand."

"You won't be dealing with them," her mom said. "There is no reason for that."

"Did you see the people at the cemetery?"

"There were a lot of people at the cemetery."

"Yes, but there were three people who weren't in our group. They watched us. I think they're Visci."

Her mom looked startled, but David asked, "Why do you think that?"

God, he had all the annoying questions. Jenny wasn't sure why she thought they were Visci. She had no proof or even a logical reason. "I just do."

"If they are, you should stay away from them," he said, his voice intense. "They won't bring anything good."

"They took off when I tried to go to them. If they were a threat, they wouldn't run."

"They're Visci," David said. "They're always a threat."

"Am I?" Jenny asked.

David's frown pulled at the corners of his mouth.

Vindicated, Jenny continued. "We don't all kidnap people and hold them against their will."

"Point taken," David said.

"You haven't told Mecca about me, have you?" The thought nauseated her.

"Not yet. It hasn't come up in conversation."

The statement felt ludicrous. On the one hand, how would it come up casually in conversation? On the other, how could he have *not* brought it up?

Her skepticism must have shown on her face because he said, "She's in the hospital. We haven't talked much beyond that."

Jenny nodded. There was something that rang false about his words, but she couldn't put her finger on exactly what. "Don't tell her."

"I'm not going to promise that."

His tone bristled under her skin, but she kept her own level. "It isn't your place to tell her."

"I'm her father. It's my place to tell her anything that might…"

She crossed her arms. "That might what?"

David glanced out the bay window.

"Hurt her?" Jenny finished for him. When he didn't deny it, she continued. "You really think I would hurt her?"

He gave a heavy sigh and rubbed one hand over his face, ending with a pinch on the bridge of his nose. "Of course not."

Jenny leaned toward him so that he had to look at her. "Then don't act like I'm dangerous to her, because

I'm not. But you need to let me have the conversation with her."

"You know she's right," her mom said. Jenny was mildly surprised at the defense.

"It is unfair that Jenny knows about Mecca, but Mecca is in the dark. There is an imbalance there."

"But they need to work it out on their own. They're not kids anymore."

The surprise at that was less mild. Jenny's first impulse was to throw her mom's hypocrisy back in her face. But that wouldn't do anything to help this situation. So she filed that bit away for later.

David sighed again. He seemed to be good at it, as much as he practiced. "All right. But tell her soon."

The words carried the threat that if she didn't, he would.

Chapter Two: Claude

Claude's hazy reflection gazed back at him from the lift's doors. With his slight build and blond, delicate features, most people underestimated him because he looked young. So young. He counted on that response in most cases and never more than right now.

The doors opened, and he stepped onto the plush carpet on the fourth floor of the Visci compound. Near the end of the hall, he would go through a stout wooden door—most of the doors were stout and wooden here—and into the lion's den where he would need to manipulate master manipulators.

He wasn't nervous.

He was very, very good.

But he was a bit anxious.

Recently, Emilia Laos, the Visci ruler of Atlanta was killed by Mecca Trenow, the young woman both he and Emilia, separately, had intended on using as a weapon. And while Claude had expected to have Mecca kill Emilia, he hadn't planned on it happening so soon. It left a vacuum in the power structure of the city that he hadn't anticipated having to deal with yet.

The tension he felt had more to do with adapting his plans than with any nerves at being in a room with Visci who were about to become very defensive and not a little frightened—though they would never admit to either.

Salas met him at the door. "She is to be released in a week. Perhaps less. I don't know whether she will go back to the college or to her father's home. But judging from the fight they had this morning, I suspect it will be the college."

Mecca suffered a bad broken leg and had been taken to the emergency room right after...the incident.

"And Will? Where did he flit off to?"

Salas inclined his head. "He is with her. He has not left the hospital."

"Interesting."

Will, Emilia's little pet human, would need Visci blood soon if he were to survive. Claude wondered how the man would get it. Anculi rarely moved from one Visci to another, and so if an anculus's normal life span had been expended, they usually died within a few weeks of their Visci's departure. "I will enjoy seeing how that plays out."

"May I be of additional service?" his man asked with a hand on the knob.

"No. I believe the rest is up to me." Claude straightened his suit jacket and gave Salas a nod.

The door opened in front of him, and he stepped through into the conference room where the Council met. A broad, oval table encircled by a dozen leather executive chairs, dominated the large room. Though there were no windows, electric wall sconces every few feet warmed the place with golden light thrown from behind amber covers.

"You took long enough," Thomas Eli said. A short man with a circle of bright orange hair ringing his skull,

Thomas complained whenever given the chance, but he was an excellent leader in Charlotte, maintaining the status quo. Claude expected that he could count on the man's support in the coming weeks, as things settled.

"My apologies," Claude said with sincerity and a short bow. He scanned the room. All the Council leaders who'd attended the Maze Party remained, along with each Visci's attendant entourage. It had been required of them, what with Emilia's demise. "I appreciate you all making yourselves available for this meeting."

Murmurs shuffled through the group. Then silence fell.

"I expect you've all heard by now, but if you haven't, let me please make the official announcement. Emilia Laos, head of Atlanta, was killed in the woods of this property. Her body has been retrieved and will be examined thoroughly. We do not know who is responsible, but an investigation is already underway, and we will find out."

"Was it a half-breed?" Tony Mercado called out. Arabella Connelly shot him daggers from across the table.

"As I said," Claude continued, "we do not know yet, but we will find out. In the meantime—"

"Who will lead in Atlanta?" Tony again. Claude would be glad to shut him up.

"Exactly," he said instead. "We need to nominate an interim head so that we don't lose the city to chaos."

"You, Claude?" Arabella asked in her lilting southern drawl. The glint in her eye and the set of her soft lips made Claude think she was being sarcastic.

"Me? No." Claude truly did not want to lead Atlanta.

He had a much greater purpose.

"I could do it," Thomas Eli said. "Charlotte and Atlanta are close to each other. It would not be too difficult." His tone conveyed honest, innocent intent, but Claude didn't trust that tone at all. And judging from the looks around the table, he wasn't the only one.

"Don't be ridiculous, Tommy," Tony Mercado said. "You can barely keep your own city under control. There's no way you'd be able to handle Atlanta."

Thomas puffed up, his face turning red. As he began to sputter, chatter started up. A few of the less powerful Visci, leaders of the smaller cities, like Raleigh and Birmingham, rumbled their discontent.

Claude raised his hands. "Please. Ladies, gentlemen. Let us settle down. I am a foreigner here. I only came to visit Emilia, whom I'd known for centuries, and enjoy the Maze Party." He paused and lowered his eyes briefly, for the effect of grief.

It seemed to work, as everyone quieted.

"I have no interest in leading Atlanta, but I do not see it as…let us be frank…*safe* in allowing any of you, as heads of your own cities, to also rule Atlanta. I am sure you will all agree that the power imbalance would only lead to instability, rather than what we are striving for — stability and peace. Yes?"

The smaller city leaders nodded, but the more powerful among them looked away with varying small, dismissive gestures.

"I propose that we name a local to step in, just for now. I am happy to stay for as long as the Council feels I am needed to help this temporary leader make sure things move along smoothly."

"And who would we choose?" Arabella asked. Her light and playful smile held something behind it, Claude knew. Cunning and ruthlessness. He wondered if she had someone in mind already.

He did. A full blood named James, whom Claude knew would be easily controlled. But he waited a moment, to see whether anyone suggested other names. It would be easier to get approval for his preference if he didn't put his choice forward first.

A commotion down the hall filtered through, the sound of at least one raised voice, a woman, coming closer to the room. Claude couldn't help being distracted, as had everyone else. They all turned to the door as it burst open.

A small, compact woman entered, dark hair perfectly flowing around her head and barely brushing the edges of her shoulders. Her gaze raked across the faces of those seated at the table until it finally rested on Claude, who stood several paces to her right. "I would speak with you about Emilia Laos and the murder of my husband."

Titters traveled around the table.

Claude only just caught his mouth before it fell open. He had not expected Carolyn Barron to show up here, at the Council meeting. How had she even gotten into the compound? He considered all the ways this could go wrong.

Or right.

"Carolyn," he said gently as he approached. "Let us step outside." He gestured toward the door she'd just come through.

"I will not be railroaded," she said to him, eyes hard.

It had been many decades since he'd been this close to her. He'd forgotten her fire.

"I am not railroading you." He wanted to see what the others were doing, but he knew looking back at them would be interpreted as weakness. So instead, he said, "Come with me for a moment, and I will tell you what's going on. After, we can return to this room, and you are welcome to be a part of the discussions." He shifted into a new plan. A potentially *better* plan.

"She isn't a member of the Council." Tony Mercado again.

Claude really wanted to tear his throat out.

"She doesn't belong here."

Claude flashed a glare at him and, judging from the other man's flinch, all of Claude's anger showed in his face. But he kept his voice level. "Carolyn and I were children together before you were even a wish in your mother's heart. She has just lost her husband. Show a bit of decorum." He laid a hand on Carolyn's shoulder and whispered to her, "Please. For a moment."

She let herself be led into the hall.

Salas, still posted out there, gave his master a deep bow of apology—Claude would deal with him later—and stepped away to give them privacy.

"I told you on the phone," Claude said, trying to sound gentle. "I took care of everything."

Her green eyes flashed. "What does that mean, exactly?"

"Emilia is dead." He looked at the closed door and back at Carolyn. He couldn't tell whether she was surprised about Emilia's death or whether she'd assumed his words had meant Emilia was dead. He found his inability to read her mildly concerning. "I cannot advise them that I killed Emilia in retaliation for murdering your husband, of course."

Her gaze cleared, and her eyes narrowed at him. "What *have* you told them?" she asked, taking half a step back from him.

He raised his hands in surrender. "Nothing, really. That she was slain the night of the Maze Gathering and that we don't know who did it."

"Where is the body?"

"Handled." Startled that she asked about Emilia's body, he suppressed the heavy feeling of alarm that her question gave rise to.

"I want to see it."

"That is not possible."

Carolyn leaned forward until he could feel her breath wave across his skin and smell the faint floral scent she wore. "You would deny your queen?"

He closed his eyes for a moment and inclined his head toward her. "I would deny you nothing, my queen. I had the body burned so that it could not be examined and evidence of my involvement found. You understand, yes?"

She studied him, and he wasn't entirely sure that she would believe. And when she finally said, "Very well," he still wasn't sure whether she believed him. But the immediate threat was gone, at least.

"Will you join us?" He indicated the entrance again. "We are discussing a temporary successor to keep Atlanta under control until a new leader is appointed. I am sure that the opinion of a royal will carry much weight."

"A royal in a Council meeting. Won't they be scandalized." It wasn't a question.

He opened the door for her, and they returned to the room.

As they entered, chatter slid into silence. Claude expected that by now they all knew they were in the presence of royalty. Not everyone understood who Carolyn was when she'd rushed in, but Claude was sure those who'd been ignorant had been schooled while he'd been in the hall with her. And that was the other reason he'd wanted to take her out there. To leave the Council to do what it did best: talk.

He offered Carolyn his own seat.

Chapter Three: Jenny

Jenny followed the room numbers down the hospital hall. The scent of antiseptic, while not strong, had been present since she'd entered. She didn't really like hospitals.

Jenny had been thinking a lot about this meeting with Mecca but still wasn't sure exactly how to handle it. She recognized her best friend was Jivaja, and she was fine with it. But Mecca didn't know she was Visci yet, Jenny didn't think.

In London, Noor, the Jivaja who killed the guy sent to meet them, had given Jenny the impression that Jivaja hunted Visci. Would Mecca be the same?

She hated that she wasn't sure.

Had Mecca's dad told her about Jenny and her mom?

She had no idea about that either.

Would this change their friendship?

She hoped not. But there was no way of knowing.

She found S609, Mecca's room. The door stood closed, but she thought she heard voices inside. Had David come?

Jenny knocked softly, opened the door, and peeked her head around.

Mecca lay in bed with one leg outside the covers. It was encased in a gigantic, bright red cast. Her hair poked out at odd angles, looking a bit wild, and she wore one of those ever-so-stylish hospital gowns. When Mecca saw her, she jerked up straighter in bed and a grin broke out over her face.

"Jenny!" She waved both her arms, motioning for Jenny to come in.

The man sitting on the recliner next to Mecca's bed stood. Jenny suddenly felt self-conscious. It hadn't occurred to her that there might be a stranger here. The confident smile she tried for failed pretty miserably, she was sure. But she made her way to her best friend, relieved to see her, even if the guy made things awkward.

When they hugged, the warmth was more than simply temperature. Jenny felt home, more so than she had in the last few days, since the plane had landed.

Even though Mecca was Jivaja, and even if that might mean they were on opposite sides, she was still Jenny's best friend. And that meant more than Visci or Jivaja.

When she pulled back, she almost felt like herself again. "What the hell, Mec?" she said. "I leave the country for a few weeks, and you get yourself kidnapped?"

Her best friend shrugged, a grin on her face. "Anything to get you home."

"Please," the guy on the other side of the bed said, "take my seat." His voice was soft and melodious. And he wasn't ugly, either, with a pale complexion, curly brown hair, and eyes that reminded Jenny of Caribbean water. She gave Mecca a sidelong glance, brow raised.

"Jenny, Will. Will, Jenny."

Will gave her a tiny bow.

A bow.

He motioned to his chair. "A pleasure to meet you, Jenny."

"Ditto," she said, waving a hand. "You don't have to give up your seat."

He beamed, and it twinkled in his eyes. "I'm happy to. I was about to step out, anyway. And that will give you two some privacy to catch up."

"Are you sure?" Jenny asked. He was already moving toward the door, so she guessed he was.

"Absolutely," he said. Then, to Mecca, "I will be back in a bit. Do you need anything?"

"To get out of here."

From his almost exasperated sigh, this was a conversation they'd had already.

Mecca rolled her eyes at him. "No. I'm fine."

"Very well," he said. He gave Jenny a parting nod and stepped out.

Jenny moved to the chair side of the bed and leaned in to Mecca. "*Who* is he?"

She shook her head. "I can't even explain it. I'll tell you later. I'm so excited you're home!" She tilted her head. "Wait. Why are you home?" Realization seemed to hit her in the forehead, and tears filled her eyes. "Oh! Your dad. I'm so, so sorry, Jen."

A slicing stab in the gut. She wished people would stop bringing up her dad. Every time, it sucker-punched her. She couldn't say anything. Her throat had gone thick and tight.

Mecca swiped away at a tear that slipped down her cheek. Her lips pursed, and she grabbed Jenny's hand. Her fingers were warm.

"I wish I could do something to bring him back. Or say something to help."

Jenny squeezed Mecca's hand and sat on the edge. Now it was her turn to swipe at tears on her own cheek. She slid her wet hand along her jeans. "I can't... Um." She took a breath and blew it out. "The funeral was last weekend. Saturday."

"I'm sorry. They wouldn't let me out. I should have been there." Another tear swelled and spilled over, onto her cheek. "You were there for me."

For a second, Jenny thought she looked very much as she had when she was twelve and lost her mom.

That death had been expected, even though it tore through all their hearts. Teresa Stone had been a second mom to Jenny. When she died of cancer, it was all Jenny could do to get through it. And for Mecca, of course, it had been worse.

"You were there in my heart." Mecca's face swam in her vision. She willed herself not to cry and released Mecca's hand. After shrugging off her leather jacket, she dropped it on the chair that Will left for her and looked at Mecca. She pointed to the bed. "Can I...?"

Mecca's face brightened, and she shifted over awkwardly. "I'll make room."

Jenny fiddled with the side rail. "How do you put this thing down?" As she said that, she found the right lever, and the rail dropped.

Jenny crawled onto the bed and laid on her side, curled toward Mecca.

"I missed you," Mecca said.

"I missed you too." She laid her head on Mecca's shoulder and tried not to think of her dad. "Tell me about what happened."

Mecca's breath stopped for a moment. "When?"

Jenny raised her head. "What do you mean when? When you were kidnapped."

The relief on Mecca's face wasn't something Jenny expected.

"What did you think I meant?"

Mecca shook her head, her eyelashes fluttering as she blinked a few too many times. "Nothing. I wasn't following the conversation. Good drugs." She gave a half-hearted grin.

Mecca had been Jivaja all her life and never told Jenny. Now, it was hard not to see her with different eyes. With a different filter. It didn't help that Mecca seemed to be keeping something from her. Jenny wondered if Mecca might be trying to decide whether to tell her about being Jivaja.

"So there was a guy who attacked me in Little Five. We'd gone outside Brew-haha, in that crumbly old parking lot, you know?"

Jenny rested her head again as she nodded.

"And I... Well, I hurt him. Later in the week, I was walking through the Tunnel and these guys surrounded me and grabbed me."

Those things didn't make much sense together. Jenny knew the Visci had taken Mecca. Was now the time to bring it up? She wished she could be sure. "Then what happened?"

Mecca hesitated for a second before she said, "They must have knocked me out, because the next thing I knew, I woke up chained to a bed."

Jenny propped herself on her elbow. She hadn't given much thought about what Mecca might have actually experienced while the Visci held her. A pang of guilt shot through her. "Chained to a bed? For real?"

"For real."

"Did they hurt you?"

"No. Not any more than being abducted and held against your will would hurt anyone, I guess." Mecca wouldn't look directly at her.

Jenny already knew why they took her, but she still wasn't sure whether she should let Mecca know that *she* knew.

But she sure as hell didn't like playing these games, either. This was so much harder than she'd thought it would be.

"How did you get away?"

Mecca shrugged. "They were transporting me in a wheelchair, and I faked being hurt. When I could, I knocked the guy out and ran away."

There had to be more to it than that, but Jenny wasn't going to say anything. She'd let Mecca have that way out. But she felt...fake. Like she was lying to her best friend.

And she was, wasn't she?

But they'd both been lying to each other for a long time.

"Is that how you broke your leg?"

Another pause, barely a beat too long. "More or less." Mecca sighed. "Look, I don't really want to talk about that right now. Can we put it on hold til later?"

"Sure. What do you want to talk about?"

"What was London like? How was it at the University of London?" Now she looked at Jenny. "Are they okay with you leaving in the middle of the term?"

"They're going to have to be. My dad died. I'm not going to class for a while."

Mecca gave a slight cringe. "Yeah. Sorry. Why did I bring that up? I'm stupid."

Odd, melancholy emotions battled in her. Sadness, wariness, maybe a little bit of anger and more than a little bit of fear. It was strange inside her heart right now.

"You're not stupid," she said. "It's just weird right now. Everything." As she stared at Mecca's eyes, she willed her friend to say something, anything, that would tell Jenny it was okay bring up all the *actual* weirdness.

But she didn't. Mecca only looked away and nodded. "It really is."

Jenny sighed and laid her head back down.

--->><<---

When Will came in, Jenny had perched on the side of the bed again, and they were discussing Jenny's adventures into British academia, as well as Brit nightlife. They tapered off the discussion, and Jenny said her goodbyes, pulling her coat on and wrapping her thin scarf around her neck.

"I'll come back tomorrow," she said, as she stepped out the door.

As she rode the elevator, Jenny replayed the strange conversation. She and Mecca had been the closest, bestest of friends growing up. They'd told each other everything, from their very first crushes in fourth grade to when their periods started and then on to more difficult things—the death of Mecca's mom and when Jenny had realized that she liked both girls and boys.

Not being sure whether to talk to Mecca about Jivaja and Visci was foreign to her. Confusing. And she didn't like it at all.

Jenny's own secret—being Visci—had been easier than this. She'd just not thought about it. It had never impacted their friendship one way or another. So it had been easy to keep.

But this one—knowing *Mecca's* secret—gnawed at her.

Outside, the sun had risen high into the sky and cut some of the bitter chill that seeped into her through her brown leather jacket. When she stepped from under the hospital awning, Jenny paused and let the sunlight warm her face. She pulled in a deep breath, the icy air filling her lungs.

She was glad for the nice day. She was pretty sure there wouldn't be a whole lot of nice days coming up.

As she walked to her car, someone called her name. "Jennifer Barron?"

When she turned, two bundled figures approached, and she recognized both. The cemetery people. The guy and the taller of the two women. Her riveting green eyes gazed from a dark face with high cheekbones. She wore that bright cap again. He was big and solid-looking with kind eyes. They came to a stop in front of her.

"Who are you?" Jenny asked, on her guard.

The guy held his hands up, palms out. "Don't worry. We're friends." He had a faint Spanish accent.

"I don't know you. That makes you not-friends. Why were you at my dad's funeral?"

"We were paying our respects," the woman said. The man's surprised, sidelong glance at her made Jenny even more wary.

"That's not what it seemed like at all. You were staring at my mom." She pointed at the man. "And you were staring at me."

"Yes. True," he said. "I'm Jorge Ramirez, and this is Helen Parkes."

Jenny glanced between them but said nothing. There was a strange scent of cinnamon in the crisp air. It reminded her of apple pie. More weird.

Jorge continued. "We're like you. Well, I am anyway. A hybrid." He glanced at Helen, his movements broadcasting his nerves. The woman gave him a slight nod, and he looked back at Jenny. "Helen is a full blood. We wanted to talk to you about what's happening here. With us. With hybrids, especially."

What the hell was he talking about? "I know all the words you used, but the way you're using them doesn't make sense."

Now he stared at her, looking dumbfounded.

"You recognize you're a hybrid, right?" Helen said. "Half human…?" The expectant look on her face finally made things click into place.

"Holy shit." She laughed out loud. So they *were* Visci. She had been right!

They both took a tiny step back. Clearly, her excitement was unexpected. But how could she not be excited? She'd never met another Visci in her life besides her mom. Hell, she hadn't even known others existed until a couple days ago. And now there were two. Right here! The wariness hovered below the surface, but she couldn't help the need to ask a million questions.

"Umm. Yeah," Jorge said, obviously having no clue what was happening with her. Surely, he thought she was crazy.

But the woman, Helen… She watched Jenny closely. "She kept you isolated, didn't she? Your mom, I mean." She had an accent. Caribbean, Jenny guessed. *Everything is coming up Caribbean today.*

Jenny flushed. She must have seemed a backwoods hick to them. "No. Not isolated, really. But I've never met others before."

Jorge frowned. "I hate that now is the time you're stepping into our community." He smiled. "But I'm glad to meet you."

"Thanks," Jenny said. She sort of wanted to crawl under her car, because she sounded like an idiot.

Helen said, "We need to talk to you. We're hoping you can help."

"Help? With what?" What could she possibly help them with?

Jorge seemed to gather himself, and he glanced around the bright parking lot. "Let's go somewhere else. There's a Starbucks about a mile down, on the corner."

"I'll follow you."

After getting drinks, they settled into the corner sitting area of the café, Jenny in a nubby-fabric armchair, Jorge at the end of a short sofa closest to her, and Helen beside him. The mocha with an extra shot warmed her hands after having stood outside in the cold.

"You probably have a lot of questions," Helen said as she pulled off her knit hat. Dozens of thin braids tumbled over her shoulders and halfway down her torso. "And we're happy to answer them for you, but first, if we can, I'd like to tell you why we came up to you out of the blue."

"How did you even know I'm..." She dropped to a whisper but felt a bit ridiculous and melodramatic doing it. "Visci?"

"Questions after, yeah?" Helen said, gently.

"Oh, right. Sorry." Jenny flushed. And then she flushed again because it annoyed her that she flushed in the first place. This wasn't the first day of high school, and these people weren't the cool kids.

So why did she feel like they were?

"I don't have any idea what your mom has told you about Visci—"

"Not much." Jenny hated that it was the truth.

Helen nodded. "There's a lot of bad blood between fulls and hybrids right now."

"Fulls?" Jorge had used that term too.

Jorge chimed in. "Full bloods. Like your mom. Like Helen too."

"Oh." She should have figured that out. *How about keep your mouth shut, Jen, and let them talk?*

"So all over the country, there's been tension." Helen had turned her body more toward Jenny as she spoke. "Even some outright fighting."

That made some sense to her. The Visci seemed to constitute an entire society, and societies have tensions. Look at the US. Plus, her mom had told her there was a lot of politics and manipulation, so what Helen was saying didn't seem surprising.

"Here, in Atlanta, we've found bodies." Helen watched her closely.

Those words shocked her. "Bodies?" *Hard to kill.*

Helen nodded. "Almost all of them hybrids. A few fulls."

"People are saying it's a civil war," Jorge said. "That fulls are slaughtering hybrids. That it's going to get a lot worse."

"But I don't think that's what's going on," Helen said, her voice level. "I think there's something specific behind the deaths."

Jenny looked between them, trying to keep up. "Why?"

Helen and Jorge shared a look. She said, "Because the two dead full bloods that I've seen have been women. That's only here in Atlanta. Reports are in from others in surrounding counties. Each jurisdiction also has one or two deaths. And all the fulls are women."

The first thing that popped into her head was "Visci serial killer?" That should have been far-fetched, but was it? "You said their 'jurisdictions.' Are you a cop?"

"No," Helen said. "I am a medical examiner in Fulton County."

Jenny's surprise must have shown very clearly on her face because Jorge stifled a laugh. Not very well, either.

"Sorry," Jenny said to Helen. "You...don't look old enough."

The other woman smiled for the first time since they'd approached her at the hospital. "You *are* very ignorant, aren't you, little sister?" Her words were soft, even kind, but the truth of them still stung Jenny deeply.

She changed the subject. "So how are they being killed? By one person?"

Helen set her paper coffee cup on the small table in front of them. "As I said, the dead fulls are women. Hybrids seem to be both men and women, so my instinct is to say that it isn't a single person."

"And there are a lot more hybrids dying than fulls," Jorge added.

"How many is a lot?"

"Almost two dozen since the spring," Helen said. "The bigger puzzle is that they had no obvious cause of death. And by that, I mean there are no external wounds."

Jenny considered for a moment.

"We don't die easily," Helen said, her tone flat.

Hard to kill. That was one thing that had already been covered.

"Disease doesn't hurt us. Well, hardly ever. We don't get cancer or anything like that. Especially as full bloods, our powers of healing happen so quickly that the only real way we can die is if there is massive bodily harm that is so devastating that the wounds overtake the healing." She tilted her head a bit and grinned. "In case you didn't know that."

"I did. Thanks." She really didn't. But Jenny was tired of feeling like the backwater country cousin. "So no heads chopped off or stakes through the heart. How *did* they die?"

Helen waited a beat and said, "It's unclear."

Jenny nodded. "Okay. Are you sure they're even related? The full and hybrid deaths, I mean."

They exchanged another glance that told her they hadn't considered that at all. That made her feel a little less like an outsider. "What do you want from me? *You* have access to the medical examiner's office and could report it to the cops. I'm only a college student."

Jorge met Helen's gaze before he replied. "Someone is blocking the investigation."

"Blocking?"

"The Visci Council has tight control over police departments in their various areas as well as other aspects of the government," Helen said. "Not just the

Council, of course, but individuals too. Powerful Visci, both fulls and hybrids. Emilia Laos was the most powerful here in Atlanta, but she's dead now. So there is something of a vacuum at the moment."

"But there is still someone in control at the PD. Because Helen's report was buried," Jorge said. "And she can't push it. Even though she's a full, it will draw suspicion."

Jenny looked between them. The initial excitement of meeting people of her kind had faded, and the mention of Emilia Laos reminded her of the slaughter of her father. It made her somber. "If you're a full blood, why are you helping hybrids?"

Helen laughed, and it was full-throated, though quiet. "Not all fulls hate hybrids. I'd argue that most of us don't." Her face became serious. "I want things to go back to normal. Fulls and hybrids have worked together for ages, millennia. We should continue to do that."

This felt so much bigger than Jenny had thought. "So who could be blocking the investigation?"

"We're not sure," Helen said.

"That's why we're here," Jorge added. "We'd like you to talk to your mom."

Jenny sat there for a long moment. She probably should have expected this, but she hadn't. They came to her because of her mom. *Do they know Mom is royalty?* Of course they knew. Why else would they ask? Jenny chided herself for thinking them approaching had anything to do with her. "I doubt she can help. She hasn't been involved with the Visci in a long time."

Helen gave a little shake of her head, making her braids wave. "She's the leader of Atlanta. At least, right now." Helen kept on, but Jenny barely registered what she said.

What? She waved a hand back and forth to get the other woman to stop. Jenny *needed* her to stop.

She did. Finally.

"What do you mean 'the leader of Atlanta'?"

That exchange of glances again between her and Jorge was getting really old.

"She didn't tell you?" Jorge asked.

No, she didn't tell me, Jenny thought. But she didn't say it out loud. She couldn't trust her voice. After all of their talking, after they'd both promised honesty, her mom was still lying.

Jorge looked sympathetic. When he spoke, compassion laced his words. "Last night, at the Council meeting. They asked her to step in to rule Atlanta until someone new is chosen by ballot."

Jenny sat back in the leather chair, her cup between her legs, and looked at the ceiling. The background buzz of the coffee shop seemed loud in her ears. "So much for one-hundred-percent honesty," she said under her breath. They could hear her. She didn't care.

"I'm sorry," Jorge said. "I assumed you knew."

Jenny nodded. "I should have. She should have told me."

"She should have," Helen said.

Jenny put away the hurt and brought her gaze back to her two new friends. Were they her friends? She wasn't sure yet. She hoped so though.

Jorge's hand closed the distance between them, and his fingertips brushed the edge of her sleeve. He withdrew. "Are you all right?"

Was she? This was all a hot mess. "What do you want me to ask her?"

"Well," Helen said, "the bigger threat is to hybrids, since they're disappearing and dying at a very high rate. Since she has you, a hybrid, she won't be on the side of the fulls who want to kill them—if it is truly fulls killing them. We're hoping she might want to help stop whatever it is that's going on."

"We don't believe the hybrids coming up dead is this 'civil war.' But others do," Jorge said, his words coming fast. "There's something else going on."

"Yes, you said. What, exactly?" Jenny asked.

Helen said, "We think the disappearances and deaths of the fulls are related to the deaths of the hybrids. But we're unsure how they're connected. That's what we're hoping your mom can help find out."

"But she has to be careful," Jorge added. "If whoever's doing whatever they're doing finds out, she could be in trouble."

"They would go after my mom?"

"Or you, more likely," Jorge said, all matter-of-fact.

Jenny blanched. She thought of her dad's murder and knew he was right.

"Jorge." Helen frowned at him.

"It needed to be said."

Helen took over, shaking her head. "If she can find out who is controlling the police, that would be of an indirect help. But the deaths and disappearances are the most important. The human police won't be able to do anything about that, anyway."

All the excitement from when she'd first met Jorge and Helen had completely drained from her at this point. She wasn't even inclined to ask real questions anymore. That numbness that had come and gone since the funeral rushed back. She welcomed it.

"All right. I'll see if she knows anything. Or can find anything out." If her mom told her the truth, that was. Probably an iffy prospect, as things seemed to be going. Weariness stole over her.

Jorge gave her a concerned smile. "Great. Umm. If you want to give me your phone, I'll put my number in, and you can call me when you hear. Or text. Text is okay too." He wrinkled his nose a little bit, and his cheeks darkened.

Helen chuckled. Jorge glared at her.

Jenny didn't want to deal with Jorge's nervousness and all this mess too. It was all too much. She fished out her phone, opened the screen to New Contact and handed it to him.

Helen watched her the entire time. Finally, she said, "You'll tell your mom to be careful? Especially when she's in there." She took a long draw from her small coffee cup, obviously finishing it.

Huh? "In where?"

Jorge handed her phone back. "In the compound. It's where Emilia Laos used to live. It's also where most of the business happens."

That name. The woman who kidnapped Mecca. Who killed her dad. "My mom went there?" Of course she did. If she was asked to be the leader of Atlanta, it was because she was there when they were talking about it. How come she was getting all this information from strangers? So much for numbness. The anger roared back.

"Yes," Jorge said.

"The Council was last night," Helen said. "They were all in town for a big party, the Maze Gathering. And then Emilia was killed. They all stayed, and your mom crashed their meeting when they were trying to figure out what to do. They asked her to step up."

Jenny didn't say anything, just took in the information, shifting her phone from one hand to the other. So that was where her mom had disappeared to. She'd said she was going to meet Claude, but she went to this Council meeting instead.

The muted mix of anger and disappointment simmered barely beneath her surface. It suddenly struck her that they had a level of detail she wouldn't have expected. She looked up at them. "That seems like a lot of information to have from a super-secret group."

"We had a friend in the room last night," Jorge said.

"A friend?"

He nodded, but remained quiet.

Jenny remembered her mom telling her about how dangerous Visci machinations were. "If you have someone on the Council, why do you need my mom?"

"We have someone in the room," Jorge said quickly. "We didn't say on the Council. But, either way, your mom can get a lot more information about what's going on in Atlanta than anyone else right now. As the leader, she can compel people to tell her things, under threat of exile. Or execution."

Jenny and Helen both stared at him.

He raised his hands. "What? It's true. She *can* have them executed."

Helen let out an exasperated sigh. "Yes, she can."

Jorge looked at Jenny. "But I can't see her doing that."

"What do you know about my mom?" Jenny couldn't see her mom doing it either, but didn't know why Jorge thought so too.

"Umm. Well, I've never met her or anything." That flustered tone had crept back into his voice. She had no idea what to make of it. "But anyone who completely leaves our craziness to love her husband and raise her kid has got to be pretty fantastic." He grinned.

How was she supposed to respond to that? Was he fanboying? Jenny supposed he might be right, regardless. But she couldn't bring herself to be as enthusiastic as he was. That now-familiar emptiness, numbness had seeped and settled into her soul again. "I'm surprised you've heard of her."

"Oh yeah! Your mom is sort of a legend. Defying her dad and leaving the line of succession to be with the man she loved. Total chick flick material."

"God, Jorge," Helen said, setting her empty cup into the table.

Jorge shaded crimson. "Sorry." He met Jenny's gaze. "Really. Sorry. That must have been creepy."

Jenny had to laugh. It wasn't that it was funny so much as it was totally bizarre. It pushed back some of the anesthetized feeling in her heart. The entire conversation had been ridiculous, but gushing about her mom was what he apologized for. "No. You're fine. I guess I'm surprised anyone knows who she is. She's just…my mom. You know?"

Jorge nodded.

"Wait." Jenny thought a moment. Her mom had told her about walking away. But…had she been supposed to rule herself? Personally? "She left the line of succession? I thought people had wanted to get rid of the royals."

"Yes and no," Helen said. "There had been some talk here and there about setting up a more democratic leadership, but that would have happened much, much later if your mom hadn't stepped down. She refused to ascend when her father wanted to retire. It only made the move to Councils easier."

Another lie. Jenny hung her head and took a quiet breath. The emotional roller coaster was getting really, really old.

There should have been some sort of pride or happiness—*something*—that her mom had given up everything for her family. But she couldn't keep from feeling betrayed by all the unnecessary lies. Even when Jenny had learned the truth about the Visci society out there, her mom *still* lied about things.

"Are you okay?" Jorge asked. He seemed so concerned about her being okay. He'd asked three or four times since they'd sat. She didn't know what to think of that. Or even how to answer it.

Jenny sat forward. "Yeah." She slid her phone into the pocket of her leather jacket. "Is there anything else?" She needed to be out of this coffee shop and away from everyone. Now.

"Umm. No. No. Nothing else," he said.

Jenny stood. "Great. I'll let you know what I find out."

Jorge scrambled to his feet. Helen watched them both and then also stood.

"Thanks, Jennifer," Jorge said.

"Jenny," she said, absently. In her head, she was already outside and in her car.

"Jenny," Jorge said, looking pleased.

She walked past both of them and pushed her way out the door.

Chapter Four: Mecca

Will settled into the chair beside Mecca's bed. "Did you have a nice visit?"

Warm fuzzies still fluttered through Mecca's heart. She hadn't realized how much she'd missed Jenny until today. She felt more grounded than she had in a long time. "Yes. It's so good to see her. I'm glad she's back. I hate *why* she's back, but I'm glad she's back."

"Why is she back?" His clear green eyes didn't show any sarcasm or deception.

He really didn't know.

Of course he doesn't know. God, I'm getting paranoid. "Her dad. Emilia murdered him."

He let out a long sigh and did a slow blink. "I'm unsure what to say."

"I don't guess there's anything *to* say. His funeral was Saturday." And Jenny had been there all by herself. She punched the bed beside her thigh. "I hate being stuck here. I couldn't be there with her on the hardest day of her life." Tears stung her eyes, but she blinked furiously to push them back. She was done crying.

They sat in silence for a long time with only the hum of Mecca's IV.

"She knows about your Gift?" Will asked.

Mecca startled. Had he lost his mind? "No."

His eyes widened a fraction. "She's your best friend, isn't she?"

Mecca didn't even have words. "How would I have ever told her? What a dumb question."

Will chuckled, which raised the anger that seemed to always be simmering below the surface.

"That's funny?" Her voice climbed half an octave higher than normal. It sounded like a screech.

He raised his hands in defeat, the smile still playing on his lips. "Hey, it was only a question. I thought women shared all their secrets with their best friends. I was just asking."

Mecca huffed and shook her head. "You know nothing, Jon Snow." She ignored his quizzical stare.

Guilt still ate at her. She'd wanted to tell Jenny so many times over the years. She never understood how to do it. It didn't help that her dad always harped on and on about how they had to keep their family Gift a secret because... Well, he never gave a reason, but telling was always a Bad Idea.

She grumbled under her breath, and Will hardly kept in a laugh.

They sat there in silence, Mecca trying to get a handle on her anger. It wasn't working. "Why are you here?"

Will startled. "What do you mean?"

"I mean, you're finally free of the Visci. Why are you staying here?" She motioned around the room. "The whole world is out there waiting. You can explore everything."

"Well, I can't, honestly," he said, his voice soft. "I will need Visci blood soon, or I'll die." He barely paused to let that sink in. Mecca had totally forgotten. Will had been Emilia's... Mecca had no idea what to call him. But he'd outlived his own life span with the help of her blood. If he didn't get more, his body would catch up to his age. "But I stay here"—he waved his hand as she had—"because I want to. I want to make sure you're okay. That you're safe."

"You think someone might come for me?" That had never occurred to her.

"No, not really." His sea-green eyes twinkled as he flashed his teeth. "I meant safe in a general way." He reached over and squeezed her hand quickly and released it.

Did that mean something? She searched his eyes. "But why? Do you feel guilty?"

The smile faded, and Mecca knew she'd hit the mark.

A knock came from the hall. They both looked over.

"No," Mecca said as soon as her dad cleared the doorway. A yucky mix of anger, betrayal, and sadness welled in her. "I don't want to see you."

He lowered his hands, the flowers he'd held now pointing at the floor. His pained expression stabbed at her heart. She didn't understand how she could still love at the same time she hated him.

She'd always been a daddy's girl. Always. But she couldn't deal with him. Not right now. Maybe not ever.

"Mecca, please—"

"No. Get out."

"I have to tell y—"

"Get out!" she yelled, pulling herself up as much as her cast would allow. A lightning rod of pain shot down her leg, and she gasped.

Will stood and crossed to her dad in four long strides. "Come on, David."

"I need to—"

Mecca grabbed the plastic cup on the bed tray beside her and heaved it across the room. Water sloshed as it went head over feet. "Get out!"

Will turned her dad and hustled him through the door.

Mecca flopped onto the pillows, her heart hammering and her belly roiling. She was going to be sick. She closed her eyes and concentrated on breathing and tried not to think about vomiting down the front of her stunning hospital gown.

Breathe in. Breathe out. In. Out.

It was a mantra that she'd always thought was stupid. But, man, it had helped her over the last week.

"Are you all right?" Will asked a few moments later.

She took one more deliberate breath, feeling the air move into her nose and into her lungs. Her chest expanded, and then she released, letting it whoosh softly out of her mouth. The queasiness receded. *Thank goodness.* She opened her eyes. Will stood beside her bed, the now-cracked cup in his hand.

"You were gone for a long time," she said.

He hadn't. Not really. Not even two minutes. She just felt belligerent.

"He wanted me to ask you to call or text him soon. He wants to share some information with you."

She snorted and rolled her eyes.

"He said it's very important."

"Thanks for taking the message."

"I think you—"

"You know," she said, leaning against the pillows and pulling up the thin blanket, "I'm tired. I'm going to sleep for a while."

"Certainly," he replied, not a trace of annoyance at her rude dismissal. "Shall I come back later?"

She kept his gaze for a bit longer than necessary, wishing that she could explain to him why she was being so...bitchy. But there was no way to explain the shame of her dad's past. "Yes. I would like it if you would." She could at least be honest about that.

The smile he gave her was genuine and compassionate. "I will see you later, then." He turned to leave but spun back. "And I'll tell them you need a new..." He held up the fractured cup with a wink.

She laughed. It felt good to laugh. For once.

Chapter Five: Jenny

She was glad that Mecca's hospital had been down in Stone Mountain, because it meant she had at least a thirty-minute drive before she got home. She needed that time to think, mulling over what she'd learned from Jorge and Helen. The things they shared with her were very different from what she'd learned from her mom.

By the time she got to the house, she wasn't sure who she could trust or what she should believe.

She checked her phone as she shrugged off her coat and tossed it on the coat rack in the foyer. One message.

Jorge: Thanks for talking with us today. It was great meeting you! :)

She puffed out a breath and shoved the phone into her back pocket.

"Hey, honey," her mom said when Jenny came into the kitchen. She'd set up at one end of the table with her laptop open. "I wasn't sure when you'd be home, so I ate. But there's a plate in the microwave for you."

Jenny approached, and her mom looked up at her.

"Where were you last night?" Jenny asked.

"I told you. I went to see Claude."

"And magically became the leader of Atlanta?" She couldn't keep the bitterness from her voice. She wasn't sure whether she even wanted to.

The surprise on her mom's face told her everything. Jenny shook her head and turned away.

"Hold on." The chair scratched against the floor as her mom stood.

Jenny didn't stop.

"Jennifer Aileen."

The mom voice.

Jenny's step faltered, mainly out of habit, and so she paused. Was she obligated to turn around?

"I did go to meet Claude. And there happened to be a Council meeting going on when I arrived."

Now Jenny turned.

"So, yes. I guess I did 'magically' become the leader of Atlanta."

"Why didn't you tell me?"

"Because I needed time to wrap my head around it. I had planned on telling you tonight." Her forehead furrowed as she frowned. "Jesus, Jen, I get to have time to figure things out too."

Jenny considered that. Maybe her mom *was* going to tell her, and Jenny hadn't given her a chance. A part of her wanted to believe that. "I guess."

Her mom took an audible breath and said, "I know that me keeping you from Visci society may not have been the right decision. But the last thing I want is for you to get embroiled in that mess. It doesn't make for a happy life."

"You don't get to choose that for me, though."

"I did when you were growing up. It's my job." Her mom's stony expression softened. "But you're right. I don't get to choose that for you now. I'm sorry."

Jenny stared at her, only blinking. Her mom wasn't big on apologies. As in, she *never* apologized.

Her mom tilted her head. "How did you even hear about the Council meeting?"

Jenny weighed whether she wanted to share her experience with Jorge and Helen. Even though her mom hadn't told her about the new "job" right away, that didn't mean she'd actively been *keeping* it from Jenny. It hadn't even been twenty-four hours yet. Was Jenny being unreasonable? Maybe.

"A couple people—Visci—approached to me outside the hospital."

As if in slow motion, her mom lowered into her kitchen chair and closed the laptop. Jenny sat in the chair beside her.

"Who?" her mom asked.

"A guy named Jorge and a woman. Helen."

Her mom shook her head. "I haven't heard of them."

"They seemed young."

A smile. "We all seem young."

"You know what I mean."

"They just came up to you and told you about the Council meeting?"

"No..." Jenny frowned. "Hybrids are disappearing."

Her mom's eyes widened a tiny bit. "What?"

Over the next ten minutes, Jenny explained what Jorge and Helen had told her about hybrids being taken and then showing up dead.

Her mom glanced at the ceiling in thought and looked back at Jenny. "There is a lot of animosity brewing right now, from what I've been told." She shook her head. "I shouldn't have stayed away so long."

"They don't think it's about that. They think it's something else."

"Why?"

"Because there's no obvious cause of death. Apparently, that's a big deal."

She'd never seen her mom chew her lower lip before, but now she was.

"It is a big deal," she said. "Because we heal so quickly, you can't poison us. Even being shot won't kill us unless it's directly in the head. Even then, we might not die, but we'll be useless mentally. So all the ways we can die tend to be violent and are quite clear after death."

"Can you find out anything about it?" Jenny asked. "The hybrids?"

"I'll try." She said nothing for a long time. "It might take some time. I'm acclimating right now. Older Visci know me, or at least know of me. Younger Visci, not so much. So I'm treading with care right now."

Jenny remembered Jorge's fangirl reaction when talking about her mom. "Why didn't you tell me that you left when you were supposed to take over for Grandad? And that the whole reason the royals stopped ruling was because you stepped down?"

Her mom's eyes widened. "Did they tell you that?"

She nodded. Jenny hoped that there was a good reason for her mom leaving that part out of the story. Her ass cheek vibrated. She ignored it.

"Wow. They've done their homework." She gave a short bark of laughter.

"So it's true?"

"Strictly speaking, yes. But it isn't as simple as that. There were things going on beyond me and our family. My stepping down was only a small piece of what happened."

"Tell me," she said.

Her mom shook her head. "It's very long and complicated. I don't want to get into it right now. It's true that I didn't want to step into my father's shoes. But I would have, if I'd had to. It worked out that I didn't have to."

Jenny let that settle in for a moment. She still wanted details. But she supposed they could wait. Other things seemed more important. "I want to go with you."

"Go with me where?"

"To wherever you go. Where the Visci are."

"No," her mom said. "Until I can get a handle on the politics and power dynamics, I don't want you there."

"But—"

"No buts. The compound is a dangerous place, especially at the moment, with everything in flux. If you *really* want to get involved with the Visci society, I can't stop you. You're a grown woman. But you have a lot to learn first." She opened her laptop, and Jenny knew the conversation was all but over. "I'll teach you, but I have to understand what's happening first. And for that, I can't have you around."

She wrenched her phone from her pocket with a loud grumble as she walked away.

Jorge: Would you want to grab dinner or something sometime?

Jenny stared at the screen as she climbed the stairs to her room.

How much more complicated was this going to get?

The phone rang in her hand as she entered her room.

Mecca.

"Hey," she said as she closed her door.

"The doctor came by. She's going to release me tomorrow!" The excitement in her voice made Jenny grin.

"That's great!"

"Want to grab dinner or something Saturday?"

"That's only a few days away. Are you sure you'll feel up to going out?"

Mecca made a snorting sound. "Yeah. I'll be fine. She is astounded at my healing ability."

Jenny still wasn't sure. "How about I come get you and we spend the night at my house?"

"Sure. That would be fun. We haven't had a sleepover in ages."

"Awesome. I'll pick you up at your dad's?"

"No. The dorm is fine." Her voice sounded frosty, cold.

"Okay. I'll text you Saturday, and we'll figure it out."

"Cool. By the way," she said, "I'm really glad you're home. I missed you."

"I missed you too."

Jenny listened as the guard who'd handed her the Visitor Pass gave her directions on how to get to the Medical Examiners' offices. Clipping the pass to her shirt, she thanked him and headed in the direction he'd indicated.

When Helen had called the day after Jenny had confronted her mom about being the Visci leader of Atlanta, she'd been wary of what the older woman had wanted. But instead of drilling for information, Helen had asked if Jenny wanted to meet to talk. When Helen said she'd answer Jenny's questions about the Visci, that was all she'd needed.

Jenny took the turns the guard had told her and found herself at a door the unappealing color of institutional puke.

Helen Parkes.

Jenny wasn't sure she'd known Helen's last name until now.

She knocked, and the musical voice from the other side told her to come on in.

The office was smaller than she'd expected; it reminded her of a college professor's office. Not a tenured professor, but the associate professor's digs. Smallish, with a couple of cheap bookshelves, three metal filing cabinets, and a matching grey desk.

Helen stood out brightly against the sad, institutional background with her cheery green and white dress. The matching headscarf let her scalp peek out, showing the origins of her thickly braided hair. The remaining long strands cascaded out the back.

As soon as Jenny entered, Helen came from behind her desk, that infectious smile gracing her lips. "Jenny! I'm so glad you came," she said, the accent thick today. She captured Jenny's right hand and squeezed it with both of hers.

"Thanks for inviting me." The pleasantry came automatically, but she found herself matching Helen's smile without realizing it at first.

Helen motioned toward one of the two barrel chairs that looked less retro and more like they had been in this office since the 60s. "Thanks for letting me change the plans at the last minute. I am sorry we're not checking out that new Japanese place though. I definitely want to do that." When Jenny settled into one chair, Helen dropped into the other. "I sent my assistant out to the food trucks around the corner for some burgers. Does that work for you?"

Jenny nodded and fidgeted with the zipper on her purse. "Thanks."

Helen came dangerously close to frowning. It looked strange on her face. "There was an apartment fire overnight, so things have been very busy here today." She shook her head. "Enough of that. How are you doing?"

"I'm okay."

"We dropped some crazy stuff on you the other day."

Jenny snorted, and Helen laughed.

"Yeah," Jenny said.

"I know. We wouldn't have come to you if it weren't a matter of life or death."

That someone would come to her in such a dire situation still blew Jenny's mind. "It's not really about me though, is it?"

Helen didn't break eye contact with her as she lifted her shoulders in a small shrug. "It's about all of us. You're no less valuable than me or Jorge or anyone else."

"Well, except my mom."

"Certainly, your mother may be able to do more things directly. That doesn't make her more valuable as a person. It only makes her situation more useful. But it's not a competition, either way. And I didn't invite you out here to talk about your mom." She tilted her head to the side and gave her a wink. "Unless you *want* to talk about your mom."

Jenny had no idea whether or not she did.

"I thought we could get to know each other and maybe I could answer questions for you about the culture, since you weren't raised in it. You can ask me whatever you'd like."

"Why would you want to help me like that?"

"I'm sure that your mother wanted to protect you—Lord knows that our kind can be…well, sometimes terrible, to be honest—but I still think it's a shame you're not familiar with anything about us, about your people and culture. So, here I am." She spread her hands. "I'll admit too, that I'm curious to hear how it was to be raised outside the Visci influence. It seems like it would be freeing."

"I don't think I would know the difference."

Helen gave a light laugh. "Well, I suppose that's true."

A soft knock came on the door, and an African American man, around Jenny's age, with a short fade cut and hazel eyes poked his head in. "Got your burgers, Doc." He stepped into the room far enough to hand a medium-size paper bag to her. The scent of charbroiled burgers came to her and woke her stomach. With his other hand, the young man offered two cans of Coke. "No root beer. Sorry." He gave a nod and a grin to Jenny as he held out one can.

"Thanks," she said, taking it.

"No prob." He dipped his hand into his pocket and pulled out a couple bills and some coins. He held them out to Helen, who was unpacking the bag.

"These smell great, Jeremy. Thanks for running over there and getting it." She noticed the money and shook her head. "Keep it."

"You sure?"

"I am."

"Thanks." He gave her a broad, pearly smile and pocketed the cash before stepping out and closing the door behind him.

Helen handed her a paper-wrapped burger and looked into the bag. "Looks like the fries are family style. They fell out all over the bottom of the bag."

"It's fine," Jenny said, unwrapping the thick burger, grease covering the tips of her fingers. She licked it off, tasting the grill. Her stomach growled, and her hand pressed on her belly instinctively. She flushed.

Helen laughed. "Eat, then."

Jenny hadn't realized how hungry she was. The burger was juicy and good.

"I came here from Jamaica for medical school. Emory. I've been here ever since." She leaned forward, almost conspiratorially. "I thought you might want to hear more about me, since I know a bit about you."

Jenny wiped her mouth with her napkin as she finished chewing. "Both of your parents are Visci?"

Helen nodded and finished unwrapping her own burger. "Yes. I'm an only child, as are most full bloods. Most Visci couples aren't even lucky enough to have one child together. A family with two full-blood children is rare."

"What was it like growing up?"

"Well, Jamaica is much different as a community than Atlanta. There are only a couple handfuls of Visci in both of the major cities and a few more handfuls scattered among the other island towns. Mostly we lived our lives like everyone else."

"What about the royals? Or the Councils?"

"Technically, Jamaica falls under the Council of the Central Americas, but I wouldn't say we're particularly active in it. We have a representative. I'm not sure who it is now, actually. But Jamaican Visci tend not to get involved in the politics of other places." She grabbed a fry from the bag and grinned. "I suppose that's why I'm not very good at all of this cloak and dagger here."

"Well, you're better than I am, I'd guess."

Helen only shrugged.

"So you did all the regular stuff like going to school, prom, working fast food?"

"Yes. Like you, I expect."

"Is that normal for Visci?"

She shrugged again. "I think so. Jorge did the same. I think in the past, growing up in a Visci household might have been different. What we would call home-schooling, not letting kids interact with humans. But I don't think that's really possible anymore. Not in the information age. So I expect that most of us came up this way. Probably more politics for some, like your mom."

Jenny ate the last two bites of her burger in silence and wiped her fingers on her greasy napkin. It would probably put five pounds on her hips, but man, it tasted good.

"You did the prom, working fast food?" Helen waved a French fry at her.

"Yep. The idea that I wasn't human—I mean, my mom didn't even tell me until I was like twelve. And even though she told me I was different, she didn't specifically tell me I was Visci. That came later, I guess." Jenny tried to remember when, but couldn't pinpoint a particular time. "She said I would be faster and sometimes stronger than others and to be careful not to let people notice it."

Helen's thoughtful look made Jenny wonder what was in her head. Was she judging Jenny's mom for telling what amounted to a small white lie?

"Did you tell anyone?"

"No. Mom said not to. I almost told my best friend more than once, but by that time, I'd worked out that I wasn't human." She looked blankly at Helen. "And then how do you start that conversation? 'Hey, let's do our nails. By the way, I'm not human.'" Jenny rolled her eyes.

"Yes," Helen said, leaning back a bit in her chair. "That is not an easy conversation."

It occurred to Jenny that Helen had grown up similarly. She must have had more human friends than Visci friends. "You told your best friend?"

She nodded, her shoulders stooped a little more than they had been before. "I wish I hadn't."

"It went badly?" That was Jenny's biggest fear: losing Mecca because of the truth. It was what had kept her from sharing her secret all these years.

"More badly than I had expected. She rejected me, and that was bad. But later, she told everyone at school that I had a dirty secret, though as far as I know, she never said what it was. But the rumor gangs only need a hint to prime their machines. People talked about all the horrible things I must have done. No one wanted to be seen with me."

"That's terrible." Jenny couldn't ever imagine Mecca doing something like that. But she guessed that Helen had thought the same thing of her friend.

"Well, luckily high school is only four years long, so it had a shelf life. I left Jamaica for college and haven't looked back."

Helen offered her the fry bag, but Jenny shook her head. "I'm good."

"You know," Helen said, setting the bag aside, "I admire your mom for pulling out and for sheltering you."

Jenny jerked her head back in surprise. "Really? Why?"

"Atlanta isn't a simple place, like where I grew up. Just working here"—she motioned around her office— "I see things about Visci culture that feel...difficult, stressful, manipulative. And that's my take as an adult. I couldn't imagine growing up in it. I wouldn't want to raise children in that environment either. She did the right thing."

Though that had been what her mom had told Jenny about her reasons, Jenny hadn't really heard it in the same way she did just now from Helen. Hadn't really seen it as a protection. Not for real.

"I don't know," she said. "Maybe she did."

The campus sounds that came through her open car windows—students yelling across the quad as she drove past, music coming from dorm room windows—reminded Jenny of her abandoned studies in London. It was weird. She hadn't thought of school in days. It's been so long that the memory of her own campus seemed distant. Old.

She sat at a crosswalk, waiting for the parade of students to go by. Her phone buzzed under her thigh.

Jorge: Still on for coffee tomorrow?

She tapped on the screen.

Me: Yep. Not sure when yet. Likely late afternoon, at the earliest.
Jorge: I'll text you the address.
Me: Thanks.

Someone behind her honked. She'd almost missed a break in the long stream of students.

Mecca stood outside her dorm building with the guy from the hospital. Will. As Jenny approached, she took advantage of the time to get a really good look at him.

He looked a little older than them, maybe in his mid-twenties. Most everything about him seemed average: his height, his weight, his build, his wavy brown hair. Everything, anyway, except his eyes, which stared out of that ordinary, average face a bright, sea green.

Mecca, beside him, leaned forward and back on a pair of crutches, a scowl on her face. His lips moved, and he broke into a lopsided grin. Jenny pulled up in time to hear Mecca say, "I don't *need* them," just like she had when they'd been six and Mecca's dad insisted on training wheels for her bike.

Jenny put the car in Park and got out. "Hey!" She and Mecca exchanged an immediate hug, the crutches trapped awkwardly between them.

Will hiked a small duffel onto his shoulder. "Where do you want her bag?"

"Back seat is fine." The small breaking wave of relief in her was surprising until she realized that she'd been afraid Will would invite himself to this overnighter. She was happy he hadn't.

With Mecca settled into the passenger seat and goodbyes said, Jenny climbed into her side and started the car, realizing by the tightening in her chest that she was anxious. When she'd texted Mecca about staying over tonight, it had been with the intention of them talking about all the secrets. She hadn't told Mecca that, of course. But that had been her reasoning.

Now, though, she didn't know how she'd bring it up. She didn't know whether Mecca would welcome her honesty. Or whether Mecca would be honest in return.

She was gonna vomit.

They sat in silence as Jenny steered them off the campus grounds.

"Do you want to get coffee? Daily Grind?"

Mecca's breathing shifted, getting shallow. She didn't speak right away, and when Jenny looked over, her best friend's features had all tightened and she'd paled.

Oh shit.

"I'm sorry!" She reached over, grabbed Mecca's forearm, and gave it a squeeze. "I forgot that's where it happened." *God, Jenny, you are an idiot.*

Mecca shook her head. "It's okay." Her voice barely came on her breath.

"Let's go straight to the house." Jenny brought her hand back to the steering wheel, feeling like a horrible, horrible person.

But that didn't stop her from still wanting to know—very badly—why Mecca had been kidnapped to begin with.

Chapter Six: Mecca

Mecca hobbled into the walk-in pantry, in search of snacks, the ache in her leg a dull thud. Jenny had dumped her duffel upstairs as soon as they'd come in and was now rooting through the fridge.

"Why won't you use your crutches?" came her muffled voice. Her head was actually *in* the refrigerator.

"I don't need them. If I needed them, I'd use them." She turned back to the shelves and grabbed a bag of tortilla chips from a high one. "This is kind of weird."

"What is?" Jenny asked.

"This." She snagged a few more things from the pantry and limped out again. "The last time we did this, we were in high school. Also, your mom never used to buy these." She grinned and tossed a box of chocolate snack cakes onto the kitchen island.

Jenny laughed. "Right? She waited until I was out of the house before she started buying the good stuff. Damn responsible parents."

They headed up, Jenny carrying all of their food, and Mecca trying to make sure she didn't fall down the stairs. The leg was getting better, much faster than the doctors had expected. But she still found it frustrating as hell not to be able to move in the ways she was used to.

"You should use your crutches."

"Oh my God, stop already. I don't need them."

"Yeah. Okay. Because you're such a spry young thing."

Mecca shot what she hoped was a harsh squint over her shoulder, but it only made Jenny laugh.

As soon as they hit the room, Mecca straggled over to the bed and flopped onto it, arms spread. "Memories of carefree days!" She propped herself on her elbows and looked around the room at the band posters on the walls. She knew for a fact that at least three of them were of bands that Jenny didn't even like. They were up because they made her parents crazy. "Your mom seriously didn't change anything, did she?"

"Why would she?" Jenny dumped her armful of chips, sweets, and drinks onto the dresser. "It's my room." She offered out a Coke, and Mecca sat up to take it. "What do you want to do?"

"Tell me about London." She desperately wanted to know why her Uncle Ken had gone out there. Or, rather, what he had gotten up to while he was there and what Jenny might have seen.

When Mecca considered that Jenny might know about the Gift, terror stabbed through her belly, making it knot up. But behind the fear was the idea that she wouldn't have to keep secrets anymore. And that felt like relief. Mecca wasn't sure their friendship would survive the searing light of truth, but a part of her wanted to find out.

They talked for quite a while about Jenny's experiences at school in London and her social life there. She talked about going to a nightclub and being able to buy beer as a nineteen-year-old when she first arrived. They both agreed that was weird but cool.

Three weeks ago, Mecca would have hung on every word. She'd never been anywhere in Europe. When she was a kid, they'd gone to Mexico once and taken a few cruises through the Caribbean, but that was as far from home as she'd ever gone.

But now…

Now, Mecca didn't care about the nightlife or the boys or the campus.

"I bet it surprised you when Uncle Ken showed up," she said.

Jenny had crammed one of the chocolate snack cakes into her mouth, so she nodded.

"What happened with that?" Mecca pulled her feet onto the bed to sit cross-legged, but when an electric jolt sent stars bursting behind her eyelids, she decided that wasn't a good idea. Instead, she shimmied back against the headboard and stretched her legs out in front of her.

Jenny swallowed her giant mouthful of chocolate and said, "It was…weird." She paused for a second and then rushed to add, "Not bad weird. Just weird weird."

I'll bet. "Weird how?"

Jenny stared at her, not speaking for a moment, her jaw moving as she chewed. Her brows had furrowed into a line over her hazel eyes. There was something Jenny wasn't telling her. Something serious.

Jenny swallowed and took a long breath. Finally, she said, "I know about Jivaja."

The pointed look that Jenny gave said that the word—Jivaja—was important, but Mecca had no idea why.

Mecca shook her head. "Well…can you tell me? What does that even mean?"

"Jivaja." Jenny waved a hand at her. "What you are."

"What are you talking about?"

"Your Uncle Ken told…" Jenny looked around the room, thinking. "No, wait. Have you talked to him? To your dad?"

A knot grew in her stomach. "No."

"That's weird. I would have thought they'd have told you."

"Dad and I aren't really talking right now."

Jenny's gaze darted to her. "Really? Why not?"

Why was everyone so interested in her damn relationship with her father? "Would you stop changing the subject? What is this thing you're talking about? This Jiv…whatever."

"Your Uncle Ken didn't know the name either. It's what you are."

Mecca couldn't keep from narrowing her eyes at her best friend. "What do you think I am?"

Jenny sighed and averted her own gaze for a moment before she leaned forward and grabbed Mecca's forearm in a gentle squeeze. "You can kill people by touching them."

Mecca jerked away. Of all the things to focus on… "I don't have any idea what they told you, but—"

"They didn't have to tell me. I saw it." Jenny drew her hand back and placed it in her lap. "Well, not your uncle, but another one like you. Her name is Noor."

Mecca stared. *Another one? What does that mean?* She realized she was shaking her head back and forth, slowly. But she didn't have any words. Turning, she swung her feet off the bed and stood. "I can't…"

Jenny scrambled up and touched her arm again but drew back. Was she afraid now? That Mecca would kill her?

The room felt tight and small. Hot. Stifling.

"Mec, it's okay."

"I should go." Her skin vibrated with her discomfort.

Jenny got directly in front of her, taking up her whole field of vision. "No, please don't. Let's just talk."

"You think I'm a murderer." Mecca's heart sank. How could she deal with her best friend thinking she went around killing people?

But you do, don't you?

"What? No. Of course I don't think you're a murderer!" The surprise on Jenny's face matched the surprise in her voice. "Don't be dumb."

"You just said I kill people."

"No, I said you *can* kill people. Not the same." A gentle smile spread across her lips. "I mean, I don't understand how it works exactly, so I can't really say what else you can do. But I feel like it's a lot, at least from reading between the lines of what Noor said."

Mecca shook her head and stepped back. "Who is Noor again?"

"The other Jivaja chick we met in London. Do you want the story? I mean...I already know, so we may as well talk about it." She dropped onto the bed and patted the mattress beside her. "Here. Sit down."

The room wasn't so tight anymore, but it was like everything was slipping away from her, like she couldn't control what was happening. Jenny didn't seem scared, and she didn't seem to be really accusing Mecca of anything.

Only because she doesn't actually know.

Mecca pushed the brain weasels aside and sat on the very edge of the bed. "Okay. What happened?"

"Uncle Ken caught up with us in London. He told Mom we were in danger. It had something to do with what was happening to you." Now Jenny did reach out again, and she grabbed Mecca's hand.

Part of Mecca wanted to jerk away. But a bigger part, the part that was terrified of Jenny hating her, held on for dear life.

"Mom was a little bitchy to him." She shrugged. "You know how Mom can be. But when we went back to the hotel—Uncle Ken was behind us, still trying to get her to let him help us—there was a guy."

"I thought Noor was a chick?"

"She is. This is the guy she killed."

Her heart raced, and Mecca suddenly felt disoriented. "She killed him? You saw it?"

"Sort of. We saw...the end." Jenny's words were slow, and she'd dropped to almost a whisper.

"This is crazy." Mecca stood again and paced in front of the bed. She had to make sense of it or else it was going to shove her right over the edge. "Keep going. Uncle Ken followed you, and then there was the guy."

Jenny watched her stomp back and forth for a moment before she continued. "Yeah, he was waiting for us in the lobby of our hotel. He wanted to talk to Mom. But it was when he left that...you know."

Mecca stopped in front of her. "Tell me exactly what happened."

Jenny's eyes searched hers, and she gave a small nod. "The man left, and we were still in the lobby. Uncle Ken started acting really weird, looking around like he was trying to find something. He took off out of the hotel. Mom rushed after him and, of course, I did too. When I came around the corner..."

When Jenny didn't go on, Mecca felt like her skin would crawl right off her body. "What? When you came around the corner, *what*?"

"When I came around the corner," she began again, slowly, not looking at Mecca, "Noor stood between a car and the wall. The guy was on the ground in front of her, but..." She finally met Mecca's gaze. "He was almost like a skeleton."

Mecca took a step back. And another.

The memory of that same vision slammed into her mind, but of herself and Hayden in the Little Five Points parking lot.

There was someone else. Someone not her dad or her uncle or her grandfather. Someone *else*.

She didn't know what to say. Or even how she felt.

"That's how we met Noor. We ended up back in the hotel room Mom had, and Noor explained some things about how...about what... Well, she told us that she—and Uncle Ken and, I assumed, you—are Jivaja. Uncle Ken was surprised by the name too. But that's what you are."

Mecca shook her head. She couldn't *stop* shaking her head. The whole idea that there was another one like her...more than one? It blew her mind.

Mecca hobbled to the dresser where all the snacks sat, grabbed the second chocolate cake from Jenny's package, and crammed the entire thing in her mouth. Her back to her best friend, she concentrated on chewing, on the hyper-sugary flavor, on anything to get her mind clear.

Jenny didn't speak again right away. The cake's thick, waxy texture, and chocolatey goodness filled Mecca's senses. She breathed through her nose and counted five breaths before she swallowed.

Clarity by chocolate. The best sort of meditation.

By the time she turned back to Jenny, she'd ridden out most of the surprise. "So what happened? What else did she tell you?"

Jenny pushed a bit of blonde hair out of her face and pressed her lips together. Now she stood. "You've had this secret all our lives, right?"

Heat flooded to Mecca's face. This was her nightmare. She'd dreaded this moment since she discovered she had the Gift. "Yes, but—"

"No, no." Jenny closed the distance between them and grabbed her hand. "That isn't an accusation. It's an observation, is all. You've held this secret."

Mecca wasn't sure where this was going. "Not all our lives. Since we were about ten, yes."

Jenny nodded. She looked away, over Mecca's shoulder. Her entire body was tense, and sweat from her hands dampened Mecca's.

What was going on? "Are you mad?"

Jenny's gaze came back to her, surprise in her eyes. She gave a short, barking laugh. "No. No, not at all." She dropped her gaze again.

Mecca didn't understand. She was relieved but confused. "Then what?"

Jenny heaved a giant sigh. She met Mecca's eyes again. "I've been holding a secret too."

"Okay, this is freaking me out now. You already came out as bi." What else could there be?

"Have you ever heard the term Visci?"

The word slammed her like ice water on her face. Mecca pulled her hands from Jenny's. No, more like she threw them down. "You are not about to tell me what I think you are."

And again, surprise touched Jenny's eyes. "You've heard of Visci?"

Mecca backed up until her ass ran into the dresser. A package of snack cakes fell to the ground.

"Clearly, you have." Jenny stepped toward her. "Whatever you've—"

"Stop." Mecca held up a hand, bile burning the back of her throat. "Stay there."

Jenny's brow furrowed, and she frowned. "Mecca, I—"

"Just stop. Stop moving. Stop talking. Just *stop*."

Jenny did.

Mecca's head fogged up and she couldn't think. Only one sentence moved through her mind.

Jenny is Visci.

Chapter Seven: Claude

Claude frowned at his computer screen. An email from Dr. Trieste, explaining another setback in the project they'd been working on for almost a decade. If the man weren't so damned valuable, Claude would have killed him himself.

A knock interrupted his anger. "Enter."

Salas stepped in and closed the door behind him. The tall man nodded his respect and said, "Carolyn Barron has come through the gate." Claude shut his laptop down. He would let the email simmer for a bit as he considered his response.

He stood and brushed off his sharply pressed slacks, though he knew there was nothing on them. "Bring a coffee tray and whatever else you think we should have as refreshments."

Salas gave a shallow bow and left the room.

Claude glanced around the neat sitting room. It would be good enough to receive Carolyn in. She no longer had the expectations of the royal blood. *Pity.* Though he had to admit that her old brazenness seemed to be returning. He'd kept intermittent tabs on her over the decades and found that she'd fallen easily into the role of human housewife and mother. In a way, he was glad of that too. He had plans.

He settled into one of the wingback chairs. He didn't have to wait long. Less than ten minutes later, a sharp knock came at the door. He knew it was Carolyn herself. Salas would never knock in that manner.

"Enter," he said.

Carolyn swept in, all purpose and drive. She still had the same immaculate style as always, though instead of the flowing skirts of their youth, she wore a deep green, well-tailored pantsuit with heeled boots. She'd already swished off her cape-like coat and laid it over the back of the matching chair opposite him.

He gave her his most welcoming smile and stood. "Good evening, Carolyn. Lovely to see you, as always."

The little incline of her head reminded him of her as a young woman, when he'd been a child. He'd always admired her.

"Good evening, Claude."

"What brings you here? I admit that I hadn't expected you for another day or two."

"I wanted to sit down with you and get a report on…the state of the city, I suppose."

"Right now? Tonight?" He certainly hadn't anticipated this intense interest in her new role. Perhaps he'd underestimated her disinterest.

She moved to the front of the chair and sat, leaning back as if she were more comfortable here, in Claude's sitting room, than anywhere else. "Yes. Of course, I don't expect a presentation of all details of all business. But an overview."

Ah yes, he *had* underestimated her. Indeed.

Salas's distinctly not-sharp knock came. Claude bid him enter, ignoring the fact that Carolyn watched him the entire time he watched Salas roll the coffee service into the room.

When the manservant came around to where they sat, Carolyn said, "Hello, Salas."

Had he been a lesser man, Claude would have taken issue with the deep bow his man gave her. But Claude was not a lesser man. Salas showed this level of respect to her for him, for Claude.

"Good evening, my lady," he said as he arranged the coffee cups on the service tray.

She chuckled. "I am no longer your lady."

He glanced at her as he raised the ceramic pot. "You will always be my lady, your highness."

Carolyn smiled, not at all flustered or self-conscious about his words. "Thank you, Salas."

"My lady."

They all remained silent as Salas poured, the gentle sound of liquid the only one in the room. When he'd finished, he looked to Carolyn. "Please enjoy the sweets and coffee, my lady." He turned to Claude. "Will you require anything else, sire?"

"No, Salas. You may go."

"Thank you, sire." And he did go. Silently.

Claude stood, went to the cart, and lifted both saucered cups. He extended one to Carolyn. "Sugar? Cream?" He hated these formalities with everything in his being, but they were required.

"Thank you, no. Black is fine."

No sugar. How strange. In the past, she'd often used all of what was available. What other things had changed about her?

"A sweet?" He offered the plate of cookies and tiny pastries for her inspection.

"Again, no. But they look lovely. Thank you."

Claude added sugar to his own cup and sat back down. "I'm afraid I will not be much help to you with your interest in what is happening here in Atlanta. I only arrived a few weeks prior to Emilia's…death. And, to be honest, I hadn't bothered trying to get involved in the workings of this city." He set his cup down and spread his hands. "I hadn't planned to stay. Only passing through."

Carolyn nodded, but he knew her well enough to assume that she didn't believe him. Or perhaps only partially believed him. "I see. Who would you have me speak with, then?"

"I only know a few of those here, but I will make inquiries." This was true. Mostly. He did have some idea of what had been happening. He'd been noting goings on in the city for several years, since he'd moved Trieste's lab here. But he didn't know who Emilia had kept in her confidence. That was something he'd been working on.

"Thank you." Now she set her own cup down, having only taken a sip or two of the very good Ethiopian blend coffee. "What have you heard of hybrids going missing?" Her emerald eyes sharpened as she waited for his reply.

"Missing?" he repeated. "I admit that I know nothing along those lines. I imagine it has to do with the growing problems between full bloods and hybrids" —

he was careful to use her term—"all around the globe. I've heard many, many stories the last few years."

She didn't respond at once, only watched him. There was a slight pulse in a vein along her forehead that he recognized as her being under stress.

"You've been gone for…a long while," he said. "Where did you hear about hybrids going missing?"

She leaned back against the leather. "It would surprise you how many come to me now that I've returned."

"Ahh." He nodded and wondered if this would prove problematic. He hadn't expected Carolyn to embrace the role she'd been given. He thought that she would have continued in her desire to be separate from them, but rule in name. His plans would likely need to shift a bit.

"You'll give me the contact information of someone I might speak with about the goings on here in Atlanta?"

He inclined his head. "Of course." He should have added some sort of honorific, but he had trouble bringing himself to adopt one with her. He never had when they'd been growing up, and even as adults, over the centuries, he hadn't felt the need to use one. But now she was back in a position of power, and he should. Even if only to underscore his respect for her new position. But still, he didn't.

"I would also like to see where Emilia lived and worked."

He snapped his gaze to her. "That is…unusual. Why do you wish that?"

Her expression had relaxed, and she looked both amused and in control. Claude didn't like that expression at all.

"Does it matter why I wish it, Claude?" The tic on her forehead had gone, and she folded her hands over her middle.

"No. Of course, it is within your rights to access anything Emilia worked on." He inclined his head. "For the city."

Her gaze narrowed but only slightly, and she stood. "I'd like to see where she worked now, if you don't mind."

This power play was most unexpected. Perhaps that was how it was with Carolyn now. She was not doing things he thought she would do. He would need to reevaluate.

He also rose. "As you wish, of course. Give me a moment, and I will get the key to her office."

⟶≫≪⟵

They hadn't spoken for most of the walk and the elevator ride down to the lower level. As Claude led her through the lush anteroom and into Emilia's private office space, he said, "Are you looking for something in particular?"

"No," Carolyn said as she moved past him and into the room, her feet silent on the deep, wine-colored carpet.

Her pace slowed as she surveyed the room: the modern, glass-topped desk in the center, wooden cabinets along the back wall, the old European furnishings. She approached the desk and surprised him by dropping into the chair behind it.

Carolyn laid her hands flat on the surface and looked over to where he remained, near the entrance. "Where is the computer?"

"In a lab, one flight up."

"Why?"

"You can't imagine Emilia shared her passwords with anyone, yes? We are trying to get into it. Probably for the same reason you're asking where it is." He smiled and hoped it looked sincere. He wasn't lying. Not much, at least. It *was* in a lab. But the lab working on it was two floors up, not one. And it was *his* people working on it. He needed Carolyn with him for his plan to succeed though, so he would be as honest as he could.

"I see. I would like it," she said.

Claude nodded.

"*Before* you break into it."

"Before? You plan to get into it yourself?"

"Do you forget who I am? What I've done?"

Ahh. Claude *had* forgotten. In the early days of computers, when shoes were tall and collars impossibly wide, Carolyn had been involved with...several of the men behind their development. Claude had always suspected she'd had more of a hand in that industry than was widely known.

"Things are different now," he said. "Computers are different."

She nodded, as if he were a child. "I know. And I would like Emilia's computer."

He tilted his head. "You don't trust me?"

She laughed. "Should I trust you?"

"I have always been on your side, Carolyn."

Claude couldn't decide whether her lack of response meant she believed him or didn't believe him. She opened the drawers of the desk, looking through items, folders, papers. Then she looked up at him again.

"Are you going to get the computer?"

She actually meant to send him on an errand. And he couldn't think of a way to get out of it. So he gave her a short bow and stepped out of the room.

Salas stood outside the door, tapping on his phone.

"What are you doing?" Claude's tone was sharper than he intended, but he didn't care.

"I received a text from the lab." His voice was measured and soft. "They need another subject."

Claude frowned and scrubbed a hand over his face. "All right. Handle it. But first, stay here until I return. I want to know if she leaves this room." Claude didn't wait for an answer but strode down the hall.

He had a damn computer to fetch.

Chapter Eight: Jenny

Jenny stood as still as possible and watched her best friend. Mecca didn't seem able to meet her eyes; instead, she looked toward the floor, somewhere in the vicinity of the bed behind Jenny.

She knew others of her kind, other Visci, had kidnapped Mecca, but Jenny didn't realize that Mecca knew they were Visci. And she'd said they hadn't physically hurt her. Jenny didn't discount the trauma Mecca must have felt just by being taken though. What should she do?

"How many people have you killed for their blood?" Mecca asked, finally looking at her. Anger shone out from her eyes.

"What? None! Jesus, Mecca—"

"Isn't that how you live? By blood?" Her tone had gone nasty, dark. Cruel.

Jenny had known this conversation would be weird, but this was getting crazy. "I don't need to kill anyone to live. Do you?"

Mecca broke their shared gaze and shoved past her, hobbling, but steady enough to ram into her arm.

"I can't fucking believe you're one of them!" She grabbed her duffel bag and tried to hike it onto her shoulder, but her bad leg threw her off balance, and she tottered.

Jenny rushed forward and steadied her. Mecca pushed her away, shifting the duffel to her hand. "Get off me!"

"I'm not *on* you, Mecca." Jenny stepped back. "Jesus, overreact much?"

Mecca spun. "Overreact? Do you know what they did to me?"

"No! I don't know what they did to you because you won't tell me!" She stared hard at Mecca, who didn't respond, only looked back, tightness around her eyes. Jenny sighed and turned to the bed. She dropped onto it and looked up. "Can we please remember that we're best friends and that we can tell each other anything?"

Mecca curled her lip. "Can we?"

"Yes," Jenny said, ignoring the attitude. "I think we can. We both had big secrets, but they're out in the open now. I think the only reason we wouldn't be able to talk is by choice. So what's your choice? Do you want to trust me? Do you want me to trust you?"

"I can't trust Visci."

"Christ, Mec, you know I'm the exact same person I was ten minutes ago, right? The same person I've always been?"

Mecca said nothing, still standing there holding her duffel in one hand.

"You are too, aren't you? You being Jivaja— someone who could kill me in a moment—shouldn't change who you are to me, should it?" That thought sent a chill down her spine. She hadn't really equated what Noor did in London to what Mecca could do. Not really.

The truth of her own words hit her like a sucker-punch to the gut, but she tried to keep it off her face.

Mecca's bag hit the floor with a muted thud.

She had said the Visci hadn't hurt her, yes, but Jenny couldn't stop thinking about what they might have done. The venom in Mecca's voice had been acidic, brutal. That sort of reaction never came from nothing.

Jenny wasn't sure that venom was gone yet.

Mecca approached. "I have a problem now."

Jenny had been wrong. The venom was gone, replaced by such a cold, flat tone that she wasn't sure how to interpret it. "What's that?" She had no idea where this was going.

"I've sworn to kill any Visci I find." Mecca stared at her, eyes hard and flinty.

Oh, for fuck's sake. "So, what? You're going to kill me? Suck the life right out of my body here in the bedroom we've had dozens of sleepovers in?"

Mecca's expression remained stony for a moment. But then the struggle that must have been raging inside her slid across her face and through her eyes.

Fear, anger, pain, uncertainty.

She finally said, "No. Of course not." She all but threw herself onto the bed beside Jenny. "I don't understand any of this. I don't know what I should do." She met Jenny's gaze, her eyes, the color of very strong tea, now earnest. "But they're horrible, the other Visci. They murder people. How do I tell the difference?"

"Is there ever a way to tell the difference between good people and bad people?"

Neither of them had an answer.

Mecca stared at her for a long moment before she pulled herself to standing, balancing on one leg. She took out her phone.

"What are you doing?" Jenny asked, standing too.

"Calling an Uber. I can't stay here."

Mecca's words punched her right in the gut. "What? No."

Mecca didn't respond, but tapped her phone screen. "Six minutes." She grabbed her duffel and limped to the corner where she'd tossed her crutches.

Jenny only stared after her, watching as Mecca struggled with holding the duffel and using her crutches. She tried holding it in her hand as she grasped her right crutch, but the weight threw her off balance. She slung it over her shoulder, but when she leaned forward to move, the duffel tumbled and almost knocked the crutch from under her.

Moving to help steady her, Jenny said, "Oh, give me that. I think you're being stupid to just leave, but I will not let you fall down the stairs because you're on crutches and are too stubborn to ask for help." She took the duffel, as Mecca gave her a look.

They said nothing as Mecca led down the stairs, one step at an excruciatingly slow time. When they got to the bottom, Jenny said, "Please don't go."

Mecca didn't quite meet her eyes. "I can't stay here. You don't understand."

"So explain it to me!" Jenny stepped toward her, but Mecca shuffled back.

"Don't. We can talk about this another time. But I can't do it now."

"Mec—"

"Jenny, seriously." Now Mecca met her gaze with fierce eyes. "Don't."

A dark blue, pristinely clean sedan pulled up outside and gave a short honk. Mecca's gaze hadn't left her, and Jenny struggled with her need for Mecca to stay. Finally, she sighed and opened the door, gesturing Mecca through.

Chapter Nine: Mecca

She'd held it together for the entire Uber ride. Will met her at the spot Jenny had picked her up. She'd had to text him because she obviously couldn't carry her stupid duffel bag up to her stupid dorm because of the stupid crutches.

Now, sitting safely on her bed in her quiet room—

"Do you want to tell me what happened?" Will asked.

"No."

He sat beside her on the bed. "Did you have a fight?"

Mecca looked at him sidelong. "Didn't I just say I don't want to tell you what happened?"

He gave her that lopsided grin of his. "Yes."

Will confused her. Some days, she didn't care whether he was around or not. Some days, she missed him when he was gone. Though, admittedly that wasn't often, because he wasn't gone often. Ever since what had happened in the woods, Will had stuck right by her side. He hadn't given her a good answer as to why, but Mecca realized, to her surprise, that she didn't really care why. She just cared that he stayed.

Mecca heaved a sigh, not sure whether she even wanted to tell him, let alone figuring out where to start. "We kind of had a fight. Not really. Well, sort of."

He didn't say anything, only waited.

"She's Visci."

"Oh."

She jerked her gaze up to him. Was that surprise or nonchalance? She couldn't tell.

"This puts a crimp in the 'kill all Visci' plan, doesn't it?"

Was he being a smart ass? She couldn't tell that either. She shimmied back until she came to the wall her bed was against. Her leg ached, and she stretched it out in front of her. "I don't really want to talk about it."

"You'll have to at least think about it though." He turned sideways to look at her. "I know you're angry. You have every right to be—"

"Aren't you?" she asked. "Angry? They held you for…decades. Doesn't that piss you off?"

"It did, in the beginning, yes. I had a very short fuse and would clobber anyone human who looked at me the wrong way."

Clobber, she thought. Who uses that anymore?

"But I got things from them too."

"What do you mean?"

"Do you think I would have lived long enough to see the internet? Wireless technology? Gene therapy? Would I have even survived the Spanish Flu?"

"So you forgive them because you can cruise porn for free?"

"What? No."

Will looked aghast, and Mecca laughed. She couldn't help it.

With a shake of his head, he continued. "No. I don't forgive them. But I don't carry that anger around anymore. I wouldn't be who I am without those years. And I never would have met you."

Scenes from every rom-com she'd ever seen flashed through her head. He wasn't looking at her wistfully, no doe eyes. She really didn't understand him.

"Okay, well, they didn't do any of that for me." She narrowed her eyes. "And don't you dare say that it was because I didn't let them do what they wanted to do to me."

He shook his head. "I wouldn't say that. What they wanted you to do was much different from what they wanted me to do."

Emilia wanted her to be an assassin. To kill for her.

Mecca closed her eyes and pinched the bridge of her nose. "I don't know what to do."

"About what?"

"About Jenny."

"What is there to do?"

Another sidelong glance at him. "What do you mean?"

"I mean: what are your choices?"

"I don't know."

"Well, are you going to kill Jenny?"

"Don't be stupid."

"I'm not being stupid," he said, his tone calm. "Sometimes when you're unsure what to do, it's easier to figure out what you're not going to do."

That made some sort of weird sense to her. "No, I'm not going to kill my best friend."

"Good, because I would have had to leave if you were going to."

She could never tell when he was joking.

"Are you going to cut her out of your life?"

That was a harder one to answer. She didn't want to cut Jenny out of her life. Well, the Jenny before today. She wasn't sure who the Jenny after today was. "I don't know."

"All right. So that's a choice. Do you want to remain friends with her?"

Yesterday, that would have been a dumb question. She wished it were yesterday. "I don't know if I can," she whispered.

"What is stopping you?"

"She's Visci."

"She's blonde too. Does that make a difference?"

Mecca glared at him, but he only gave her a gentle smile. How was he so damn patient?

"I'm saying—"

"I know what you're saying. Jenny is the same as she was yesterday, and being Visci is just one aspect of her. She said the same thing." She sighed and leaned her head against the wall. "I just don't know if I can say it."

Chapter Ten: Jenny

Jenny turned off the car, grabbed her purse and opened her door. A crisp wind sliced in, blowing her hair around her head in a frenzied mess. She shivered. Temperatures had dropped drastically over the past two weeks, barely above freezing at night. The holiday season was definitely on its way.

The upscale condo community where Helen lived featured multi-level brick townhouses each with a one-car garage. All the tiny front yards looked like strips of perfectly proportioned quilt squares with expertly manicured lawns.

Jenny had parked in front of Helen's place. A dark red four-door sedan that had seen better days took up the single driveway. With rust spots on the fenders and windows so dirty they looked frosted, the car couldn't have been Helen's. Helen was way too neat and fastidious.

Jenny climbed the flagstone steps and rang the bell.

When Jorge opened the door, he broke into a bright grin. "Jenny! I'm glad you made it. Come on in." He stepped aside and let her into the house.

The exterior, which had looked sedate and cookie-cutter-normal, gave way to brightly painted walls and lots of simple wood decor. A living area opened to the right, and stairs led up on the left. In the living room, the young woman from the cemetery sat on a dark blue overstuffed chair across from a burnt-umber colored sofa. This room had had bright blue walls with ocher accented trim. A large-screen laptop perched on the natural-wood coffee table in front of the woman, and the light scent of lavender drifted on the air.

"Jenny, this is Zoey."

"Hey," Jenny said. "Nice to meet you."

Zoey gave her a nod but didn't say anything. She returned her attention to the phone in her hand.

Jorge shrugged. "Conversation isn't her strong suit. Here, let me have your jacket. Helen's in the kitchen, making some tea. I always ask for coffee," he said as he slid her coat off her shoulders, "but I always get tea."

He led her toward the back, stopping at a coat closet beneath the stairs. Helen stood in front of the island in the bright, airy kitchen, pouring steaming water from a kettle into a teapot. The scent of jasmine reached Jenny's nose.

"Ah, Jenny!" Helen gave her a radiant smile. "I am glad you're here."

Helen wore a dark-yellow blouse beneath a red sweater. Her braids hung free and swung as she turned to put the kettle back onto the stove.

"Thanks," Jenny said. Even though she and Helen had been texting over the last two weeks, Jenny hadn't realized Jorge, Helen, and Zoey had become an organized group. But here they were. And they'd invited her over. She couldn't help the thrill that ranged through her when she thought of being included by "her kind."

Jorge picked up three mugs by their handles from where they sat on the counter and stopped at the fridge to grab a Coke. As the door closed, he grinned at her. "Zoe won't drink anything that isn't carbonated and caffeinated."

The all returned to the living room, just as Zoey came in from the front door.

"Forgot my charger." She held up a small battery pack and plopped back into her chair.

Helen poured out tea for herself, Jenny, and Jorge. Zoey took the Coke from Jorge and unscrewed the top as she hunched over the laptop. Helen had also brought a plate of pastries. They seemed a bit like tiny pecan pies, but the topping was definitely not pecans. Helen called it *gizzada* and when Jenny took a bite of one, she delighted in the coconut flavor.

Jorge had already eaten three. Helen didn't offer the plate to Zoey.

"They're too fancy for her," Jorge said, when Zoey declined the offer from Jenny.

Zoey shot him a narrow look. "I don't like coconut, okay?"

He laughed. "Okay."

"Let's get down to business, shall we?" Helen said. "Jenny, we appreciate you coming out."

"Thanks for inviting me." Jenny tried hard not to gush over them being her very first Visci friends. She chided herself for feeling like a twelve-year-old at a new school. She sipped on the jasmine tea to cover her nerves.

"How is the Skype coming, Zoey?"

Zoey remained bent over the laptop. "Your network is really slow."

Helen sighed, but clearly not with exasperation. She looked more amused than annoyed.

"But I sent Arabella a message that we're ready when she is. She said she'll call in a few."

"Who is Arabella?" Jenny asked.

"She is our person in the room," Jorge said.

"She's on the Council," Zoey chimed in. "Runs Memphis."

Jenny raised her brows and looked at Jorge. "I thought you said your person wasn't on the Council?"

He grinned at her. "No. I said that I hadn't *said* our person was on the Council. And I hadn't."

"Let's not get bogged down in the details," Helen said.

Jenny felt like Jorge was teasing her, especially because of the twinkle in his eye when he winked at her. Was he flirting? She couldn't tell, but her cheeks heated, and she looked away.

The familiar Skype ringtone chimed, and Zoey connected the call. A beautiful, pale woman with thick chestnut hair and dark, intelligent eyes came onto the screen.

"Afternoon, y'all," the woman said.

Zoey turned the laptop, so it faced Helen and, next to her, Jenny.

"Good afternoon, Arabella. How are things over there?" Helen said.

"As good as can be expected," she said. "I see we have a new face."

"This is Jenny. Carolyn's daughter."

Thin eyebrows raised as a wide, very white smile broke out on Arabella's pink lips. "So you're the daughter! Very nice to meet ya. I've known your mom for a long time."

Jenny wasn't sure how to feel about that. In a way, it seemed flattering that this woman knew of her. But she couldn't help also being reminded that her mother had an entire circle of people around her that Jenny had no clue about.

"Hey," she said, self-conscious.

"Is there any additional news?" Jorge asked.

"Another full blood is missing. Sami Cabel." Arabella's voice went soft, somber. "She's new to town, but a friend of hers came to me yesterday and told me that Sami couldn't be reached. Had missed a meeting for a new start-up"—with her accent, she pronounced this *staht hup*—"and that isn't like her at all, from what he said."

Helen let out a heavy sigh. "What about hybrids?"

"No. We still haven't had any disappear or come up dead, thank God. That seems to only be there, in Atlanta. At the Council meeting, I spoke privately with Thomas and Tony. They've both had issues with fighting among fulls and hybrids, but no hybrid deaths that they know of. Although they've had a couple full bloods disappear also."

"Who are they?" Jenny whispered to Jorge.

"Thomas Eli runs Charlotte," Jorge replied, matching her volume. "And Tony Mercado is Miami. He's a dick. But Thomas isn't bad."

"Tony *is* a dick," Arabella said. She followed this with a light, tinkling laugh.

"Jesus." Zoey scowled. "So what's the plan then?" she blurted, her tone sharp. Apparently, she was done with small talk.

"Was that Zoey?" Arabella asked.

Jenny had forgotten that the other woman wasn't on screen.

"Of course," Jorge said, that same twinkle in his eye.

"Yes, of course." Arabella laughed again. "All right, the plan. Carolyn is going to be key, I think. As the current leader of Atlanta, she's gonna have a lot of power. Plus..." She paused for a moment. "She has history with Claude."

His name was coming up everywhere.

"Why is that important?" Jorge asked.

Jenny found him watching her out of the corner of his eye.

"Because I believe Claude is somehow involved in whatever is going on," Arabella replied.

That got Jorge's full attention. "You think he's the one killing hybrids?"

Arabella sighed and shook her head. "I don't know. But he's as slick as a greased-up eel on a kitchen floor."

Jenny looked at Jorge and then Zoey. They had matching looks on their faces, which was probably the same as hers. She mouthed, "greased-up eel?" and they all held back the guffaws, which left them looking as if they were trying to contort their faces to fit into a small box.

Helen chuckled, though whether it was because of Arabella's words or their expressions, Jenny wasn't sure.

Jenny cleared her throat to cover her amusement and said, "You've met Claude?"

"I've had the dubious pleasure of his company, yes. You know how some people invite that creepy feeling up your spine? He's that guy." Arabella swept a lock of hair up into a clip, looking at herself in the camera. "I got word that he'd come to Atlanta a few weeks ago. He and Emilia were...old friends, from what I hear. He attended the meeting on the night of the Maze Gathering. That was the first time I'd met him. It was just before..." She frowned. "Before Emilia was killed."

"Do you think he killed her?" Jenny asked. She wanted to learn everything about him.

Arabella's delicate brows knitted closer together. "I don't know. I haven't been able to get any information on how she died. Her body seems to be gone. There were no witnesses." She smirked. Somehow, it looked lovely on her, though her eyes had hardened. "At least, according to Claude."

Zoey sighed, clearly done with this line of conversation too. "Okay, Emilia's dead. Check.

Claude's slimy. Check. *What* is our next step? What do we do?"

Arabella's lips ticked upward on one side. "Emilia had been my main point of contact in Atlanta, so I'm afraid I may not be as useful as in the past."

Wait. What? "Hang on," Jenny said. "Emilia was helping you?" She brought her gaze to Jorge, then Helen, and back to the laptop.

Emilia Laos—the evil woman who'd kidnapped Mecca.

"Not everyone loved her, but she didn't want this war any more than any of us do. Emilia is the one who told me to be careful of Claude." She gave a short, wry laugh. "And she knew him the best of all."

Arabella stared at the camera, and it felt, to Jenny, as if the woman were looking straight into her.

"At least, until now," Arabella continued. "I suspect yer mom may know him better. Or perhaps at least as well."

Jenny had no response to that. *Did* her mom know Claude better? She'd told David that Claude had wanted to marry her. Did that mean they'd dated?

What did dating even look like in the Visci world? Jenny scowled at her own ignorance. Again.

"Okay?" Jorge whispered, leaning in.

Jenny glanced at him before turning back to the laptop. "Why don't you reach out to my mom yourself? You're on the Council."

"A fair question," Arabella said, her tone gentle. "I don't rightly know if Carolyn *is* close enough to him. Not for sure." This came out as *fo' shuh*. Arabella sat very still as she continued. "And the second reason... It's also possible that she could be working with him."

"What?" Jenny almost jumped up from the sofa. "She would never!"

Helen laid her hand on Jenny's forearm. She leaned forward. "Calm down," she said under her breath.

"No! You asked for my help and now she's accusing my mom of—"

"She's not accusing your mom of anything," Helen said, her voice level and quiet. "Arabella's position is important and in some ways precarious. She can't take frivolous risks. Until we can be sure—100% sure *for ourselves*—Arabella cannot let anyone discover that she allied with us."

Jenny clenched her fists and stared at Helen. "How could you think that of her?"

"I don't think that of her, Jenny. We're being cautious with Arabella. That's all. It has nothing to do with your mom in particular. It would be the same with anyone."

"Not with me."

That kind smile came across Helen's face. "You believe we didn't discuss and work out whether it was safe to let you meet Arabella before Zoey connected this call?"

Jenny stared at the woman. That hadn't crossed her mind. "You talked about me?"

"Oh my God, of course we did," Zoey said, tilting her head back til she gazed at the ceiling. "We don't invite random people here." She looked again at Jenny and rolled her eyes.

"Zoey," Helen said.

"What? She's not even thinking about any of this logically. She's acting like a dumb kid."

The words struck Jenny hard, particularly because, even though Jenny was only twenty, Zoey looked much younger.

Jenny glared across the coffee table at Zoey. She sat draped across the chair, one leg over the arm, the other flung carelessly on the floor. Her blonde, spiky hair had been tipped with a pink so pale that Jenny hadn't noticed it earlier. She returned Jenny's look with one of boredom.

Blood crackling hot under her skin, Jenny rose. She would slap that boredom right off the bitch's face.

Cool fingers wrapped around her forearm. "Jenny."

She looked down at Helen, whose own eyes had grown hard.

"Sit down, please."

Glancing between Helen and Zoey, who, looking at her phone, seemed done with the entire situation, Jenny pulled away. "No. I've heard enough. If you don't trust my mom, then I assume you don't trust me." Heartbeat thrumming in her ears, she snatched up her purse and made her way out of the room. Jorge jumped to his feet.

He followed her. "Wait."

"No." How had she thought these people would be her friends? She glanced around the foyer. "Where's my coat?"

Jorge came up and got in front of her. "Please. Just hang on a second."

"Why? So you can try to convince me to get my mom to help, even though you don't trust her? Where is my coat?" Heat burrowed beneath her skin. If she didn't get out of here…

Jorge shook his head, but he turned to the closet under the stairs. "Your mom is still an unknown. That's all." He pulled her coat off a hanger. When he turned back, he gave her a pained stare. "Please understand. It's only a precaution. Believe me, if I had my way, she'd be here right now. But we have to be careful." He held her coat out for her to slip into. "People are *dying*."

They faced each other for a long moment. Then, she turned around and jammed her arms into her coat sleeves. He hiked it up over her shoulders.

"Can I call you tomorrow?" he asked as she turned back around.

She wanted to say no. She wanted that so badly. Her anger still simmered, hot and immediate. But if what she'd learned today was true, he was right. People were dying. "Yes. Fine."

He walked her out onto the small porch. "Jenny."

She looked back from the bottom of the steps.

Jorge's solid frame engulfed the opening to the steps, and he watched her with an intense look.

"Thank you."

Chapter Eleven: Mecca

"He's at the bar, sitting on the corner. Red shirt, black pants. He looks like a throwback from the eighties," Will said, as he closed the car door and settled into the driver's seat. They'd parked in the side alley, just to stay out of the way. "Oh, he's bleached his hair, but otherwise, he's like the photo."

Mecca smoothed her blouse. She'd chosen a low-cut cami top and a black leather miniskirt, with a long, open trench coat over top. She'd wanted to wear big heels, but Will forbade it. Normally, she'd have flipped him off and done what she wanted. But while he was out of the room, she'd tried her lowest heels and found that she couldn't walk in them. Could barely stand. She still favored her bad leg when she walked, but she could cover the limp pretty well. Not so much with the heels. She'd walked two steps and the pain bolting through her had almost knocked her down.

So she'd reluctantly settled for flats and decided to get the guy's attention with her cleavage rather than her legs.

"Are you sure you want to do this?" Will asked, his voice low but intense.

"Yes. I'll get him out here, get him on the ground, and you can use your modern medical miracles there" — she nodded at his black medical bag that they'd gotten at a thrift store—"to get what you need from him. Then we'll rid the world of him for good."

Will didn't meet her gaze.

Mecca sighed. "Don't tell me you're feeling guilty."

He turned toward her. "This is going to change you. I want you to be sure."

Her heart pounded in her ears. "Hayden changed me when he attacked me in the parking lot. Emilia changed me when she kidnapped me from campus." Mecca heard her voice rising in pitch but couldn't control it. "If she had left me alone, I'd be worrying about midterms right now." She narrowed her eyes at him. "I'm already changed."

Will didn't answer at once but didn't look away either, his eyes bright as he held her gaze. Finally, he sighed. "All right. Let's get it over with."

—⇒⫸⫷⇐—

The bar was a dive. Let's get that right. Hazy smoke hung above her head, grey in the dim light of the room. All the scents you'd expect to be in the air—stale beer, grimy sweat, and the sour smell of desperation—had made an appearance.

The man stood right where Will said he'd be, alongside the bar. Smoothing her top again to cut her nerves, she set out with her best saunter in his direction. She'd only gotten halfway there when he stood and pushed through the crowd, moving away from her. She cursed under her breath and followed, trying not to be obvious.

He disappeared into the men's room.

"Dammit." *Of fucking course.*

Mecca changed direction and found a spot near a pillar where she could see the bathroom door. Bodies crowded in around her, the scent of beer and aftershave heavy in her nose.

"Can I buy you a drink?" The voice came from over her shoulder. When she glanced back, a man at least twice her age—maybe three times—shifted his gaze from her ass to her eyes.

Gross. "No, thanks. I'm waiting for my boyfriend." She returned her attention to the bathroom door. It hadn't opened.

"He lets you out in that?" The guy smirked, his thick lips curling up into a leering grin.

"Seriously, if that's your best line, you need to fast forward into the current century."

He scowled. "Bitch."

"Yeah. Now go on."

He groused under his breath but went away. She was glad he hadn't made a scene. She didn't want that sort of attention.

When she brought her own attention back to the bathroom, the men's door was swinging shut and a tall figure slipped into the crowd. As she watched him move away and toward the door, she recognized his walk. She looked back at the bathroom door. It remained closed.

"Oh no. No, no, no." Mecca rushed after the retreating figure, shoving her way through the crowded bar. Her leg throbbed. She stopped treating it carefully, limping as she rushed to follow.

She broke through the crowd and out the door into the cold night air. Her breath steamed in front of her, and cool air iced her lungs.

"Dad!"

He turned, and her heart sank. It *was* him.

"Mecca." He looked up and down the street. "What are you doing here? And why are you dressed like a hooker?" He hurried to her.

"You killed him, didn't you?" She barely kept her voice a whisper. Past his shoulder, she saw Will jogging toward them from the car.

The wide-eyed, open mouthed expression on her father's face would have been funny if the situation weren't so dire. The shift from surprise to anguish happened so quickly, Mecca almost didn't track it.

He took a step toward her and reached out a hand. "Mecca, I'm glad—"

Moving out of his reach, she said, "Why were you even here? How did you know who he—" She looked from her dad to Will, who'd just made it to them, and back to her dad.

Things clicked into place. Only one reason he'd be here. Why he'd kill the Visci in the bathroom.

"Claude?" She stared at Will, who lifted one shoulder but gave a single nod of agreement. She looked into her dad's eyes. "You're working for him."

He kept her gaze but didn't respond.

"That's why Claude's left me alone, because you took my place. *You're* his assassin."

The defeat on her father's face, in his posture, left her confused. She wanted to hug him. She couldn't. But she wanted to. He was still a liar, though. And a killer.

"It's the only way for you to live your life safely," he said, his voice quiet, resigned.

She scoffed and shook her head. How did he not get it? "I'll never be safe as long as he's alive. Neither will you or Gramps or Uncle Ken."

"I'm not worried about us. You're the one who's important."

"I can't believe you're killing for him." She gave an exasperated snort. "I don't know why I can't believe it," she said, only half under her breath.

"What were you doing in there?" He took a step forward, reached out and fingered the strap of her camisole. "And looking like that?"

She jerked away. "It's not your business what I'm doing. Or how I dress."

"Mecca, come on," he said. "Can we talk? Please?"

"No." The word came out louder than she'd intended, but she was so angry.

"I think we need to move this off the street," Will said, stepping between them.

"No," Mecca said, getting her tone under control. "We're done here." She gathered her anger and leveled her gaze at her father. "I will kill him." She didn't bother to name who she spoke about. Her dad would get it. "And every one of them I can find." The thought of Jenny came to her, but she locked it away. "You can warn him or not. I don't care. But as long as you're his pawn, I don't ever want to see or speak to you."

She spun on her heel and winced as sharp electric pulses arced up her leg. But she didn't stumble. There was that.

When Will opened the driver's side door, she was already sitting in the passenger seat, fuming. She didn't look up as he slid in.

"You shouldn't be so angry at him."

"Please just start the car. I'm freezing."

The motor hummed to life, and Mecca pointed all the heater vents toward her. She thanked the car gods that the engine was still warm.

"He said he had information you needed to know."

"I don't care. Wait. You were talking to him?" Anxiety spiked through her gut. What would she do if Will took her dad's side? The thought freaked her out more than she wanted to admit.

"He told me as I left after you. That's all he said." He touched her elbow. "He's only trying to protect you."

"I don't want to talk about it. I only want you to help me keep my promise. I want to kill them all."

"*All* of them?"

When she looked at him, she could tell he hadn't pushed the thought of Jenny aside. "Shut up and drive, would you?"

--->>><<<---

As Mecca parked in the dorm lot, her phone buzzed. She glanced at it as she got out, the ache in her leg much more pronounced than it'd been earlier. She'd definitely overdone it. Not that she'd ever admit that, though.

*Dad: I'm sorry. Please call me. There's something you *need* to know.*

"Jesus," she said under her breath as she turned off the screen and shoved the phone in her pocket. They took two steps from the car, and she stopped.

"What's wrong?" Will asked.

She grabbed onto his shoulder for balance and pulled her shoes off one after the other. "Nothing. Just need to get these off." The asphalt chilled the bottoms of her feet.

He narrowed his eyes at her as she straightened. "How is your leg?"

"It's fine." It really wasn't. The throb had gotten worse and worse during the ride home.

"I don't believe you."

She shrugged. "Doesn't matter if you do or not. Let's go."

The hall was relatively quiet as they made their way down. Rock music blare from behind one door. A tall blond guy, towel wrapped around his waist, came out of the men's shower at the end of the hall. Mecca ignored it all.

When they got to the room, her dorm-mate, Josie, sat on her bed with two books and a bunch of papers spread around her. She looked up as Mecca limped in, shoes in one hand, keys in the other.

Josie tilted her head a bit as she looked Mecca's outfit up and down. Finally, she said, "You okay?"

Mecca nodded and threw the shoes into her closet. Will followed in behind.

Josie scrambled out of her academic nest and looked at him. "Hey, can you give us a minute?"

Will didn't hesitate. "Yes. No problem. I want to get something from the snack machine, anyway."

He wasn't going to get anything from the snack machine. He hated junk food. But she watched him go and close the door behind him. When she looked back to Josie, her friend stared back with an expression that told Mecca they were going to have The Talk.

"I didn't mind Will crashing here for a couple days, especially right after you got out of the hospital," she began.

Mecca dropped onto her own bed and sighed. *Here it comes.*

"But, Mec, he can't stay here."

"I know."

"He's a nice guy and all, and I get that you like him—"

"What?" Her toes curled, and she wrinkled her nose as heat flushed her skin. "I don't like him. Not like that."

Josie rolled her eyes. "Right. Okay, whatever. That doesn't actually matter. What matters is that he *can't* stay."

"Fine."

"The room isn't even big enough."

Mecca pulled herself up with the foot of the bed frame and went to her closet. "I said fine. We'll be out tomorrow." She grabbed a duffel from the floor and tossed it on her bed.

"What do you mean 'we'?"

"Exactly what I said." She started throwing clothes into the bag. "We'll find somewhere else to stay. You can have the room to yourself, since it's so small." Mecca understood she was being melodramatic and unreasonable, but it didn't matter. She couldn't stop what came out of her mouth right now. She didn't have the energy to try.

Josie sighed this time and shook her head. "That is not what I meant at all, and you know it."

Mecca lifted her shoulders in a shrug.

"So you don't like him 'like that'"—she even did the air quotes; Mecca saw it out of the corner of her eye—"but you're *moving out* because he can't stay here. Yet you don't like him."

"You wouldn't understand."

Josie grabbed Mecca's arm and turned her until Mecca had to meet her friend's gaze. The green eyes staring at her had an intensity she'd never seen in them before. "Well, *tell* me. I *want* to understand whatever it is you're going through."

Tears burned her eyes, and she clenched her jaw. God, she hated this… Angry one second, crying the next.

She blinked back her tears and stared at Josie, trying to get control of her emotions.

Josie had lent Mecca her car when Mecca had escaped from Emilia. She had asked no questions when Mecca had begged her not to. Mecca wanted to share with her so very badly. Josie had been her best friend on campus since Jenny had gone to an Ivy League college in the northeast and on to London this semester.

But telling her roommate would only put her in danger. Mecca did *not* want that. So she shook her head and steadied her voice. "I can't."

Josie glared at her for a long moment and then shook her own head. "No. You can. You just won't. I don't know what your deal is, but I don't understand you anymore." She returned to her bed and crawled back among her notes.

Mecca hung her head, all the fight drained out of her.

"Go do what you want," Josie said, her voice thick. "But he can't be here anymore."

Mecca looked at the mess of the duffel, fabric spilling out. Then she left the room.

Chapter Twelve: Claude

The girl laid on the bed, studying him as he buttoned his shirt. Claude ignored her. He ran a finger over his lips and found blood, so he slid his handkerchief out of his pocket and wiped his mouth. He'd moved the girl into the compound a few days after Mecca had killed Emilia. It was easier to keep her on hand.

"I'm pregnant," she said, her voice low.

Claude paused for only a moment before he turned and gave her a smile. She still stared at him with fearful eyes, but as he approached, smiling, her expression shifted slowly, becoming tentatively hopeful. Her hand fluttered to the place at her neck. His place.

"That is lovely, my dear. We will need to make sure you're perfectly healthy. I will send my doctor to you."

"You're happy?" She sat up, the fabric slipping to reveal a tanned breast.

He dropped to sit beside her and laid his hand on her sheet-covered thigh. "Of course. Why wouldn't I be happy?"

A relieved sigh slipped from her lips. "Thank God. I was worried."

He patted her leg and stood. "Nothing to worry about, my lovely. Now, I must run, as I am late for a meeting. I will take care of everything. Do not worry."

He left her smiling behind him.

Salas met him in the hall.

"Get Trieste. She's with child."

Salas nodded solemnly. If he had questions as to why Trieste should see the girl, he didn't ask. Claude doubted he had questions. Claude would never tolerate a half-breed child. They waited for the lift.

"Your video call with Carolyn Barron is in ten minutes. I've set up your laptop in the sitting room."

"Very good."

Salas left him at the door to his rooms.

He'd been true to his word. The laptop was ready for him at his writing table, flanked by a cup of tea. It would have honey and not sugar, of course. He settled into his seat, woke the computer, and had just taken a sip of the slightly cooled tea when Carolyn Barron rang.

"Good afternoon," he said after the video call connected.

"Hello, Claude." She sat in a modern-looking kitchen, with stainless steel appliances and marble counter tops. "Thank you for taking my call."

He tilted his head in acknowledgment. "It is my pleasure my queen."

Carolyn waved a hand. "That is unnecessary."

"As you say. Have you found the information you were looking for on Emilia's computer?"

The slight pause before she spoke interested him, but Claude wasn't sure what it meant.

"Yes, things are on course. But I have a question for you."

He nodded. "Go on, please."

"I want to know who controls the police department. Who's calling the shots?"

"I believe it was Emilia herself."

"Certainly someone has taken over."

He watched her carefully. "Yes, I imagine so."

"I'm surprised that you don't know who it is, Claude."

"Things have been chaotic since Emilia…" He let the sentence trail.

"Indeed," she said, her eyes narrow. "You have your finger on the pulse of any city you're in. Particularly when in a position as you are now."

She was digging. "I assure you, my queen, my lack of knowledge is only because of the circumstance. You wish me to find this out for you?"

"I do."

"Very well. I shall discover what I can."

"Quickly, please, Claude."

"As you wish, my queen."

She gave him a curt nod and closed the call.

Chapter Thirteen: Jenny

"He looks much younger than I expected," Jenny said, as she stepped over to where her mom sat in front of her laptop in the kitchen.

"Yes. His family has the gift of youth. Some bloodlines have that. It is both a blessing and a curse."

"How old is he?"

"We are the same age."

"Wow. He looks like he's in high school." And her mom looked like a soccer mom in her early thirties, though her real age numbered in the hundreds.

"Yeah. But I wanted you to see him so you recognize him. Just in case…"

"In case? You think he might, what? Try to do something to me?"

She shrugged. "I don't know. He is hard to anticipate. But at least you know what he looks like now."

Jenny nodded, still not sure what she would do with that information. "Do you believe Claude is running the police department?"

"I wouldn't be at all surprised."

"But he wouldn't tell you if he was."

"No. He'll deflect, redirect."

"You don't expect to get a real answer out of him, do you?"

Her mom smiled at her. "The rule to dealing with Visci, especially those with power, is 'don't trust, and always verify.'"

Jenny nodded, considering. She tilted her head toward the computer. "So you're going to talk to the Council?"

"I want to get with them individually. If I'm going to come back in, I need to understand the field I'm entering."

She'd never seen her mom's eyes so bright and full of life—excitement, even. Definitely not since her dad died, but maybe even before.

"You've missed it, haven't you?"

Her mother looked startled for a moment and considered this before answering. "I suppose a part of me has missed it, yes." She reached out and squeezed Jenny's forearm. "But I would make the same decision. I was so much happier when I wasn't around"—she waved a hand toward the computer—"all this."

Jenny nodded as her phone buzzed in her pocket.

Helen: See you at 1.

Jenny texted back, "Looking forward to it!" To her mom, she said, "I have lunch plans and after, I'm going to visit Mecca for a bit, but I can stay around for a while, if you want." She'd been surprised that Mecca had reached out to her. Surprised, but relieved.

"I've been trying to give you space, so I haven't asked til now. Have you and Mecca talked about…things?"

She'd considered telling her mom about the huge blow out the night Mecca was supposed to sleep over, but she hadn't. She'd kept the music on loud and the door closed and locked. "Sort of. I'm sure we will talk more about it today."

If her mom thought she was hedging, she said nothing, but her look told Jenny that she knew *something* was up. "Who's lunch with?"

Jenny hadn't shared the meeting she'd had with Helen and the others, either. Any of the meetings. But she didn't see a reason to lie about her plans. "Remember the people I met? The ones who told me about the hybrids disappearing? One of them."

Her mom seemed as if she wanted to ask questions, but she only said, "All right. Let me know how it goes."

Was her mom finally accepting that Jenny wasn't a kid anymore? "You too."

They exchanged a smile and Jenny left.

Since Mecca's Uncle Ken had told her that her father was dead, she had felt empty and angry at intervals. For the first time, it seemed as if she had some purpose, a reason to move forward.

Chapter Fourteen: Claude

Claude tapped his keyboard with the hunt-and-peck method, answering yet another email from Trieste. The project's progress had been lethargic, and Claude wasn't happy.

A gentle knock came on the door.

"Enter," Claude said.

"I've put him in the library," Salas said after closing the door behind him.

"We'll let him sit for a while."

"As you wish," Salas said.

"I will want the car later. Let us pay a visit to Trieste and see where the issue lies."

His man bowed. "I will make the arrangements."

Claude sent the email he'd been working on and closed the laptop.

Salas held out a pair of exquisite lambskin gloves.

He pulled them on as he stood. "Come," he said, moving for the door. "Let us meet our guest."

Claude entered the library precisely fifteen minutes after their arranged meeting time, the thick carpet swallowing his footfalls. He had chosen a different time, and David Trenow had dictated this time in response. It had been a power play that Claude had allowed the other man to win. There would be plenty of time to show him who held the power in this relationship.

"Mr. Trenow. Good evening," he said, as he approached. "Thank you for taking the time to meet with me."

Salas followed and moved off to the sideboard, where a decanter of brandy and four small glasses sat.

"I think we both know that I wouldn't be here if there was a way I could *not* be here."

Claude chuckled and inclined his head toward David. "That is so. You completed the request?"

"I killed your man, yes."

Claude twinged at the vulgar words, and one corner of David's mouth quirked up.

Salas, always adept at ignoring conversation as he served, presented a silver tray that held two snifters, both half-full of the sweet amber liquid. David shook his head as Salas offered the tray to him first. Claude took his own glass. Salas withdrew.

"Did you take a photo?" Claude asked, watching David closely as he sipped his drink.

David blanched. "No, I didn't."

"In future, I would like proof of death."

David watched him for a moment, his eyes narrowed. "I'm not going to leave a photographic trail of my misdeeds. So, no, I don't think I will be doing that."

"You will." Claude easily suppressed his urge to destroy David because of his refusal.

Centuries of manipulating people and events had given him the control to resist. But time had had no effect on the urge itself. Defiance of his wishes always created rage in him.

"Otherwise," he continued, "our deal is in jeopardy. I cannot know whether you've completed the task. If I do not have proof of death, I wouldn't know if you hadn't done as you're told until someone came along and became a problem." He smiled. "And so it would be worse for you. And then it would be worse for Mecca." He motioned to Salas.

The man stepped forward, produced a smartphone, and offered it to David.

"It is untraceable, as long as you are careful with it," Claude said. "There is one telephone number programmed in and one application installed. You will take a photo, send it to the number, and delete the photo. It will be encrypted and deleted from the application's servers once it has been viewed."

"Great. Murder Snapchat," David muttered. He took the phone and slid it into his jeans pocket.

"Keep it off unless you get a message on your usual telephone to turn it on," Claude continued. "Understood?"

"What happens to the picture that the phone number—your number, I assume—receives?"

Claude enjoyed the fact that David thought he had any authority in this situation, demanding answers. He smiled again. "It will be stored to ensure you comply as we arranged."

Alarm flashed through David's eyes but disappeared in a second. "I don't like this at all," he said in an even voice.

Claude took another sip of his brandy, enjoying the sweetness on his tongue. It paired well with the sweetness of dominance. "This is how it is to be. It can be you, or it can be your daughter. That has always been your choice."

David's anger filled the room like a scent. Claude did so enjoy the smell of an opponent who realizes he has been checkmated.

Claude motioned his man forward again. "I brought Salas here so that you might meet him. He will be your main contact point." Salas bowed to David in the manner Claude expected.

David shook his head, jaw set. "No."

The corner of Claude's mouth quirked up. "Excuse me?"

"I won't have an intermediary. I will deal with you directly."

Claude crossed one arm over his chest, leaned the other elbow in that hand, and raised his glass to his lips. He took a small sip. "You think you are the one in charge?"

"There is no 'in charge,'" David said. "We have made an agreement of equals. In return for leaving Mecca alone forever, I consented to do a series of tasks for you—*you*. Not an intermediary."

"You do not get to decide how I choose to communicate." Claude found this entire conversation amusing. Though David's brashness annoyed him, a small part admired the human's tenacity.

David leaned toward Claude. His breath, smelling of mint, brushed against Claude's skin like a feather. Salas tensed, but Claude raised a hand to still him.

"Let's be honest, Claude. Straightforward," David said. "The tasks you wish me to do will mean killing someone. I don't relish these tasks, and so I will tell you clearly, right now, that I will not kill someone for you at the request of an intermediary." He eased back. "Because I did not make this deal with an intermediary. I made it with you. So, by all means, send someone, if you'd like. Understand, though, I will only fulfill a request made by you, directly."

Claude studied the man before him. David's dusky blue eyes and stiff posture spoke of being resolute about his words.

"Very well," he said. He inclined his head. "I suppose that is not terribly unreasonable. However"—now Claude leaned in and lowered his voice—"when you hear from me, I shall expect *immediate* results."

Chapter Fifteen: Jenny

Jenny sat at Manuel's Tavern in the Highlands, a glass of tea centered on the dark wooden table in front of her. She turned on her phone to check the time. 1:12. She didn't know Helen very well, but she didn't seem the type to be late. Or, at least, not without giving a heads-up.

Me: Traffic?

She ran a finger through the cool sweat on the glass. Patience had never been a strength.

"Still waiting on your friend?" the server said as she approached. Her hair was pulled back in a ponytail with one errant dark brown lock tumbling over her forehead.

"Yeah. I'm sure she'll be here soon. She's coming from downtown, so she probably hit traffic."

"Want an appetizer or anything?"

"No, thanks. I'll wait."

"Okay. Holler when you're ready."

"Thanks."

What her mom said about Claude flitted through her mind. *"Just in case…"* Was there a cause for "just in case"? Would he come after her?

Her mom had never been one to panic or overreact in a situation. She had always taken things in stride, calmly, carefully. So there had to be something her mom thought might happen.

Was Claude behind the disappearances? Was he responsible for Helen's investigation into the deaths being quashed?

She tried to envision the small, blond boy—he really reminded her of a high school art kid—as a cold-blooded killer. It was difficult. He didn't look dangerous. He looked like he should be making a silk-screen Warhol T-shirt.

There were too many questions and not enough answers. She didn't know whether Helen had anything more on what was happening, but Jenny was impatient for the older woman to arrive. Even if there was nothing new, Helen had such a greater understanding of Visci politics and culture. Jenny was eager to learn from her.

She checked her phone again. No text from Helen. 1:28.

Calling people was not her favorite thing in the world. She often got anxiety about talking on the phone. But that would probably be the best way to get Helen. She couldn't very well text if she was driving.

The phone rang four times before going to voicemail.

Okay, now Jenny was getting concerned.

Maybe Jorge had heard from her. She sent him a text. Ten minutes later, he replied that he'd texted her during the morning, but not the afternoon.

Me: She's more than half an hour late. I'm worried.
Jorge: That's not like her. Did you call?

Me: Yes. No answer.
Jorge: I'll try.

The ice in her tea had melted into a clear layer of water on top. Jenny waited, edgy. Her phone rang. She snatched it up, hoping it was Helen, but Jorge's name flashed.

"Hey," she said.

"I tried her cell and her landline. No answer on either. I'm going to her place."

"Me too. She texted me around eleven to confirm lunch."

"I'll meet you there."

"'Kay."

Another text came through as she disconnected the call. Mecca, sending an address for their meet later.

Me: Might be late. Something came up. Not sure how long it'll take.
Mecca: K

Jenny didn't know whether to read into that short reply. She brushed it aside, dropped a five on the table, and headed to her car.

Chapter Sixteen: Mecca

"Are you sure this is a good idea?" Will asked as they approached the brownstone.

They were on a side street in Little Five Points, and Mecca didn't think this was a very good idea.

"Probably not, but we don't have another choice," Mecca said.

He grabbed her arm and stopped. When she turned, his sea-green eyes flashed with intensity. "*You* have another choice. You do not have to leave. Go back to school. I'm a grown man, you know. I can take care of myself."

"How? Your name is the name of a man born like a hundred years ago. How will you get a place to live, exactly? How will you pay your bills? With what money from what job? Do you even have a social security number?"

He let go of her arm. "I don't need to be taken care of, Mecca. You have an entire life to live. Go live it."

She frowned. "Who will help me kill the Visci?" She left the question sitting there in the air like smog over a city.

Finally, he said, "You don't have to kill Visci."

How could he say that? After everything he'd seen? After everything she'd lived through? She turned away and stomped up the steps to the brownstone. She couldn't even look at him. He heaved a sigh and followed her as she rang the front bell.

The *Star Wars* theme rang somewhere deep in the house.

They stood there, looking like idiots, she was sure, and waited. After a few minutes, she rang again. She didn't even let the theme song end before she hit the button a third time.

"Look, she's obviously not home," Will said.

The door opened. Sara stood there in a pair of dark grey cargo pants and a tank top. Her short black hair poked out in different directions, and Mecca thought she saw dark green folded into the ebony streaks. Sara's expression clouded for a moment when she made eye contact with Mecca. She glanced at Will. Then she saw the duffel back over Mecca's shoulder. "Oh, hey... Mecca, right?"

"Yeah, hey. Thanks for opening the door."

"No prob. I was downstairs. Took me a minute." She shifted her weight from one combat-booted foot to the other. "So, what do you need?"

"Could we come in for a minute? I need to ask a huge favor."

"Favor." She seemed to be weighing her options, but finally she stood to the side and held the door open. "All right. Come on."

Once they'd settled into the living room—it looked the same as before, except Sara seemed to have acquired a lamp that looked exactly like the stocking leg lamp from that Christmas movie her dad loved to watch every year.

Sara must have noticed her staring at it because she laughed and said, "Heh, I won it in this weird Christmas hack-a-thon."

"Hack-a-thon?" Mecca said, turning back to her.

"Yeah. A bunch of computer people get in a room, break into teams, then write code for some project they each come up with. We were runners up, so we got the leg lamp. Get it? Runner up?" She shrugged, obviously also not appreciating the humor in it. "Anyway, come on in. What's going on?"

They all settled down on the second-hand furniture, and now Mecca found herself even more self-conscious than before.

"Sara, this is Will," Mecca said, pointing at him as he sat down.

"Oh, yes, hi, sorry." Will stood again and held a hand out to Sara.

Sara shook it. "Hey. Nice to meetcha." She dropped back into the over-sized recliner and looked at Mecca again.

Oh man, why am I doing this? "Okay, I get that we're not friends enough to even ask this," Mecca said, "but I don't have anywhere else to go." She paused, not even sure how to ask for what she wanted.

Sara waited and tilted her head. "Uh huh. You haven't actually asked anything."

"Yeah." Mecca laughed and cringed at how high-pitched and nervous it sounded. Will watched her calmly, but she was sure he was saying he told her so in his head. *Okay, get to it, Mec.* "I was wondering if it would be okay for me and Will to crash with you for a little while. I can give you some money for rent."

Sara gave a surprised flinch. "Oh. Wow. Not sure what I was expecting, but that wasn't it." She looked from Mecca to Will and back to Mecca. "Your dad doesn't want you shacking up?"

"What? No! I mean, we're not shacking up. That isn't… No." Mecca's cheeks flushed hot, and she shook her head belatedly.

Sara laughed and held up her hands. "Okay, okay. Don't flip out. That was the only reason I could think of why you wouldn't be crashing at your dad's. I imagine he has room."

"I'm not… He and I are not really speaking right now," Mecca said. She hoped Sara wouldn't ask about it. She was also glad that Will was staying quiet for once.

"Not speaking, huh?" Her eyes bored into Mecca but then looked away. She shrugged. "He's not speaking to me either."

Mecca didn't feel the need to correct Sara about who wasn't speaking to whom.

Sara looked again at Will. She leaned back in her chair and pulled her legs up under her. "So why don't you have anywhere to stay, Will? New to town?"

"Not really," he said. "My previous employer had provided lodging, but that situation has ended."

Sara nodded, as if she bought that entire thing. Mecca didn't think she had, even though technically it was true. Of course, that situation ended because she, Mecca, had killed Will's employer.

It was complicated.

"You can't get an apartment? No savings?"

"Look," Mecca said, "if you're wanting us to sign a lease, we could have gone anywhere else. We only need a place to crash for a week or so." Mecca could figure out the rest later.

"Well, you couldn't have gone anywhere else, could you?" Sara's eyes twinkled. "You said that on my front porch."

Mecca bit back an exasperated snarl.

Sara grinned—part friendly, part competitive, if Mecca read it right. "You're welcome to stay. But there's one condition."

Mecca narrowed her eyes. "What condition?"

She leaned forward, all seriousness now. "I want you to tell me what happened to you. When we found you on that property. Your dad would never give me all the details, and I helped him a lot. I mean a *lot*. He told me some stuff, but I want to know what really happened. All of it. You tell me that, and you can stay as long as you want." She settled against the back of the chair again.

Mecca looked at Will. He wasn't any help. She'd avoided telling Josie to only now have to tell Sara. Mecca couldn't win. Sara *had* been the one to lead the people trapped in the maze to safety. And she had helped her dad do…whatever. So she at least had some idea of the level of danger involved in what was going on. *What had her dad told Sara when he'd been here?*

Sara sat there, watching her, as she warred with herself. But even as she weighed the pros and cons, there wasn't much choice. Will had no money; she only had the money her dad had given her, which she hated using.

"All right," Mecca said, finally.

Sara grinned and sat forward in her seat. "Great! Now, you were kidnapped, and I know where they kept you, obviously. Who are they, and why did they take you?"

Well that's straight to the point. Mecca looked at Will again. He raised his eyebrows, and she took it as, "You're the one who agreed to this." She scowled at him.

"They're a group called the Visci. They're... Okay, you're not going to want to believe this, but you wanted the truth. Are you *sure* you want this?"

"Yes," Sara said, without hesitation. "I want to know."

Mecca sighed. "Okay. They're not vampires, but they seem to be *like* vampires. They drink blood, and it somehow keeps them alive. They're super strong"—the memory of Claude lifting her without so much as a bead of sweat came back to her—"but I don't know a whole lot more beyond that." She looked at Will sidelong. "That's going to change soon."

"And why did they take you?" Sara's clear eyes watched her with interest.

Mecca thought about that for a longer time than she intended. "That isn't something I am ready to share with you." When Sara began to speak, she raised a hand. "Because it's very personal for me, and I don't even know you. So I'm not going to tell you that right now. I may share it with you in the future if I come to trust you.

But right now…" She shrugged. "If that means we can't stay here, then we can't stay here." She hoped she was playing this right. She wasn't lying. But she really hoped her guess that Sara would accept her reason was spot on.

The other young woman stared at her with suspicious eyes. She gave a small nod. "Okay, for now. Let's hear the rest, and I'll decide."

Mecca hoped that was a good sign.

"Why did you go back?" Sara asked. "I've been asking myself that question ever since it happened. Was it to rescue those people?"

Mecca shook her head. "I didn't even know they were there. That whole maze thing? That was crazy. I literally had no clue any of that was out there. Somehow, I'd missed the entire thing when I escaped."

Sara nodded, but didn't say anything.

"I went back because I was stupid. I thought I could end things by myself. I thought they'd never expect me to come back, so I could sneak in and have the upper hand." Mecca shook her head. "It was really, really stupid."

"I never understood why your dad didn't call the police."

Will finally chose this moment to jump in. "The police wouldn't help. They'd have come to the gate, been told everything was fine, and left."

"Even with a kidnapping?"

Will gave a soft snort. "If the officers who came to the gate tried to press, they'd have gotten an order from a superior sending them off. Calling them wouldn't have helped Mecca at all."

Will's words brought Sara's attention squarely to him. "And how do you figure in to this?"

"I was one of her captors." Will's simple explanation surprised Mecca. She hadn't thought he'd say anything at all.

Sara leaned away from him, surprised. "So you're one of these Visci?"

"No, but I was with them for a long time. Something of a prisoner. A trusted one, but still a prisoner." His voice, soft and matter-of-fact, made Mecca admire his self-control. He wasn't emotional about any of this.

"And you escaped with Mecca?"

"Something like that."

Sara looked back at her. "And your dad won't let you stay with him?"

"I told you," Mecca said. "I don't want to stay with him."

"Yeah." Sara looked thoughtful. Finally, she said, "All right. You can stay. But whatever it is you guys are up to, I want in."

That was not something Mecca wanted to hear. "What do you mean?"

Sara rolled her eyes and stood up. "I'm not an idiot. There's something going on. The things I did for your dad to help get you out are not things that happen if nothing is going on." She glanced at Will and back to Mecca. "And my guess is that whatever was going on then is still going on now. Maybe a bit different, but still going on." She crossed her arms over her chest. "And I want in."

How had her dad put Sara off? She was absolutely determined. Mecca looked at Will. He only shrugged. She frowned at him.

"She wants in. I say let her in." To Sara, he said, "How are you with killing people?"

Mecca stared at him. What the hell was he doing? "Will…"

Will put his hand up and continued to address Sara, who also stared at him. "Because that's what the plan is right now, to kill any Visci we identify. That's regardless of whether the Visci is good or bad. We're killing them all."

So that's how it is. "You're doing this now?" Mecca said, turning to face him. "Here? You couldn't brought this up privately?"

Now Will looked at her and Mecca, for the first time, fully felt their age difference. He was decades older than her, no matter how young he looked.

"I tried to speak in private, but you have been dead set against talking about it. If Sara wants in, I want to make sure she knows what she's actually getting into."

Mecca hated the feeling of needing to defend herself that welled up. "Fine. Sara, there are no good Visci. They all feed from human beings to stay alive, period. So they're all a danger."

"Every living thing eats other living things, including humans," Will said. "And you know at least two who are good."

Mecca was vaguely aware that Sara had dropped back into her chair, watching them, but she didn't care. How could he be arguing with her like this? He'd been held captive for ages!

"Why are you defending them?" she almost shouted. "How can you be defending them?"

"I'm not defending them, Mecca." His calm, level response only made her angrier. "I'm trying to tell you that they're not all like Emilia. You already *know* that though. I'm not sure why you're so intent on ignoring it."

"I'm ignoring it because I can," Mecca said, crossing her arms over her chest. Her tone sounded petulant, and she hated that.

"So you're going to kill her?" Will asked, his gaze still on her.

Why was he doing this? And in front of Sara!

"You promised you'd help me."

"I did. And I will. But you're painting all of them as evil, and they are no more or less evil than we are. Each one is their own person."

Heat burned Mecca's cheeks. In truth, it burned through her entire body. She wanted to leave. Wanted to slam through the door and disappear.

But where would she go? Back to the dorm?

And how would she hunt Visci?

"So," she said, "what are you saying?"

Will shook his head and sighed. "I'm only saying that you are coming at this without thinking. You want to be judge and executioner." His face softened now, as did his tone. "I am afraid of what being judge and executioner will do to *you*."

She knew what it would do. It would make her feel amazing for ridding the world of the Visci stench. But he obviously didn't want to consider that.

"Fine. What are you asking?"

His shoulders lifted. "I don't know. Only not to be so quick to decide who is worthy and who isn't, just by sight."

"Okay." If that was what he needed her to agree to in order to keep him on board, then that is what she'd agree to.

His gaze didn't waver, but he also didn't respond right away.

If Sara felt uncomfortable, she didn't show it. She sat, leaned back on the chair, watching them. It made *Mecca* uncomfortable to be on display like that.

Will finally gave her a nod. "All right. I feel as though you agreed to that entirely too quickly, but I will take you at your word."

When neither of them spoke again, Sara said, "Well, that was interesting." Her broad grin showed no malice. Mecca wasn't sure what sort of unicorn-fairyland Sara lived in, because she never seemed upset or angry.

Mecca was tired of being the center of attention. It was her turn to ask questions. "How do you know my dad? It's weird, him 'hanging out' with someone our age."

"He was married to my gran before she died." Sara shrugged, as if it were no big deal.

Bells rang in Mecca's head. She'd learned of her dad's previous wives while in captivity. Emilia had left files of information for Mecca to read in the periods when they'd allowed her to be awake. She'd discovered his horrible secret while chained to a bed.

"Your gran?" Mecca asked. "Grandmother?"

Sara nodded. "My mom was a kid when she died, and Dav—your dad made sure she was provided for. He still sends her checks every month." She looked around the living room. "That's how I have this. She put all the money away for me for college."

Mecca followed Sara's gaze around the room, but only heard her through a funnel. She looked back at the pretty young woman with the short-cropped curly hair that was sticking up everywhere. "What's your last name?"

"Harrington. Why? Did he mention me?"

Susan Harrington. The woman her dad had been married to before her own mom. The last woman he'd killed.

How could he be friends with the granddaughter of a woman he murdered? Her head spun, and she couldn't think clearly. She pulled in a deep breath to try to clear it.

"Mecca?" Will put a hand on her forearm.

It brought her back to herself. She shook her head. "Sorry. Sorry." She looked at Sara, who had a mixed expression on her face: concern and hope. "I was trying to work out whether I'd heard that name before, but I don't think I have."

Sara tilted her head. "It didn't seem like you haven't heard it before."

Mecca smiled and hoped it looked reassuring. "That was my thinking face. It looks funny to people who are not me."

Sara didn't look convinced but didn't pursue it. "Well, there's only one spare room, so you'll have to share it or one of you can sleep here on the sofa. Don't go in the basement unless I invite you down." Her face went serious. "That's a hard rule. Understand?"

They both nodded almost in unison.

"Thank you, Sara. I know this is weird," Mecca said.

Sara stood and gave her a brilliant smile. "This has been weird since I met your dad. Good thing I like weird."

Chapter Seventeen: Jenny

Jenny parked in the same spot she had when she'd first come to Helen's place. Jorge's small pickup truck sat in the driveway, and he was taking the porch steps in one bound.

Jenny got out of her car and hurried over, right as Jorge was unlocking the door. He met her eyes, looking grim.

They tumbled into the house together.

Everything looked perfect, just as it had been the first time she'd been here. The silence deafened her though.

"Helen?" Jorge called, cutting through the quiet.

"If she texts me asking me where the hell I am, I'm gonna feel stupid," Jenny whispered.

Jorge began moving through the downstairs, occasionally calling Helen's name. They found nothing.

"I have a terrible feeling," Jorge said as they mounted the stairs.

"Me too."

Helen's bedroom was decorated in pale yellow and dark blue. A high queen-size bed took up one wall, and a natural wood armoire graced another wall. The thick carpet underfoot dampened their steps. The room was immaculate.

To Jenny's right, the bathroom door sat ajar. Something tiny and square and black lay on the floor just inside.

"Hey." She still whispered but had no idea why. No one was here. She went to the door as Jorge turned to her.

Jenny picked up a small plastic fob with what looked like a red button. It'd been smashed. She turned it over in her hand.

"Shit." Jorge came behind her. When she glanced back, she saw him looking into the bathroom over her shoulder. Then she looked up.

The room looked like a tornado had come through. A towel rack hung halfway off the wall, the coral towels in a heap beneath it. The shower curtain had been torn down, exposing a giant jetted tub. On the counter, a stoneware bathroom set lay strewn, the lotion dispenser cracked and oozing pearly white liquid onto the granite countertop.

"Shit," Jenny echoed quietly, the plastic in her hand forgotten.

Jorge snatched it from her. "Oh no. Where did you get that?"

"It was on the floor. What is it?"

"Shit, shit, shit!" The forlorn look on his face scared her more than the disaster in the bathroom.

"Jorge! What is it?"

He reached into his collar and pulled out a corded necklace. On the end hung a plastic piece just like what she'd found, except his was intact.

"It's a panic button. Once we realized people were disappearing with regularity, Zoey set each of us up with one. If we hit it, it sends a text out to all our phones with our GPS coordinates." He looked around the room. "She must have been in the shower when they came. Maybe it was on the counter."

That would explain how it was shattered on the floor.

"I don't understand though," Jenny said. "Is she one of the ones who disappeared? Or was she taken because of what we are doing?" What *were* they doing?

Jorge shook his head. "She's a full, so…"

When he didn't finish, she followed that thought. The fulls who disappeared were never found. Always women.

She looked at him. "What do we do?"

"I don't know. I'm going to text Zoey. I'm hoping she can trace Helen's phone."

"We should call the police."

He brought his gaze up from his phone. "Really? Because they've cared about every other missing Visci woman?"

Jenny bristled under his sarcastic tone. "But Helen was one of their own, in a way."

"I don't think it works that way," he said as he looked back to his text. "But if you really think that will make any difference, we can make an anonymous call after we leave."

That made sense. If a powerful Visci ran the police—she was beginning to be paranoid enough to think they ran everything now—then she and Jorge couldn't be there when the cops arrived. If Helen were targeted like the other Visci women, it wouldn't matter. But if she were targeted because of the questions she was raising about the disappearances, she wouldn't want them to risk being captured too.

They went back downstairs, and Jorge made a stop in the back of the house. When he returned, the laptop they'd used to call Arabella was tucked under his arm.

"We don't need them finding this," he said. "There probably isn't anything on it. Helen was good about that. But it's better to be safe."

Jenny nodded.

"Zoey texted. Helen's phone is on, but it'll take a little while for Zoey to find it."

"What do we do in the meantime?"

"Go home. I'll let you know when we get anything."

"No way. I want to help."

"There's nothing to do, Jenny. I promise I'll tell you when there is."

She didn't like it. But he was probably right. Until Zoey could figure out where Helen was, there was nothing any of them could do.

Helpless. Again.

This shit was for the birds.

Chapter Eighteen: Claude

His cell phone vibrated against his chest and Claude took it out of his inside jacket pocket. Treiste.

"Yes?"

"Your problem has been taken care of."

"Did you sedate her?"

"I did. And she has been returned to her room. She must rest for a day or two, but she will be fine. I will check on her again tomorrow."

"Very good. And the other?"

"The new test subject may work out. It is too soon to tell. I have made advances with each one and we are closer than we have ever been. It's quite exciting." That, Claude could hear in Treiste's voice. He sounded almost like a small child.

"When will I see your results?"

"Give me a few days. I want to make sure it's taken. There will not be much to see in these early stages, but as long as she remains strong, we should have good results."

"Excellent. I look forward to seeing those results. Soon."

"Of course."

Claude clicked off the call. He had never particularly liked Treiste, but the German was the only one for this project.

If this new test subject worked out, then Claude could move on to the next phase. The one for which he would need Carolyn Barron.

He turned his attention back to the security film he'd paused. The image was grainy, but he zoomed in on the frozen frame.

A long-shot of a residential hallway, looking through a house from the front door to the far end where the kitchen was. Several people stood in the frame. None of the faces were familiar, but he would have Salas rectify that. Well, none except one. And that one he recognized immediately.

"What are you up to, Mecca?" he whispered.

Chapter Nineteen: Mecca

Mecca crammed a couple T-shirts into the top drawer of the oak dresser. Will had stayed downstairs to talk to Sara. Had he been right? Should she let all this go? Stay at the dorm, finish her schoolwork?

She didn't understand how he expected her to do that. These creatures were monsters who preyed on humans. Who'd preyed on her. How did he expect her to just let it go?

She grabbed another handful of clothes from her duffel, not paying any attention to what went where.

The doorbell rang below, and footsteps sounded along the wooden floor. She was only registering these sounds on the outskirts of her mind. She'd started thinking about how they would find other Visci to kill. And before her dad found them for Claude.

The rage at her father simmered below the surface, like a surging tide trapped by a dam. She didn't know how long the dam would hold.

Voices filtered through from the hallway and a knock came at her mostly closed door. Will pushed it open.

"Jenny's here." He stepped in enough to let her best friend through. "I'll be downstairs." When he left, he closed the door behind him.

They stood, looking at each other, the awkward sitting in the air like humidity, heavy and thick.

Jenny glanced at her duffel and the half-open drawer. "You moved out of the dorm."

"Yeah…" Mecca turned back to the duffel and fiddled with some socks, finally scooping them up and going to the dresser. "Things have gotten weird."

Weird. That was the word of the day, wasn't it?

Jenny nodded. "No kidding." Thunder rumbled overhead.

When Mecca faced her again, Jenny stood, watching her, expectant.

"I just…" Mecca pulled in a deep breath and pushed on. "I didn't like the way we left things."

"The way *you* left things."

She nodded. "Yeah." She didn't know what else to say or how to fix it.

So they both stood there.

As the awkward silence grew, Jenny said, "Why did you call me here, Mec? To make me watch you unpack?" She waved an arm around the room. "I don't have time for this right now." She stalked toward the door. Rain hammered on the roof above them.

Mecca flinched. Jenny had never dismissed her like that. "I was trying to apologize."

Jenny whirled and her eyes flashed. "So fucking apologize! There is too much going on for me to spend an hour pulling your feelings out of you." She paced toward Mecca, stopping two feet from her and spreading her arms. "So if you want to apologize, I'm right here. Apologize."

Mecca blinked slowly. "What the hell is up with you?"

Jenny pinched her lips together and shook her head. Her voice came low and quiet. "My dad is dead. The people my mom comes from did it. My best friend, who can kill anyone I care about—me included—by just touching them, isn't sure whether I'm a real person or 'one of them.' And 'one of them' who has become my friend is now missing and may be dead too. That's what the hell is up with me."

Mecca could barely follow everything she said. "You think I'd kill you?" How had this become their normal conversation?

"You haven't told me you won't."

"Don't be stupid. Of course I won't."

"What about my mom?"

"Huh?"

"She's Visci. Are you going to kill her?"

"No!"

"And my frien—" Jenny stopped and then flinched as if Mecca had slapped her. She blew out a short breath and blurted, "Did you kill Helen?"

"Huh? Who's Helen?"

Jenny narrowed her eyes. "Maybe you're the reason Visci are disappearing and coming up dead."

"Jenny. What...in...the...*hell*...are you talking about?"

Mecca couldn't make heads or tails of any of it.

A voice from downstairs yelled, "Jenny!" And then, not quite so loud, "Where is she? I know she's here!"

The voice wasn't one Mecca recognized. Sounded like a woman. Jenny glanced at the door, her brows squished together and a frown pulling down the edges of her lips.

Mecca followed her gaze. "Who is that?"

"I'm not sure," Jenny said, already distracted and opening the door.

Chapter Twenty: Jenny

When Jenny got toward the bottom of the stairs, she found Zoey in the foyer, dripping wet, standing almost nose to nose with Will. He stood rail-straight, an intense expression of control on his face.

"…know she's here." She waved her phone to the side and pointed at the screen. "See?"

"Zoey," Jenny said, rescuing Will from having to respond. He stepped back as she reached the foyer and Zoey turned to her.

The other woman's short, usually spiky hair lay plastered to her head, the tips, currently blue, looking purple black. Her words came in a rush. "You need to call your mom right now and find out what the hell is going on with the hybrids."

"And how did you find me?" Jenny hadn't even known she was coming here.

Zoey waved a hand in the air, as if she had better things to do. "Tracker on your car."

"What?" A tracker? They were spying on her?

"Never mind. You need to call your mom. Jorge is missing."

"What do you mean, missing? Helen is missing. Not Jorge."

Zoey huffed and rolled her eyes. "They are *both* missing." The smell of cinnamon floated in the air. "He was supposed to meet me at the apartment, but he hasn't come home, and I can't find him anywhere."

Jenny stared at her.

"We're roommates." Zoey spoke slowly, as if Jenny were four years old. "He was supposed to come home. He always comes home. And he isn't answering texts. He *always* answers texts." She pointed a finger at Jenny. "You need to talk to your mom. See if she can find out where they've taken him."

A girl stood from the overstuffed chair in the living room and moved to the edge of the foyer, watching intently. Her black spiky hair shot through with emerald green seemed a strange juxtaposition of Zoey's usual style.

"Who the hell is Jorge?" Mecca asked from behind her. "And why would you need to talk to your mom?"

Jenny wanted to scream. This was not how she envisioned telling Mecca about the other pieces of this mess. She didn't turn around, but raised a hand to hold Mecca off for a moment.

Zoey looked back and forth between Jenny and Mecca, her brow creased between the eyes. She shook her head. "Doesn't matter," she mumbled. Zoey didn't seem to be talking to her. Then those green eyes focused back on her own. "You need to talk to your mom."

"I doubt she knows anything. I don't think the Council is after you guys."

Zoey took half a step toward her and wagged her finger between them. "You mean 'us guys.' And if you believe they're not after us, you're stupid." Her voice lowered again. "Of course, you're probably protected because of who you are."

Mecca burst forward from behind her. "Jenny, what the hell is going on?"

"That's a great question," said the chick with the dark hair. "I'd love to know what's going on and who's dripping in my front room." So this was her place that Mecca was crashing in. The young woman gave Zoey a grin, and Jenny thought hearing those words coming out of most people would be snarky as hell. But they hadn't been. She turned her gaze to Mecca. "And your friend, too."

Mecca sighed. "This is Jenny."

She noted the lack of "best friend," which they'd been appending to their introductions of each other since they were seven. A piece of Jenny's heart broke at that tiny, little thing.

"Hi, Jenny. I'm Sara." She extended her hand with what seemed a genuine smile.

Jenny shook, hoping the awkward didn't drop off her. "Um... Hi."

"And your friend?" Sara spoke as if they'd run into each other at a restaurant. Not all crowded into the entranceway of her house, acting like a bunch of lunatics.

"This is Zoey," Jenny said.

Zoey raised a hand in wave to Sara. "Hey." Also as if it were the most normal thing in the world.

Was Jenny actually the one acting like a lunatic? Everyone else seemed like this was all perfectly normal.

"Great to meet you. Now what were you saying about someone being missing?"

The blank look on Zoey's face was almost comical. She gave her head a little shake and turned her gaze back to Jenny. "You need to talk to your—" A weird siren-sound came from her jacket. It rang out like a foghorn for a few seconds, getting louder when Zoey yanked it from her pocket.

"That's him!"

"You have a siren as a ring tone?" Sara asked.

Zoey looked at her as if she were the biggest idiot in the room. "No. He hit his panic button." Her attention went to the phone. She unlocked it, swiped, and tapped a couple times. "I've got his coordinates. I have to go." She turned toward the door, never looking up from her phone.

Jenny peered at the others, especially Mecca, and she was sure the weird panic that had welled in her showed in her face. She grabbed Zoey's arm. "You can't go alone."

Zoey paused, surprised, and yanked her arm away. "I have to go."

"We're coming with you," she blurted.

Zoey stared at her, shock clearly etched on her face. And when Jenny glanced around at the others, the same expressions were reflected there.

"We can't let her go alone." Jenny grabbed her coat from the hook on the wall behind her. "Come on."

Sara grinned now, her wet floor forgotten. "I'm in!"

"Mecca?" Jenny said. She hated the begging quality of her voice.

"I don't even know what the hell is going on."

"You can prove you're not the one who's kidnapping and killing hybrids by helping us find Jorge." Jenny didn't believe Mecca could be behind the disappearances. Not really.

"*Who* is Jorge?" She all but threw her hands up in the air.

"He's a friend," Jenny said. "Is that enough?"

Mecca stared at her, eyes hard. And for the first time, Jenny wondered if their friendship would survive their secrets.

Zoey huffed. "Oh for fuck's sake. Kiss and make up or don't. But I'm not waiting around."

Jenny waited for some response from Mecca, but her best friend—former?—said nothing.

"Who has taken Jorge?" Will's voice slid through the heavy silence.

"We don't know," Zoey said. "But I'm betting her mom knows."

Jenny spun on her heel. "She doesn't. The Council isn't taking them."

"You can't be sure of that," Zoey shot back.

Will ignored the back and forth. "Is he Visci?"

At the word, all eyes shifted toward him.

"We all know they exist. And I can't think of any other reason that she"—he pointed a finger at Zoey—"wouldn't call the police."

Zoey turned on Jenny. "Who in the hell are these people?"

"*You're* asking that?" Mecca almost shouted.

Jenny puffed out a breath. "Would everyone calm down for a second, please?" How had this gotten so out of control? When they all looked at her, she continued. "Jorge is a friend. Yes, he is Visci. A hybrid."

Sara, who'd been leaning nonchalantly against the wall, straightened up and seemed to listen more closely.

"Visci have been disappearing from the city. And other cities too. Earlier, another friend, Helen, was kidnapped too. Cops seem to be in someone's pocket. But we don't know whose yet."

"Can we *go*?" Zoey said.

"Yes," Jenny replied, her gaze skimming everyone else's. She pulled her jacket on. If they had to rescue Jorge themselves, they'd try, at least. She really wished her best friend could support her. But if Mecca didn't, then she didn't.

Jenny tried not to think about that bit, though. She couldn't stop it from hurting her heart.

"Do you have any weapons?" Will asked, looking at Sara.

"Oh!" Sara squealed. Well, maybe it wasn't an actual squeal, but it sounded close enough. "I get to use my TASER again! Oh man...yay! I'll be right back." Her eyes shone brightly as she rushed to the door beneath the stairs. She pressed her thumb to a keypad and the metallic *clunk* of a lock disengaging sounded. Then she was gone, through the door.

Will looked at the others. "I doubt a TASER is going to do much good. If they're snatching Visci, they'll be armed and there won't only be humans doing the job." The intensity of his gaze made a little ball of dread settle in the pit of Jenny's stomach.

Since she'd developed her Visci strength and quickness, she'd never feared for her safety. But Will's words made her wonder how much good those benefits would be up against another Visci. Perhaps an older, stronger, more experienced Visci.

"I don't have anything but myself," Zoey said.

Sara bounded up the basement stairs and pushed the door shut behind her, as she waved the TASER she held in her hand. "Got it! Man, this is gonna be awesome."

"Do you have anything else we can use to defend ourselves? Any guns?"

Sara gave him a blank look. "Um. No. Not a gun person."

"A TASER person," Zoey said, flatly.

"Yep," Sara said with a grin.

Jenny didn't think Sara got that Zoey was mocking her. Or maybe she did but just didn't care.

"Can we go now?" Zoey asked, moving to the door.

Will looked at Mecca. After a long moment, she gave a long sigh and nodded.

Jenny held in a gasp of relief.

Will tossed a coat to Mecca and pulled on his own bomber jacket. "This is a really bad idea."

-->>*<<--

They'd piled into Zoey's car, an old maroon sedan that had looked almost black in the rainy darkness. Jenny sat beside Zoey while the other three crammed into the back. Dark grey seats had threadbare patches. Nicks and cuts marred the dashboard, and the entire car smelled like pickles. Jenny cracked the window as they made their way toward the highway. Fresh air and raindrops hit her face.

Zoey hadn't spent much money on the car, clearly, but on her gadgets...

A full tablet-sized screen sat on a mount between their seats, with a mapped-out route on the night-dimmed display. Zoey's phone was in a second mount on the dashboard near her door, its screen dark. Zoey herself clutched the wheel tightly, with the occasional glance at the map.

"Cool setup," Sara said from behind Jenny. "What is it?"

Zoey rattled off a name and some specs that Jenny couldn't follow.

"Nice," Sara said.

"Has anyone thought of what we'll do when we get there? Wherever 'there' is," Will said. He'd been crammed in the middle.

Zoey said, "Rescue Jorge."

"Ah," Will said. "Well, that's that, I suppose."

"He's right," Jenny said. "We don't know what we're walking into. We can't go running in. If he *is* in danger—"

"He is," Zoey said. "He wouldn't have pushed his panic button if he weren't."

"Why do you guys have panic buttons?" Sara asked.

"Because people like us are being kidnapped."

Mecca muttered, "Not people." And Will put a hand on her arm. She glared at him.

If Zoey heard her, which Jenny was pretty sure she had, she didn't act like it, instead continuing. "About a year ago, we started noticing a pattern when the bodies of hybrids turned up."

Jenny's adrenaline spiked as Zoey spoke. She hadn't even gotten to tell Mecca anything about hybrids or full bloods or the tensions between them. But Zoey kept going.

"We discovered that there were more hybrids missing than had been killed. So we connected our phones, so we could track each other's movements and we created secret panic buttons for ourselves." She reached beneath her sweater and pulled out a pendant.

Jenny had seen that before. "Helen had something like that, but it was a key fob. It was broken on the floor of her bathroom."

Zoey cut her a sidelong glance. "Yes. I just told you we created them for ourselves."

Jenny sighed. "I mean that I don't see a button."

Zoey flipped hers over. "It's on the back. A big button on a necklace wouldn't be so secret, would it?" She snorted. "Duh."

The constant ridicule was getting on Jenny's nerves.

Sara chimed in from the backseat, saving Zoey from Jenny's wrath. "What exactly does the button do when you hit it?"

Zoey dropped the pendant behind her sweater again and said, "It pings the satellites. Then it connects to the nearest cell tower and sends a single text to all of our phones with our coordinates at that moment."

Silence settled for a moment as they pulled up to a red light.

"Okay, that's pretty cool," Sara said.

"Thanks, I guess."

Jenny thought about Jorge, grabbing that pendant he'd worn and pushing the button. "We still need a plan, though. If we don't get an idea of what's going on wherever we're going, we could end up in the same situation as Jorge is. If that happens, we won't be able to rescue him at all."

Zoey shoved the car into Park and turned bodily in the seat. "I'm not an idiot." She tapped the tablet a few times, which brought up the satellite view of a house marked by a big purple dot. "We'll park there" — she pointed to a street around the corner — "and cut through the side yard here." Her finger traveled the path as she spoke. "There are enough of us to circle around the house and have a look before we go in. It's not very big."

The screen changed to a web page with photos of both an aerial view and a front view. It was a small ranch house with a single-car garage on the left, along with a gravel driveway. She was right. It didn't look very big.

Zoey pointed to data on the right side of the page. "Three bedroom, one bathroom. Fourteen hundred square feet. Three-quarter-acre lot, but it looks like most of that is trees." Her finger tapped the overhead photo, and it got bigger. "Just a couple hundred feet through the side yard." Three more taps and the map came back up.

She swiveled and grabbed her phone. She unlocked it and tossed it at Sara, who scrambled to keep it from hitting the floor.

"Put your number in there. I'll make a group text." The light turned green, and she faced front again, putting the car back into gear. "And for God's sake, turn your phone sound off. All of you."

The four of them looked at each other. *Where had all that come from?*

And then they were moving again, into the turn lane to get onto the interstate.

"Apparently, we do have a plan," Will said, as Sara handed the phone to him.

Chapter Twenty-One: Mecca

Zoey parked the car exactly where she had said, and they all tumbled out into the cold, damp. The rain had slowed as they'd driven, and Mecca was glad. Her coat was warm, but not waterproof. As it was, getting rained on when they'd left Sara's had made the coat wet enough to send a chill through her when the wind hit as they gathered on the driver's side. She pulled the coat tighter.

"Hang on," Zoey said as she tapped on her phone. She looked at Mecca. "Which one are you?"

"What?"

"Sara or Mecca? Which one are you?"

Seriously? "Mecca," she said, her voice flat. Why was she even *here*?

Zoey went back to tapping frantically and then said, "Okay, check your phones."

Mecca's vibrated in her pocket as she reached for it.

Unknown: test

Mecca didn't bother adding Zoey to her contacts. She wouldn't be talking to the chick after tonight.

"Now, everyone reply with your names."

More texts came in, but only one from an Unknown. Sara. Mecca did add her to the contacts list.

"All right," Zoey said. She had taken on a much more mature and stable demeanor than before. It irritated Mecca as much as the bitchy demeanor. "You guys break into pairs. One pair goes round the far side of the house, one the near side. Check the windows and see if there are any doors. If you see anything, text. I'll check the front."

"That's not very good, tactically," Will said. "That leaves four people in the back and one in the front."

Mecca stared at him. Why did he care if a Visci wanted to put herself in extra danger?

"I'll be fine," Zoey said.

Now Mecca turned her gaze to the Visci. "What are you hiding?"

Zoey only stared back.

Jenny stepped in. "Will is right. It doesn't make sense to split up that way."

Zoey made a disgusted sound in her throat. "There is more ground to cover around the sides. Didn't you look at the photos? It's short in the front and long behind."

It *was* short in the front and long behind, now that Mecca thought about it. But she hadn't noted that when she'd looked at the photos. A glance at the others told her that they hadn't either.

"Okay," Sara said. "So snoop at the windows and the doors. Are we going in if something is open?"

"No," Zoey said quickly. "Text if something is open. We can decide what to do once the entire place is assessed." She waited a short moment. "Any other questions? Or can we actually go now?"

"Let's go!" Sara said, a grin on her face.

Mecca didn't get her enthusiasm. Sara's life must have been spectacularly boring if she was so excited to run into an unknown situation for a complete stranger. And a Visci, at that.

The whole situation stank to high heaven. Mecca wished she hadn't come. In the end, the only real reason she had put on her coat and joined them was because Jenny went. Mecca didn't have any idea whether it was because she felt guilty or because she didn't want Jenny to get hurt. Everything about this was confusing.

Their small group began to move through the trees of the side yard. Mecca dropped back and fell into step with Jenny. She still didn't know how she felt about Jenny being Visci. "You could have told me," she said. And she wished Jenny had. Then maybe she wouldn't feel so torn, so betrayed.

"We both could have told each other," Jenny whispered.

Old, wet leaves underfoot brought the sweet, sickly smell of rot to her nose. Jenny was right, of course. She swallowed past the thickness in her throat. "Yeah." They walked in silence for several moments, both of them watching the others in front. Finally, Mecca said, "I don't know how to relate to you now."

Jenny sighed. "What do you want me to tell you? Maybe I should not know how to relate to you too."

"None of my kind kidnapped you."

"No, you only got my dad murdered."

Mecca gave a pained sound, but said nothing. What could she say? Jenny was totally right. She had gotten Jenny's dad murdered. Mecca blinked back tears and sped up her pace until she'd moved ahead and joined the others.

An open yard ahead led to a small ranch with a gravel road leading to the single attached garage. The house sat a couple hundred feet off the road. The narrow front was much more obvious in person, with only the garage, a door painted a dark color, and a double window. Though small, the front also had a wooden porch with a tiny patio table and two chairs tucked into the end.

Droplets of cold rain fell from the leafy canopy.

"You guys ready?" Zoey said. "Don't forget to make sure your phones are on vibrate."

"Ready!" Sara said.

"I don't think this is a good idea," Will said, quietly.

Zoey swung her gaze to him. "We have to get Jorge out. If he leaves here, he will end up dead."

"I'm still going with you," Will said. "But they're likely to have weapons. We have nothing. What if there are more of them than us?"

"Let's see what's in there and then decide, okay?" Jenny said. "We can't be sure what we're up against until we look."

Will nodded. "Very well."

Sara gave him a weird face, but Mecca didn't care anymore. Not about any of it. She wanted to get this over with. The irony that she was helping the very beings that she wanted to eradicate was not lost on her. But it was no longer that simple. How could she eradicate Jenny? She couldn't. And now where did that leave her?

Mecca pushed the thoughts away. She didn't have time to get all wrapped up in it now.

But she didn't disagree with Will. This was a bad idea.

They sprinted across the yard on silent feet. The wet ground helped with that. Mecca broke off with Will and moved to the far side of the house, Jenny and Sara the near side. Zoey started up the five porch steps slowly.

Right as Mecca and Will had gotten to the corner, she heard the crunch of gravel. A car was coming!

She and Will both crouched low and peeked around. A black sedan pulled up and stopped in front of the garage door. Mecca looked past the car and saw Zoey frozen on the front deck. She was in plain sight.

The driver's door opened, and a man got out. He wore something like a trench coat over what looked like blue hospital scrubs with white tennis shoes. He closed his door and opened the door of the back seat. As he reached in, Zoey hopped over the side banister of the porch, into a bush. Mecca released the breath she hadn't realized she'd been holding.

Jenny's head was peeking around the other corner of the house, right beside where Zoey now crouched in the bushes.

The man took a large black satchel out of the car. He took the porch steps two at a time and knocked loudly on the door. It opened, but Mecca couldn't see who stood in the doorway. Whoever it was invited the man in and the light from inside scissored to black as the door closed behind him.

Her pocket vibrated. She pulled her phone out as Will did the same.

Unknown: Keep to the plan.

She looked at him. He shrugged. She shoved the phone back in her pocket with a scowl. Before they made their way down the line of the house, she glanced back to the porch. Zoey straddled the banister as she climbed back onto the porch. Mecca shook her head.

"That girl is gonna get killed," she whispered.

Will had already started down the yard. She caught up with him at the first window, which gave them a view of the garage. Inside sat a light-colored passenger van with writing on the side. She couldn't make out what it said. She looked at Will, and he shook his head.

They moved on. She couldn't shake the ominous feeling that seemed to be settling over her. The next three windows had blinds inside, which had been closed. Mecca searched for breaks or misalignment in the blinds, but they were all perfect. She swore under her breath.

Will put a finger to his lips, and she scowled at him. He pulled her close and put his mouth right against her ear. His fresh, clean scent filled her senses. "They have heightened hearing." He spoke in such a low tone, it was barely a breath against her skin. "Don't say anything unless you have to." When he pulled away, he gave her an intense stare.

She nodded.

The last window on their side did not have closed blinds. Light shone bright onto the grass in front of them. They both approached cautiously. Mecca leaned to the side to get a view.

Inside was a kitchen. The cabinets, wood painted a stark white, lined three of the walls on the other side of the room. An old white refrigerator was tucked into a crevice between two counters. It had a pull-down handle and rounded corners. It probably wasn't an inch taller than she was.

A scuffed wooden table with four spindly chairs sat closest to their window. The man from the car stood beside it, his satchel on top. He was in the middle of shrugging off his coat, and Mecca had been right. He wore hospital scrubs.

She glanced at Will, but he was studying the man, or maybe his satchel, with intensity.

Another man must have been just out of sight. Mecca thought he might be in the doorway to the kitchen. The sound of their conversation could be heard, but Mecca couldn't make out any words.

The men spoke for another minute, and the man from the car draped his long coat over a kitchen chair, before he palmed the handle of the satchel and hoisted it off the table. It must have been heavier than it looked. He left, following the other man out.

Mecca looked at Will again. His eyes were a bit wide, but he said nothing. He nodded toward the corner of the building. Turning that way would take them to the back of the house where the others should be. She nodded.

When they rounded the corner, Jenny and Sara had already arrived and Zoey was coming around the other corner at the same time. She motioned them to her side and a few feet away from the house.

"The living room is empty," she said. "But there is a covered window between there and here."

Jenny and Sara nodded.

Will told them what they'd seen on their side.

"Most of our windows had blinds too," Mecca said.

"Not blinds. Covered. With a blanket."

"That seems weird," Jenny said. "Why blinds in the others and a blanket there?"

"Sound reduction?" Sara asked. When they all looked at her, confused. "Podcasts. I put up blankets in the corner for when I'm recording. They dampen sound."

For the first time, Zoey seemed at a loss. "I don't know. Maybe?"

"What do we do now?" Sara asked.

Before Zoey could respond, Will spoke up. "I have an idea."

Mecca was glad that she didn't have to listen to Zoey talking again. Though the Visci looked at Will with a veneer of contempt, she didn't interrupt him.

"There are three options for where he might be. We had three windows with blinds on our side. One is likely a bathroom." He looked at Zoey. "It's only a one-bathroom house, right?"

She nodded.

"So we can rule one of those out. We just can't be sure which one. Then there's the other window. The one with the blankets." He paused for a second and seemed to decide what he wanted to say next. "If I had to bet, I would bet that is where he is. But there's no way to be sure until we get inside."

"I think that's where he'd be too," Zoey said. Her haughty look had been replaced by one of agreement.

"Did you guys see anyone? We saw the guy from the car and one other."

Jenny shook her head, as did Sara.

"So we don't have any idea how many people are in there besides Jorge," Will said, the frown reaching deeply into his eyes. "I don't like this."

"We have to do something," Zoey said.

Will nodded. "I know. But I don't like it." He ran a hand over his face and nodded again. "Okay, we'll need a distraction. We don't have a lot of options, so let's go old school."

Mecca grinned at his use of slang. Will still spoke pretty formally most of the time. And since his real age was…well, old, him using "old school" was especially funny. It sounded weird coming out of his mouth though.

"The plan is to break windows in different places, spaced apart by five or ten seconds. Zoey, you'll throw a stone into the first window on our side. It's the garage. That will get them as far away from the room with the blanket as possible without bringing them outside. It will keep them moving while I pick the lock on the back door."

"You know how to pick locks?" Sara asked.

"I had a questionable childhood."

Sara grinned. "Cool."

He gave her a quizzical look and shook his head. "Okay, Zoey, you'll break the window in the garage on that side." He pointed to where he and Mecca had come along the side of the house. "Jenny, you'll do the living room window on the other side. And last, Sara will take the other living room window." He pointed at her. "As soon as your glass breaks, you get back here."

"What about Mecca?" Jenny asked.

Mecca wasn't sure whether it was because Jenny was concerned about her or… *Or what, Mecca? Jenny wants to sabotage me?* She didn't like her own thoughts, but had no idea how to stop them.

"Mecca's going to be back here with me," Will said, turning his sea-green eyes on her. "She's going to coordinate the timing via text message."

Zoey rolled her eyes. "That's dumb. We can throw after we hear the previous window break."

"What kind of lock is on the door?" Will asked.

Zoey looked taken aback. "I don't know."

"Neither do I. If it takes longer, we will need space between the breaks. And there is no way for any of you to know whether it is taking longer."

He seemed really sure of himself in making this plan. Mecca wondered whether he'd done something like this before. She made a note to ask him about his "questionable childhood."

Zoey nodded, but didn't say anything more.

"We go in as a group. Sara, because you're last, we may already be inside by the time you come around. That's okay. Stay outside."

"Why do I have to stay outside?"

Will looked at Mecca. It took a moment for her to realize what he was trying to convey. Sara knew Jenny and Zoey were Visci, even if she didn't know that meant they were stronger than humans. But Sara didn't know about Mecca's gift.

Mecca sighed and said, "You're the only one without defenses."

Sara stared at her for a long moment. She gave a glance to Zoey and Jenny and then looked back at Will. "Fine."

He nodded and continued. "We get in, get Jorge, and get out. Deal?"

Mecca wondered what they'd do once they got Jorge out of the house. It was still a long way to the car.

"Okay," Sara said. "So, rocks." She started searching around the yard.

"Or wood," Mecca said, nodding toward the trees that edged both sides of the property.

"Mecca will send you each a text when it's time for your distraction."

Various nods and sounds of agreement, and then the other three set off on their search for something to throw and to get into position.

As they headed toward the back door, Will pulled a wallet from his back pocket and slid two small, thin metal tools from inside a flap.

"You have lock-picking tools in your wallet?" Mecca asked. *Who does that?*

Will shrugged. "I was too old to be a Boy Scout, but I like their motto."

"Not being a boy…" Mecca shrugged.

"Be prepared."

"Ah. Still. Weird."

He smiled. "Well, we do know weird in this group, don't we?"

That was a fact.

"Send a text," he whispered. "Ask if they're ready."

Mecca did. After a moment, they'd all responded. "Yep."

"Okay, let's go. When I nod, send a text. Remember, Zoey first, then Jenny, then Sara."

Adrenaline made her skin feel jumpy. Now that they were doing it, it struck her that he'd been right. This was a bad idea. She was a live wire.

Light splayed a white box onto the concrete patio that they walked through. Mecca hoped it was enough for Will to see. He crouched and looked at the doorknob. She bent down beside him, not wanting to be seen through the window if anyone came into the kitchen.

Then he nodded.

Mecca sent the first text. As soon as the crash of glass came to them, Will had his tools in the knob and fiddled with them. No noise came from inside, but

Mecca couldn't imagine there wasn't a response. The pull to peek through the window was strong, but she stayed beside Will.

He continued to do whatever it was a lock pick did, but it felt like it was taking way too long. Finally, he nodded again.

Mecca sent the second text.

Glass crashed from the other side of the house as Zoey rounded the corner and stepped onto the patio.

This time, the vibration of boots along the floor inside was obvious. Someone ran toward the front of the house.

"That's two," Zoey whispered, and she crouched beside them.

Mecca thought that was a dumb observation. Of course that was two windows.

"Shh," Will said. And he nodded for the third time.

Mecca sent the final text and Jenny came around her corner. The crash of Sara's window came to them.

Finally, a soft *click-click* came from the lock, and Will let out a breath. He looked back at them as he wrapped his hand around the knob. One final nod and everyone nodded with him. He turned the handle, and they barreled into the brightly lit kitchen.

Chapter Twenty-Two: Jenny

In the chaos of them blasting inside, the weirdest thing came to Jenny. The place reminded her a bit of the shotgun houses they'd been to over Spring Break last year in New Orleans. The kitchen took up the entire back of the house and a narrow hall went straight to the other side. She could see the front door from where they stood.

Zoey, who'd entered before her, made a mad dash for the hall. A guy stood inside an archway to the left — a dining room? He raised a gun. But Zoey, like a tiny, spiky-haired bolt of lightning, got to him first. She ducked her head and plowed her shoulder right into his gut. They fell in a crashing tangle of limbs.

Jenny started in the same direction when a man suddenly appeared in the hall on the other end of the house, close to the front door. From here, it looked as if the hallway opened into a living room and that was where he'd been until a moment ago. Now *he* raised his gun.

"Get down!" Jenny yelled as she took cover around a corner. Will grabbed Mecca and dove to the other side, around a cabineted corner.

From her angle, Jenny saw Zoey wrestling with the man she'd tackled. They grappled their way into the hall. This made the man by the door pause in his shots. But then the two on the ground rolled into the dining room. A bullet whizzed just above Jenny's head. She jerked back to safety. Her heart thumped everywhere—her ears, her throat, her chest. Sweat sprang up on her skin.

"How are we going to get by him?" Jenny called to Will.

He didn't respond right away, only gave her a grim glance before he peeked around his corner very quickly. "We're pinned. I don't know how we're—"

Th-th-th-th-th!

What the hell?

A bullet shot threw the kitchen and lodged itself high on the wall behind her. Then nothing but the *th-th-th* sound, and Zoey, several feet away, punching the other guy.

Jenny peeked around the corner, but all she could see was the feet of the man who'd been shooting at them. He was on his side on the floor, with his lower legs sticking into the hall. His calves and feet were still, but straight as a board.

There seemed to be movement across the hall from him, and in the split second it took her to shift her gaze, another shot rang out from a barrel she could just see. A scream from the living room. A female scream.

There was no time to think. She raced down the hall. She needed to get there before this new person had time to pin them again. Visci blood sang in her veins as she put on more speed than any human.

The man stood at the inside door to the garage, and he was just shifting to face her direction when she slammed into him. The gun flew from his hand as they fell back onto the concrete floor. It skittered beneath the van parked there.

The man's head slammed against the floor hard enough that Jenny thought it should have cracked right open.

It didn't.

His brown eyes clouded for a second but quickly cleared. He drew back his arm. Just as she realized he was going to hit her, fire exploded in her jaw. She flew backward through the doorway.

Ragged pain ripped up her torso as she landed squarely on her hip.

The man got to his feet so fast, Jenny didn't even see him. He came at her. Everything moved like lightning. She skittered away on her backside, trying to get to her friends. To safety.

But he was on her, the weight of him pinning her, keeping her from moving. His fingers wrapped around her throat. Her heart felt like it would explode. She kept trying to move down the hall but now he was squeezing her, and she couldn't get air. Couldn't get breath.

Voices yelled from far away. Voices she thought she recognized.

She beat against the man, but even with her strength, she couldn't match him. His face contorted above her, until it looked like a fun-house apparition, all swirls and weird angles. Except his eyes. Dark eyes. Black eyes.

Black dots. At the edge of her vision. She tried to gasp, but there was nothing there. Her hands flailed uselessly against his.

She wouldn't close her eyes. If she was going to die, she'd make sure he'd see them. Her eyes. Make him watch.

His grip tightened more. As if it really could. She struggled beneath him, but his weight... His weight.

She wished her mother was here.

"Jenny!"

She tried to call out to her mom, but there were no words. Because there was no breath.

The blackness around the edges of the man closed in. Taking over.

No air. Just his weight, his crushing weight on her body, on her neck.

Air.

She gulped in a thin mouthful.

His grip had loosened, but only a bit. Barely enough.

She opened her eyes. She didn't remember closing them. She hadn't meant to close them.

Above her the man—he looked smaller, older—struggled with...someone.

The vision swam.

Brown skin.

Brown hair.

Mecca.

No! He'll kill you! You're human!

She gasped again, and the air was still there. All there. Plentiful. She sucked it in, her throat on fire.

And the man got smaller.

His eyes.

He looked back at her, and his eyes held panic. Raw fear. A part of her fed on that.

Beyond his shoulder, Mecca stood, her hands on his back. Her eyes were wide open, but she didn't seem to be seeing Jenny. Or the man. Her eyes focused on something in between Mecca herself and the man withering beneath her.

The weight on Jenny lightened, and she had enough wits to scramble away, her heels skidding on the linoleum floor of the hall.

Then someone was behind her, hands touching her shoulders. "Shh," came the male voice. "It's okay. You're okay."

"Holy shit." A woman.

Jenny couldn't make her mind recognize the voices, but she knew them, she was sure.

Everything was quiet, except for soft sobs coming from somewhere. What direction were they even coming from? Everything was so confused.

When Jenny finally swung her gaze up, Mecca stood over…

A waterfall of information clicked in her head. Noor, in London, standing over the dead Visci sent by her mom's old friend Claude. Mecca's Uncle Ken, who discovered there was a name for their kind: Jivaja.

Telling Mecca that she knew what Mecca was, and it was okay.

Jenny hadn't connected Noor to Mecca. Or, rather, she hadn't connected what Noor did to what Mecca potentially could do.

Until now.

Until Mecca killed a Visci in the same way Noor had killed the hotel man.

Her best friend met her gaze, and they stared at each other. Mecca's eyes were both defiant and searching at the same time.

"Thank you," Jenny said.

Mecca's expression softened, and the corners of her lips raised. She nodded.

"Holy shit," Zoey said again.

Yes. Zoey. The weird, rude woman who'd led them there in the search for Jorge.

"How did you do that? Actually, what the fuck is it that you *did*?"

Jenny swung her gaze around and looked at each of them. Except...

"Sara," she said. "Sara is hurt." She struggled to stand, and Will helped her.

Mecca's forehead creased. "What? No. She's outside."

"Yes."

Sara was supposed to have gone to the back of the house. But Jenny knew she hadn't. That scream. It came from the side, not the back.

Jenny staggered toward the kitchen with Will all but propping her up. She was glad he hadn't tried to stop her, because he could have. Easily. Her body barely moved the way she wanted it to. And that took all her concentration. She had no energy for anything so luxurious as resistance.

She heard Mecca coming up behind, and she was glad. There was no way she'd be able to help Sara the way she was, hardly able to even walk on her own. A faint throb in her hip walked with her the entire way.

"I'm staying here with Jorge," Zoey said.

Jenny was almost past the dining room. She spared a glance toward the room beside her as they made their way. Jorge lay on a table, straps holding him down. One sleeve of his shirt had been rolled up, and a rubber tourniquet lay trapped between his upper arm and torso, as if it'd been unfastened after use.

"Someone is under the table," Jenny said, the incredulity in her voice matching her emotion.

"Yeah," Zoey said. "That's the guy from the car. He's fine. I've got him."

And then they'd made it to the kitchen.

Cool autumn air met her at the door, chilling her throat with each breath. It felt good. Somewhere, someone had been burning leaves or maybe a bonfire. It was the weather for it. Jenny peered through the darkness as she walked.

By the time they'd gotten halfway around the house, Jenny had her feet more firmly under her and didn't have to lean as heavily on Will.

"You okay?" he asked when she straightened.

"Yeah, I think so. We need to get to Sara."

"I'm here," came Sara's voice.

She sat on the ground, cradling her left arm with her right. The living room's light barely reached her, so Jenny couldn't make out details until they got closer.

"Sorry," Sara said. "I passed out after that asshole shot me."

Will squeezed Jenny's arm. "You okay to stand?"

She nodded as Mecca came up on her other side.

"I'm right here," Mecca said, barely meeting her gaze. "If you need me."

Jenny gave her a smile, and Mecca returned it—probably the most honest, heartfelt expression they'd shared since Jenny had gotten back from London.

Will moved to Sara's side. "Let me see."

"He fucking *shot* me," Sara said again. "Asshole."

Will tended to Sara and Jenny pulled in a lungful of the cold fall air. It burned her throat, but she was glad of the burn. It meant she hadn't died under that man's hands.

She was alive.

Chapter Twenty-Three: Mecca

Mecca watched as Will checked Sara's wound. She was acutely aware of Jenny beside her.

How did her best friend in the world view her now, after watching her kill someone? She didn't know.

Jenny had thanked her, but did that mean anything besides what the words said? Was there something beyond that? She didn't know that either.

Sara let out a yelp. Will had pressed hard against her wound.

"It took a chunk out of her arm, but it's mostly just a bad graze," Will said. "That's good, but we need to get her to a hospital. I can bandage her up inside."

Mecca nodded. "Can you walk?"

"I got shot in the arm," Sara said. "I don't walk on my arms."

They all looked at her, surprise in each of their features matched Mecca's reaction one hundred percent.

Sara gave a rueful laugh. "Sorry. I think I was channeling Zoey right then."

Now Will laughed, but a true one. One he didn't use often. "Yes. Yes, you were. Come on. Let me help you." He got her to her feet, being careful of her arm.

"Was that the front door?" Jenny asked.

"I didn't hear anything," Mecca said. She listened, but still heard nothing.

They made their way around to the back of the house and inside.

In the room beside the kitchen, the guy who'd been under the table was now sitting in a chair beside the table Jorge lay strapped to.

Zoey stood leaning against the table, staring at the man. When they came in, she nodded toward him. "He's the dude from the car. Medical guy."

"Scientist," he said.

"Yeah, yeah. Now he talks." She looked over to them. "Been trying to get him to talk since you went outside. I think I've been too nice." Then she noticed Sara. "What happened to you?"

"Shot," Sara said. "In the fucking arm."

Zoey nodded. "Cool."

They shared a strange grin.

Wait. Are they…flirting?

Mecca shook her head. She didn't actually care if they were.

Will had disappeared, coming back a few moments later with gauze and an athletic wrap. He set about bandaging Sara's wound.

Jenny, who had walked on her own the entire way back, that badass, took several steps down the hall. "Where's the other guy? The one from the living room?"

"Yeah," Sara said. "He's my guy. My TASERed guy." She grinned.

"Let him go," Zoey said.

"What?" Mecca could imagine him running back to wherever, talking about the meddling kids who ruined their operation.

"Jorge needed a snack, so we borrowed the guy for a few minutes. But we don't need him long-term, since we've got the medical du—"

"Scientist," the man interjected.

Zoey barely glanced at him before continuing. "So we didn't need the other guy."

"You didn't kill him when he…fed?"

Genuine surprise showed in Zoey's arched eyebrow. "Why would we kill him?"

A flush heated Mecca's cheeks. Zoey's tone made it sound like Mecca was an idiot. She thought Claude would have killed him. Or Emilia. She glanced at Will, and he gave her a little shrug and a smile. A gentle *"I told you so."*

Zoey pushed off the table into a stand. "He took off out the front door. He might be half a mile away by now, as fast as he was running."

"We have to get out of here," Will said. "Whoever this place belongs to, when our runner gets to them, they will come back. We need to be gone."

Mecca didn't have any argument with that.

"It's going to be hard to get out while Jorge is napping," Sara said.

"He was just awake." Zoey spun around. "Dammit."

Jorge had definitely passed out.

"Anything in that bag," Will said to the guy in the scrubs, pointing at the satchel beneath the table, "that will wake him up?"

He didn't say a word. Zoey took a step toward him, and he flinched. But he still kept silent.

"Oh, for Christ's sake," Will said, grabbing the black satchel on the floor beneath where Jorge's head was and hoisting it onto the table. He rifled through it for less than a minute, grabbing things and looking at them, before pulling out a syringe and a particular glass vial.

He set them on the table beside Jorge and tightened the rubber tourniquet around the unconscious man's arm. Will tapped around the crease of his elbow for a moment and grabbed the vial. He filled the syringe.

As he bent over Jorge's arm and positioned the needle, he said, "The trick to giving Visci a poke is to go really, really fast." He thrust the needle into a vein, pushed the plunger, and slid the entire thing out in less than two seconds. As he wiped the area, he looked up. "They heal very quickly."

Mecca stepped forward and looked. Jorge's arm was smooth and unmarked. "Wow. That's crazy."

All of this reminded her way too much of her own captivity. She was ready to get out of here.

"No crazier than you sucking the life out of him," Zoey said, throwing her hand in the direction of the withered corpse. "A lot less crazy than that, actually. You still haven't explained what the hell you just did." As she said all this, her face became stony.

Will spoke again, his voice louder, a bit more firm. "We can sort that out later. We need to go. How long until the one who ran brings others?" He glanced around, but no one answered. "Exactly. We don't know. So let's go, while we can."

Mecca had never seen his take-charge attitude before. It was interesting. Good. Especially if it shut Zoey up, which it did. For now.

"What happened?" Jorge struggled to sit up from the hard table, and Zoey rushed to his side.

"Hey. You're okay. We came to get you."

"Oh. The panic button. Yeah. I'm glad it worked."

For the first time tonight, a gentle smile played along Zoey's lips. "Me too. Come on. Let's get you moving."

Will was scrounging through the satchel. He tossed Mecca a pair of black latex gloves. As he shoved a second pair into his jeans pocket, he said, "You're with me, in his car." Will motioned to the guy in scrubs. "Jenny, your guy had a gun. Did you see what happened to it?"

"Under the van in the garage, I think," she said, watching him.

Will came back with the gun and approached Mecca. He leaned into her ear. "Confirm that scientist guy over there isn't Visci for me, please."

Mecca nodded and opened her sight. Their captive sat on one of the dining room chairs, only one of three, against the wall the room shared with the living room. The man's cavern overlaid the reality of the scene.

His soul glowed bright gold, but not entirely. Grey veins snaked through the warm pulse of light. She wasn't sure what that meant. She mentioned it to Will.

"He's an *anculus*, most likely. A Visci has influence over him, like Emilia had over me."

Mecca nodded and filed that away.

They spent several minutes working out the logistics of leaving. Mecca, Will, and scientist guy would take the car in the driveway. The others would go in Zoey's car. Zoey left Jorge with them while she went to get it, so he wouldn't have to walk.

"Where are we taking him?" Mecca asked, giving a nod to the silent scientist guy. Her dorm room was out, of course. She looked at Sara, who stood against the wall, holding her injured arm gingerly. Mecca realized both Jenny and Will had also turned toward Sara.

Sara shook her head and winced. Blood had soaked through the makeshift bandage Will had made. Her face looked paler than normal. "No. I don't want him in my house." Apparently, getting shot had given her her fill of adventure.

Will said, "Of course. We need to get you medical help anyway." He eyed the bandage. "What about Zoey's?"

"We can go, but it's small. We'll have to get really tight with each other," Jorge said. When everyone's gaze swung to him, sitting on the table, he gave a weak grin. "We're roommates. It's a tiny, shitty apartment."

"We can take him to my house," Jenny said abruptly.

Mecca thought about Carolyn Barron, Jenny's prim and proper mother, watching over their hostage. "Are you sure that's a good idea?"

"I think it's the only option we have. My house is big. We can take him down to the wine cellar my parents never use. It's full of boxes—Halloween and Christmas stuff—but we can clear enough space." Jenny looked at Will. "What are we going to do with him?"

And now Will fixed his gaze on scientist guy. "Well, we need information."

The other man remained silent.

Did Will mean they were going to torture him? He couldn't mean that. That was…crazy.

Zoey came in the front door. "I've got the car. Jorge, come on." She got beside him and helped him off the table.

As Will filled Zoey in on the plan, Mecca took the opportunity to approach Jenny.

"What's your mom going to say?"

Jenny shrugged. "I don't know. Maybe we won't tell her."

She tried to imagine explaining that to Jenny's mom.

"Sooo…we've got this guy we need info from. Mind if we tie him up in your wine cellar? He won't be a bother. Promise."

Yeah. That'd work.

"Did you plan on telling her about all this?" Mecca asked.

"Maybe? I'm not sure. Once she told me about the Visci—the ones besides us, anyway—I thought our relationship would change. That she'd… I don't know. Trust me more. Include me more?" Her voice had gone sullen, hurt. "But she's still keeping secrets." She raised her gaze, her hazel eyes clear. "So if I have some secrets too…" She shrugged again.

Mecca knew that feeling. She knew it really, really well. Her dad had kept some terrible secrets. Really horrendous ones. She could never decide which of his secrets was the worst. But the one that had hurt her the most was the one where he'd lied her entire life about their family Gift. About how he didn't have it.

She wanted to hug Jenny, but she wasn't sure their new relationship allowed for it. So she only nodded and said, "I feel you."

"Could we, y'know, go please? I think I..." Sara's eyes rolled back in her head. She slid down the wall and listed to her left.

"Shit!" Will rushed to her, but Jenny was already there, easing her to the floor. She'd moved so fast. Jenny leaned Sara against her own chest to stabilize her.

Movement caught the corner of Mecca's eye. She whirled and found scientist guy out of his chair and inching toward the front door. She pointed at him, hoping he'd seen her kill his boss, hoping to scare him. "Do...not...move."

He froze.

That was cool.

His dark eyes blinked rapidly in his ashen, pallid face. Mecca could feel his terror.

She pointed to his empty chair. "Sit."

He took the five steps back to the chair in jerky movement.

"Don't you worry," she said. "You'll be leaving very soon."

Beads of sweat glistened on his forehead, and he dropped his gaze to the floor.

Her chest tingled. She could get used to that sort of reaction.

"Ah, damn it," Will said from behind her. "Mecca, here take this." Will held the gun out.

Mecca shifted her body so she wouldn't lose sight of the frightened man in the chair and took it from him. It felt dangerously heavy in her hand.

Will had leaned Sara forward a bit and was looking at the back of the bandage on her arm. "It's soaked with blood. I didn't realize she was losing it so fast. Change of plans. We have to get her to the hospital right now." He glanced around until his gaze rested on Zoey and Jorge, who'd only made it to the hall before Sara had passed out. "Zoey, you need to drive. I'll go with."

"No," she said. "I'm taking Jorge home. We can drop her off at the hospital after."

"We can't wait that long. She's losing blood too quickly. Jorge can go with the others."

Before Zoey could protest, Jorge said, "I'll be fine. Go."

"No," Zoey said to him. "I'm not—"

Jorge's soft voice became stern. "This isn't a debate." He disentangled his arm from Zoey's. "She got shot helping to save me. I don't even *know* her. Take her to the hospital."

"What if they come after you?" She'd dropped to a whisper, and Mecca had a hard time hearing, but she couldn't believe this was even an issue.

"Would you just take her to the hospital?" she shouted at Zoey. "God! Jorge is *fine*. Sara is dying because she wanted to help your damn friend." She waved her hand in Jorge's direction. "A perfect stranger! The fuck is your problem?"

Jorge squeezed Zoey's hand and said softly, "Go."

She nodded to him and shot Mecca daggers with her eyes. Mecca didn't care. If Sara didn't make it through this, Mecca wouldn't forgive Zoey. Or herself.

"Make sure everyone going in his car wears gloves," Will said as he stood and hefted Sara into his arms. "We don't need to leave fingerprints behind."

Mecca hadn't even thought of that.

"Good luck," Jorge said.

That seemed to startle everyone. Will gave him a nod, gratitude in his eyes. "Come on," he said as he passed Zoey and headed toward the door.

"Will," Mecca called.

He turned.

"Text me when you know something."

He nodded again and stepped through the still-open door. Zoey followed.

Chapter Twenty-Four: Jenny

As they parked in front of the garage, Jenny, seated in the passenger seat, turned to their captive driver and said, "We're going to take you inside. Don't give us any problems, and we won't give you any problems, okay?"

He didn't look at her, only stared straight ahead and nodded.

Mecca, sitting behind him with the dead Visci's gun pointed at the driver's seat, added, "Get out, slowly. And don't make any sudden movements. Open your door now."

Jenny hated the idea of the gun. She'd have argued against it if she'd known Mecca had it. She'd never seen Mecca like this. Of course, nothing in their high school years involved kidnapping or a gun, either.

The man did as told, and Mecca opened her own door at the same time. Jenny got out herself and helped Jorge to stand from the back seat.

"I'm okay," he said. "Just a little wobbly."

Mecca walked their captive around the car, and then they all moved to the door in a small huddle. As Jenny fished for her keys, the man dashed from between them and ran in the direction of the garage, on the other side of the car they'd driven.

"Shit," Jenny said, under her breath. She took off after him, putting on a burst of speed that let her easily overtake him. She launched onto his back, and they both toppled half on the grass on the other side of the driveway.

Her hip screamed at her, still tender from her earlier landing on it. Tomorrow was gonna suck.

The man grunted beneath her and scrabbled to get away. She grabbed him by the back of his coat and hauled him to his feet. She spun him around and got in his face.

"I can knock you out and toss you over my shoulder like a sack of potatoes." She focused on his dark eyes. "You know I can do that, right?"

He tightened his jaw but nodded.

"I don't *want* to do it, but I will if you don't cooperate. We don't plan to hurt you. We only want information." She shoved him toward the front of the house. "Let's go."

She wasn't sure where all that bravado came from. Perhaps she was just afraid that her mom would hear and come out demanding answers. How would she explain all this?

"You should have gone out for track," Mecca said. "We'd have won every meet."

Jenny smirked.

He didn't give them any more trouble as they entered the house. Jenny had them stop inside the doorway. She passed the closed door of her dad's office—neither of them had been able to go in there since they'd been back—and down the front hall to the kitchen. When she saw the way was clear, she motioned them forward.

She led them through the kitchen and into the laundry room in the back. The door there, the one to the wine cellar, always remained closed and locked. She turned the deadbolt, yanked the door open, and flipped the light switch on the wall just inside.

A faint yellow light shone up from below. "Go on," she said to their captive.

He moved down the stairs with slow steps, Mecca behind him, still holding the gun. Jenny hated that they had to use it.

Jorge went next and Jenny came behind, pulling the door shut.

The wine cellar wasn't a place Jenny usually spent time. The rest of the house was well-appointed and clean and bright. But the cellar was more like a cave. Not that the walls were stone—they were concrete block— but the floor was rough cement and it reminded her of something out of a horror movie. So she'd always avoided it.

The temperature dropped as she descended, and the single light hanging from the ceiling created weird shadows among the boxes and old things her parents had stored down here. She suppressed a shudder.

"I'd forgotten how creepy this is," Mecca said. "Remember when we tried to come down and tell ghost stories that one Halloween and we freaked ourselves out so much, we ended up running screaming up the stairs?"

Jenny laughed. She hadn't thought of that in a long time. "And I ran right into Mom bringing down apple cider. I ruined her new silk blouse."

The men stood looking at them, and Jenny shook her head. "Never mind."

Boxes piled high along the walls, some of them big plastic tubs, others cardboard moving boxes. A stack of extra patio chairs stood in one corner beside an old footlocker her dad had said was from college. The musty smell of old paper hung in the air.

Everywhere, Jenny saw memories of her dad. The tricycle she'd ridden when she was a kid. There was a picture in a photobook of her toppled over and crying, with him crouched beside her. She didn't have any memory of that, only the old photo.

Even her dad's old aquarium stood on its side nearby. He'd gotten into his head that he'd wanted saltwater fish, but ultimately decided it was a lot more trouble than it was worth.

Her eyes prickled.

"Hey," Mecca whispered from beside her. "It's just stuff."

Jenny nodded and pulled in a deep breath. "Yeah. Okay. We need a chair." She got one from the stack and put it on the cement floor with a *thunk*. Pointing at their captive, she said, "You. Sit."

He did as she told him but didn't break eye contact with her.

"What's your name, anyway?" When he didn't respond, she sighed. "I can keep calling you 'You,' or I can use your name. It won't kill you to share your name."

"Oliver," he finally said.

"Huh. Oliver. That's a good name. So, Oliver, we're going to have to tie you to the chair," she said, as she looked around for something to do that with.

Jorge saw what she was doing and began searching boxes too. Mecca kept the gun trained on Oliver.

"Hey," Jenny said as Jorge rooted through a box near her. "I'm glad you're okay."

He gave her a smile. "Me too. Thanks for coming to find me."

"Well, we still need to find Helen, so I couldn't be losing you, right?" She didn't want to make a big deal about it, so she continued her search.

She found a ball of twine in a box labeled *Old Dishes*. Why twine would be in a box of dishes she wasn't sure, but she also wasn't going to complain, either.

She tied him as best she could and stepped back. "Okay, Oliver, we need some answers. Why did you kidnap Jorge?"

Oliver only looked at her. His mouth remained closed.

Mecca wagged the gun in front of him. "Answer her!"

He cringed away, but still said nothing. His hands shook.

"He might not be able to answer," Jorge said.

Oliver's dark gaze darted to Jorge.

"What do you mean?" Jenny asked.

"He might be under the control of a Visci."

"He is," Mecca added.

Jenny couldn't make sense of what they were saying. "Hang on. Are you saying that some Visci is controlling him right now?" She looked between Jorge and Mecca.

"I only know that there are signs of Visci in his soul," Mecca said.

"That doesn't add any light to the situation," Jenny said, her voice flat. She didn't understand any of this. Feeling this confused made her angry.

Jorge's chestnut brown eyes turned to her and held concern. "You really don't have any idea about what you are, do you?"

Jenny flushed and then frowned at her reaction. "You don't have to keep throwing it in my face."

"What? I'm not—" He scrunched his nose and continued, his tone level. "I didn't mean to throw it in your face. I'm sorry. It's not direct control, like a puppet, but he probably has a Visci he answers to who can directly influence his behavior." Jorge looked at Oliver. "If I were doing something horrible and had to bring a human in, I'd have a standing order on him about not speaking of whatever I am doing to anyone outside the project."

Oliver's eyes glistened.

Mecca stepped forward and put the gun barrel to Oliver's temple.

Jenny gasped, her heart suddenly pounding. "Mecca!"

"So even if I did this," Mecca said, "he wouldn't say anything?"

"He wouldn't be able to. Even if he might really want to."

Oliver hadn't stopped staring at Jorge, but the trembling in his hands had traveled to the rest of his arms.

Mecca pulled the gun back. "I wouldn't shoot him. I can't believe you think I would." She gave Jenny a pointed look.

What was she supposed to think? She swung her gaze back to Jorge. "So how do we get him to talk?"

"We bind him more tightly to one of us than he is bound to the other Visci."

Terror traveled through Oliver's eyes.

Jorge's brows knitted together. "It'll be kinda gross," he said to Oliver. "But it shouldn't hurt."

"It always hurts," Oliver whispered.

Jenny hadn't expected him to speak, and he surprised her. He seemed more afraid of the process than of them doing something to him directly. It occurred to her she didn't actually know what the process was. So perhaps his fear was logical.

"How does it work?" she asked, a bit wary of the answer.

"Blood," Mecca said.

The surprised look on Jorge's face pulled a wry laugh from Mecca.

"What? You think you're the only one with super-secret Visci knowledge?"

"Um. No. I wasn't... I didn't..."

Mecca waved a hand at him.

"Would someone clue me in, please?" Jenny asked. She was so out of the loop even Mecca knew more than she did.

"He has to drink your blood."

Drink her blood? That seemed gross. Her mom had been feeding her blood for years, but that didn't feel as disconcerting as sharing her blood with a stranger.

"How much he must drink to override the other Visci's power will have to be determined."

"Or you could inject your blood directly," Mecca added.

Jenny stared at her. *Gross.* And not particularly practical. "Where would I get something to do that with?" She skimmed her gaze over the rest of the room. "Unless we find needles and syringes in a box of dishes down here."

"It was just more information," Mecca said.

Dread uncoiled itself in her gut. "Do we really have to do this?"

"If we want to figure out why they took me, I think so," Jorge said. His voice was calming. "I would do it, but I don't know what they drugged me with. I'm not sure if that would affect him."

"You're not up to one hundred percent anyway," Jenny said. This was going to be her lone responsibility. "It could hurt you more than it would me."

"Okay, so we're going to do this?" Mecca said.

"We?" Jenny didn't feel much like it was a group effort.

"We're not a team?" Mecca asked.

That had been unexpected. They'd always been a team before, but Jenny thought maybe now that the truth was out, they wouldn't be. She wasn't sure whether Mecca would accept her anymore. She'd already said as much. But... Maybe something had changed?

Jenny nodded. "All right. Let's do it. But I'm going to need a knife. I'm not interested in cutting myself with any old dull pocketknife we might find down here." She went to the stairs. "I'll be right back."

When she got into the kitchen, she stopped dead in her tracks. "Oh. Hey, Mom."

Her mother was at the stove, taking the water kettle off a burner. A mug sat on the counter beside the stove, with a tea bag inside and a spoon right next to it. "Hi, honey. I've got something to share with you." She poured steaming water into the mug, and the scent of peppermint came to Jenny's nose.

"Okay," she said. She wasn't sure what else to say.

When her mom turned, Jenny was surprised at the excitement coming off her.

"Don't ask me how, but I got hold of Emilia Laos's computer. I've been doing some digging—"

"How do you know how to dig on a computer? I had to teach you how to do the coffee pot."

"Computers are easier for me than coffee pots. Someday, I'll tell you about the work I did in the earliest days of computers." She put the kettle back on the stove and waved her hand at Jenny. "But anyway, I found evidence that Emilia knew about the disappearances."

A jolt of excitement hit her. "She was behind them?"

"No. She was tracking them, though. It looks like she was trying to figure out what was happening to the hybrids as well." She put half a teaspoon of sugar into her tea and stirred. "But that's not all. She had some information about full bloods being taken too."

"Did she find out who was taking them?"

"No. But Emilia suspected that someone was doing something with them and killing them after. She also suspected that whoever was behind it was trying to feed into the idea of a war between hybrids and fulls."

Jenny thought about this. "So it's not actual targeting for the war?"

"Well, I don't know, but Emilia thought not. I'm still working through it upstairs." She lifted her cup and headed toward the hall. "I'm going to get back into it. I'll let you know what else I find out, okay?"

Jenny nodded absently.

After her mom had left, she remembered why she'd come up here. She grabbed a knife from the block on the counter and headed back to the basement.

Chapter Twenty-Five: Mecca

Oliver hadn't moved the entire time that Jenny had been gone. He'd only sat there and waited in silence. Mecca still didn't understand how she'd gotten caught up in helping Visci. She sighed.

"Okay, got it," Jenny said as she came down the stairs. "And Mom was in the kitchen. The Visci apparently knew about hybrids disappearing. And the fulls." She said this last while looking at Jorge.

"Hybrids?" Mecca asked. Why were they talking about cars?

"There's someone or some group, more likely, kidnapping Visci like me: half human," Jenny said.

Jorge nodded. "And then they turn up dead."

"What?"

"That's why Zoey was so freaked out when Jorge disappeared," Jenny continued. "Jorge, Zoey, and Helen had figured out that the deaths that everyone thought were just deaths were actually something more."

"You guys," Mecca said, "I am not getting what you're talking about. What deaths?"

Jorge slowed. "There are full-blood Visci and hybrids—those who are born with one human and one Visci parent."

"Yeah, I got that."

"Okay. Visci have a lot of trouble having children between themselves. That's why there are many more hybrids than there are full bloods."

"And you're a hybrid." Mecca pointed to him.

"Yes. But for the last five or ten years, there has been growing tension between full bloods and hybrids. No one really knows why. We've worked together, lived together, for centuries with no problems. But hybrids started showing up dead. We're easier to kill than full bloods. Not much easier, but a little easier. And then the occasional full was found dead as well. Each side blames the other. So now, there's crazy tension all over."

"Zoey and Jorge realized that in many of the cases, the person was missing for several days, sometimes longer, before they were found dead."

"So we think there's something else going on."

Mecca looked at Jenny, considering all of it. "Is this what you were talking about at Sara's? What you were asking me about?"

She nodded and looked sheepish. "I knew it couldn't be you. But at that moment, I was mad and freaked out."

Mecca nodded. She didn't know how to respond to that, her feelings in a messy, muddled ball.

Jorge looked at Oliver. "I'm betting he can give us something really helpful."

Oliver looked both relieved and terrified. Mecca understood that feeling.

Jenny looked at Jorge. "Emilia Laos…"

Mecca didn't hear the rest of the words. Just the name brought back a vision of those last moments in the forest. The dank scent of rotting leaves. The feel of Emilia's old, hollowed-out Cavern. Freshly fallen snow—the taste that had come onto her tongue when in the Cavern.

Emilia's shrieks as she died.

"...so like we thought, it's not only hybrids. I'll even bet that the few full bloods that came up dead, all of them had been missing before they were found. The good news is that it means we might still be able to save Helen."

Mecca blinked a few times to clear away the awful memories. She just wanted this done. "All right. So let's get to work. You got the knife?"

Jenny nodded. "I'm not sure if I can cut myself."

"I'll do it," Jorge said.

Mecca wasn't sure if she'd have trusted him, but Jenny nodded again. She kept the gun trained on Oliver, even though she thought the fight had left him. She wondered if he would be glad to be out from under one Visci's thumb only to be under another. Though she was sure that Jenny was a better person than Oliver's current "master," the whole idea made Mecca's skin crawl. She'd come very, very close to being in his shoes.

"Oliver," she said, as another thought crossed her mind. He looked older than her, but not much. Late twenties, maybe.

He'd been watching Jorge and Jenny and now his eyes jerked up to meet hers.

"How old are you?"

"Fifty two."

The corners of Jenny's mouth turned down in a frown.

Mecca nodded. Not as old as Will but still older. At least he wouldn't die once the Visci blood had filtered out of him. Mecca thought Will was starting to feel his "age," but he hadn't actually started aging again. He said that as soon as the Visci blood in his system burned off, he would die. Mecca didn't want to think about it.

She didn't understand what their relationship was. They weren't really romantic. They'd never even kissed. But they'd lived out of each other's pockets since the confrontation with Emilia.

Jenny swore. "Why isn't it working?"

Jorge bent over Jenny's upturned wrist. The knife pressed against her pale, thin skin. "You have to concentrate on not healing," he said. "Otherwise, it won't be open long enough to get blood."

"I get it. But it's hard. I've never done that before."

He laughed. "I can't imagine when you'd ever *want* a wound to stay open under usual circumstances. Ready?"

"Yes."

He bore down with the knife, and she gave a soft grunt as it cut through her skin. Mecca gaped, both fascinated and horrified, as blood began to well. He quickly moved her wrist to Oliver's mouth.

Oliver hesitated for a moment, but then he latched onto her wrist and began to suck.

Mecca turned away. Watching vampire movies where people drank each other's blood was one thing. But this... She couldn't watch this.

"God, that feels so weird," Jenny said.

"Concentrate on keeping the cut open."

"I am. It's just...ugh."

The sucking sounds became louder, and Oliver whimpered. Mecca glanced back and saw Jorge had drawn Jenny's wrist away.

"I don't know how much this is going to take," Jorge said as he wiped Jenny's wrist with his hand. "The cut has already closed. He couldn't have gotten much. Ask him again, Jenny."

Jenny looked down at Oliver. "Why did you kidnap Jorge?"

The man in the chair didn't respond. He stared at them with wide, blinking eyes.

"All right. We'll try again," Jorge said, returning the knife to Jenny's wrist.

It suddenly struck Mecca that she might be able to see a change in his soul if it worked. She shifted her vision. She'd gotten so much better at doing it over the last few weeks. Oliver's Cavern appeared over the scene in the cellar.

His golden soul still held those grey veins worming through it. Perhaps it wouldn't change at all.

"Okay, keep it open," Jorge said.

When Mecca looked at the other two, their Caverns came into view. Jenny's looked like it had when she'd peeked at it earlier. Jorge's, whose Cavern she'd never seen, looked much like the man she'd killed several weeks ago, Hayden. That event had started this entire mess.

It looked exactly like Emilia's had. And Claude's. Dark, with only a small glowing soul held by smoky grey tendrils.

She wished she could choose to only see one Cavern. She didn't like seeing Jenny's Cavern with her friend knowing. But that wasn't how all this worked. So she focused on Oliver and tried to avoid the other two.

Behind the Cavern, he watched Jenny eagerly as Jorge sliced her wrist again. When Jenny moved to Oliver, he had no hesitation. He immediately started drinking.

Mecca tried to ignore the sucking sounds and the vision of Oliver latched onto Jenny's wrist. Instead, she focused on his soul and those grey snakes of Visci that wound through it.

As Jorge encouraged Jenny to concentrate on controlling her healing, Mecca saw a slight change in the grey veins. They seemed to be developing a mild green tint. Not the entire thing, but occasional reflections of the golden light on the grey looked different.

"I think it's working."

"How?" Jenny said, looking at her.

At that moment, Oliver groaned. "It closed," he said.

Jenny pulled her wrist back and looked at it. "Dammit." She held her arm out to Jorge. "Mecca, how do you know—ow, dammit—how do you know it's working?" She offered her wrist to Oliver and closed her eyes as he latched on again.

"Because his soul is changing. The parts that are Visci are different."

That had gotten Jorge's attention. His dark eyes bored into her. "You're not human?"

"I just have a Gift," she said. It occurred to her that even two months ago, she'd never have been okay saying that. And she certainly wouldn't have looked at anyone's Cavern.

He stared at her, a thoughtful expression on his face. "I have a lot of questions. I would like to hear about your Gift," he said, "once all of this mess is handled."

Mecca didn't say anything. She wasn't sure whether she wanted to share anything about herself with Jorge. She didn't even know him. And he was Visci.

Oliver's soul was shifting again. The veins had a definite dark green sheen to them now. And he was still sucking on Jenny's wrist, so she must have gotten the hang of keeping the cut open for him.

Jenny's phone made a weird-pitched, buzz-farting sound. That was the notification of her mom texting. Mecca choked out a laugh. She'd forgotten about that sound.

Jenny jerked, but Oliver kept at it, so Jenny was getting better at concentrating. She got her phone out with the other hand and read the text.

"Shit." She held the phone out to Mecca. "Would you text her back? She wants to know where I am. Just text, 'I'll be in in a minute.' Hopefully, she'll assume I'm out by the pool."

Mecca smirked, but started typing. "Swimming in November. Because you're the smart one."

"We're both the smart one."

That had been their standard back and forth since they were young teenagers.

"Okay. Done," Mecca said. She handed the phone to Jenny.

"Yeah, and you're done too," Jenny said to Oliver.

Jorge sat, quietly observing all of them. "Ask him something."

Jenny focused on Oliver. "Why did you kidnap Jorge?"

"I didn't kidnap him," Oliver said.

Jenny rolled her eyes as she wiped the remaining smears of blood with her hand. "Okay, fine. What were you going to do with Jorge?"

"Sedate him and take him back to the lab." Oliver's lips widened into a big smile. "I'm so glad this is working!"

Mecca shook her head. "You're the worst bad guy ever."

"I'm not a bad guy. You think I want to help them?" He shuddered and looked at his arms, still bound to the chair. "Can these come off? I'm not a threat to you."

They looked at each other, none answering at first. Finally, Jenny crouched and began untying the knots around his arms.

The upstairs door opened. "Why is this light...? Jenny?"

Everyone froze. The expression on Jenny's face when she looked at Mecca reminded her of the time they'd gotten caught with her dad's whiskey bottle in the upstairs bathroom.

That hadn't ended well, either.

Chapter Twenty-Six: Jenny

Jenny tried not to freak out as her mom looked from person to person. When she spotted the knife in Jenny's hands, those green eyes looked at her with such intensity, Jenny wanted to run away, hide, whatever.

"What's going on here?" Her mom's gaze moved down Jenny's arm to the knife she still held and then to Oliver. Jenny cringed when she realized blood still smeared Oliver's mouth. Her mom grabbed her by the elbow and pulled her aside, near the wall.

"What the *hell* do you think you're doing?" Her whispered words came in an impassioned rush.

"It was the only way to get him to talk!" Jenny said, her voice low to match her mom's.

Mecca came up, and Jenny wasn't sure she'd ever been so glad of her best friend. "One of Jenny's friends is still missing, Mrs. B."

Her mom glared at Mecca and back at Jenny. "You don't have any idea what you're doing. You don't—"

"Whose fault is that?" Jenny blurted.

Mouth clamping shut, her mom looked between them again. She pursed her lips and drew in a long breath through her nose.

Jenny snuck a glance at Mecca, who shrugged.

"You're right," her mom said. "That is my fault."

She only had a moment to feel a measure of satisfaction before her mom continued.

"But it doesn't change the fact that you don't understand anything about what you're doing." She looked Mecca up and down. "You two obviously have shared some things."

Mecca huffed. "Good God, does everyone know?"

Carolyn swung her gaze back to Jenny. "What the hell is happening?"

She wasn't sure what to do. Mecca wasn't much help. She only raised her eyebrows and shrugged. A tap on her forearm brought her attention back to her mom.

"No secrets, remember? It works both ways."

Jenny sighed, but before she could even begin to explain, Mecca spoke.

"Jorge was kidnapped. We rescued him, but when we found him, it was clear they were doing something medical. So we grabbed Oliver over there when we left. He was the one in charge of the"—she waved a hand in the air—"medical things. But he's not in charge for real. He's tied to one of the Visci who are doing...whatever they're doing, so Jenny decided to try to override that connection and create one of her own, so we can find out what's going on." Mecca met Jenny's gaze. "Did I miss anything?"

"Nope. I think that's about right." She wanted to kiss her best friend.

Carolyn glanced between them and brought her gaze to Oliver. "And did it work?"

"It seems to have," Jenny said.

Her mom groaned. "God, I hate this. It's exactly what I *didn't* want for you. This is what I was protecting you from."

"You can't protect me from who I am," Jenny said.

Her mom stared at her, silent. Then she nodded.

The doorbell chimed faintly upstairs. Carolyn took her phone out of a pocket and pulled up the doorbell app. A thin, young-looking man with blond hair stood in front of the camera.

"Shit," her mom said.

"Is that Claude?" Jenny asked. It *looked* like Claude.

Mecca closed the distance between them and looked over her mom's other shoulder. "Shit." A shudder ran through her best friend.

Her mom looked at Mecca. "You know him?"

"He's one of the ones who…" She didn't finish the sentence but just nodded.

"Why is he here?" Jenny asked.

"I have no idea. But I should go find out. You guys stay quiet." She met each of their gazes in turn with an intensity that conveyed the importance of her words. She mounted the stairs, pausing for a moment near the top to stare down at them. Then she shook her head and continued, closing the door behind her.

"We can't stay," Jorge said. "Especially if Claude is here. That can't be a coincidence."

His face had gone pallid in the time her mom had been downstairs. "You okay?" Jenny asked.

He nodded and stood, keeping a hand on the stack of boxes beside him. "Yeah. But we need to go."

"Where?" Mecca asked.

"We can go to my place for now," Jorge said. "I don't know if it's safe, but...I'm starting to think nowhere is at this point."

They all nodded.

"We'll have to be quiet," Jenny said, going to the stairs.

Chapter Twenty-Seven: Claude

Claude rang a second time. He was sure Carolyn was home. At least, her cell phone was. After a moment, footsteps sounded beyond the thick wooden door.

Carolyn didn't look surprised when she opened it to him. Leaving the screen door between them, she inclined her head. "Claude. You'll forgive me for being surprised that you would show up at my home."

He beamed. "I hope you will forgive my forwardness. I've brought some of the information you requested. It occurred to me that you may want it at once."

She studied him for a moment, in that way she used to do when they were children. That way that told him she was scrutinizing, evaluating, his every movement. He shook off his apprehension as she unlocked the screen door.

They'd come a long way from childhood.

"Very well. Come in." Her gaze never left him as she stood aside to allow him to pass.

Claude wasn't used to feeling on edge like this. It was always he who had the upper hand. Carolyn had been out of the game for a long time, and he'd forgotten how it was to have someone as old and experienced as he in play. He needed to be sure he adjusted for her.

As the latch clicked shut, she gestured to a set of closed French doors off the foyer. "Please, we can talk in there."

The office they entered was nicely appointed, with a formidable cherry wood desk at the far end, and a leather seating arrangement in the center. Dark bookshelves lined most of the walls. The areas without bookshelves housed some strangely out of place neo-art deco framed prints. Curious.

"So, you have something for me?" Carolyn said from behind him.

He turned his back on the desk and held a manila folder out to her. "I am still tracking down your request about the police, but here is information I've gathered on other influence within the city. You may be particularly interested in the sections about medical influence, in light of your inquiries about hybrids being killed."

Carolyn took the folder and held his gaze for a moment longer than necessary before flipping it open and fingering through documents. She scanned the pages of printed material. When she looked at him again, he saw the question in her eyes before she spoke it.

"You believe Arabella Connelly controls the medical franchise in Atlanta? The leader of Memphis?"

Claude paced to his right, giving a grave nod. "That is what everything points toward. She seems to have a strong hand in Emory, but also the public health sector. We've seen her influence within the county systems, especially Fulton."

"I see."

Claude faced her again. "I do not know whether or not it was with Emilia's blessing. Obviously, I have not spoken to Arabella herself about this."

"Obviously."

The word was not spoken sarcastically, but then, Claude had never been able to read Carolyn perfectly. Outside, he picked up the sound of an engine starting.

"Thank you for this, Claude," she said as she closed the folder. "I will look into it more closely tonight. Do you have any update on the police situation?"

The soft rumbling engine died away.

"I should have something for you soon. I have a name, but...there is not enough information to be sure yet. Or even confident in the name. So give me another day or two, if you would, and I will have something solid."

"Very well. Is there anything else?" Carolyn motioned to the still-open doors, and Claude returned to the grey-tiled foyer.

"No. That was all."

As Carolyn opened the door, Claude pointed to an empty spot in front of her garage, beside where his own car sat. "There was a car there when I arrived. A sedan. Did I interrupt?"

Carolyn's eyes darted to the driveway, and for the first time, Claude felt something less than the composure she'd displayed since he'd arrived. It was gone almost at once, but he was positive it had been there.

"No, not at all. That's my daughter's car. She went out with friends."

Claude studied the tic at the corner of her left eye. "That is a shame. I was hoping to meet her. I've heard lovely things."

"Have you?"

He laughed. "Well, no, not really. I've heard nothing about her." He leaned in. "That is why I was hoping to meet her."

She didn't smile right away, and when she did, it seemed an afterthought. "Thank you again for bringing these to me. In future, you may email, and we will appoint a time and *place* to meet."

Claude bowed. "As you wish, of course."

He was barely on the porch when she closed the door behind him without a sound. His driver stepped from the car and moved to the back of the vehicle and opened Claude's door.

"What did you see?" he asked.

"Three young women and two men. They piled in to the car and drove off."

Claude nodded and slid onto the leather back seat as he removed his phone from his breast pocket.

The map app lit the screen, showing a little red dot moving along the road out of the subdivision.

Chapter Twenty-Eight: Mecca

Zoey, Will, and Sara beat them to the apartment complex parking lot—Mecca had texted the grand escape to Will. The level of relief at seeing them came close to alarming her. She shook it off and left the others to get out of the sedan. Sara gave her a huge grin as she approached. The woman's left arm lay in a blue sling, the upper part wrapped in a thick layer of bandages. Her smile made her seem a lot happier than Mecca thought she should be.

"Hey!" Sara said, nodding down to her arm, a glint in her eye. "Cool, right?"

"Um. I guess?" Mecca couldn't keep the tiny laugh from slipping out. She didn't get Sara at all. But she was definitely glad to see her.

More glad to see Will, who'd come across from the driver's side. "Everything okay?" He gave her a partial embrace. It was the only real PDA they engaged in.

Mecca shrugged. "Nothing is okay. I've been with a bunch of Visci all night. Sara got shot. I watched my best friend feed her blood to a human. And a Visci I definitely don't trust showed up at the house we were at. I don't think anything will ever be okay again." As she said it, the truth of her words hit home and an oppressive cloud laid over her, dispelling the relief she'd felt a moment ago.

Will put a hand on her arm. "It's going to be okay. But…" He glanced over at the other group who were making their way toward the building, Zoey under Jorge's arm, helping him along. He looked even more pale than he had when they'd left. "Why was Jenny sharing her blood with someone? And who showed up?"

Mecca nodded. "I'll explain inside."

They filed into the apartment after Zoey fumbled with the keys and finally got the door open. It was a normal-looking two-bedroom, but the living room had been turned into more of a bedroom. A hide-a-bed was open in the center of the room, with pillows strewn across it and disheveled sheets. A giant television took up one wall. Game controllers lay discarded across the surface of the cheap coffee table in front of it.

"Do you have another roommate?"

"Huh?" Zoey asked as she lowered Jorge onto the bed. He sat hunched over, his back rising and falling with his breath.

"The bed."

"Oh. No. I use my bedroom for something else."

As Will closed the door behind them, Jorge said softly, "I'm not feeling…" He tilted forward and toppled to the floor.

"Jorge!" Zoey cried as she dropped to her knees beside him.

Jenny also ran to his side. She looked up at Oliver. "What's happening to him?"

Mecca felt the concern in the room, but she couldn't get herself to really care. He was Visci, after all. She watched.

Jorge's breaths came in shallow rises and falls of his chest.

Will stepped past Mecca and joined Jenny and Zoey. He crouched and pressed his fingers against Jorge's neck. He looked at Jenny. "Let's get him up."

She nodded at Zoey, and together, the two of them lifted Jorge as if he were a child and laid him gently onto the hide-a-bed.

Mecca sucked in a breath. Even more than the blood-sharing, watching Jenny lift a full-grown man... That drove home, straight into Mecca's gut, how not-human Jenny was. Her breath caught in her throat. How had she never noticed it?

She turned away and moved into the kitchen, past the small island with its pizza boxes piled on the trash can and the empty Chinese takeout containers on the counter. Her heart pounded too fast in her chest.

She stopped in front of the refrigerator, her back to whatever was unfolding in the living room. Sweat exploded across her skin and her vision narrowed, black pinpricks popping along the edges.

Fear—or something very close to it—gripped her heart.

Her breath tried to run away, leaving her gasping with soft sounds. She put a hand on the refrigerator door. The cool metal on her palm felt in stark contrast to the burn of her skin. Panic galloped through her.

"Hey." Sara's soft voice startled her. "Breathe with me. Take a breath in."

Mecca couldn't get her bearings enough to argue. Or tell her to mind her own damn business. Or even turn around.

She matched Sara's "in" breath.

"Out now. Slow. Everything is okay. In." Sara didn't touch her, but Mecca could feel the woman's presence at her back. "Out. And in."

Mecca's heart slowed, and her lungs didn't seem like they were controlled by someone else anymore. She breathed with Sara a couple more times. Her vision widened. The black spots went away.

"You're okay," Sara said. She moved around so that she was in Mecca's field of vision but still didn't touch her. The other woman smiled. "You're okay."

Mecca pursed her lips. "Thanks," she said, her voice weak. She hated that weakness.

"No worries at all. I've been there. It sucks. But you really are okay."

Mecca wasn't sure whether that was actually true. But she was too tired to argue. And it didn't matter anyway, did it?

Mecca looked over her shoulder. "Is *he* okay?"

Sara frowned. "I don't know."

"It would suck for you to have gotten shot in his rescue just for him to die on us now."

"Oh, I dunno. I did get to use my TASER, after all. And how cool is it to have a story about getting shot?" She pushed her slinged arm forward a bit. Then Sara's grin faded. "But I don't want him to die. That really would suck."

A new-agey warbling sound came from Sara's pants. Her cheeks flushed pink as she pulled her phone out of her pocket. "Hey, Aunt Tea." She gave Mecca a grin and a little half-shrug. "No, I can't today. Can it wait til next week? Okay, I'll call you tomorrow and let you know when is good. Love you too." After she disconnected the call, she said, "My aunt. She needs computer help. I'm pretty much her tech support."

"I get that," Mecca said absently. She stared at Sara for a moment. "Why are you helping them?"

Her eyes widened a bit, and an unsure little grin spread across her lips. "They're your friends."

Mecca couldn't stop the shake of her head. Only one of them was truly her friend. "But you hardly know me."

"Okay, okay. It's exciting." Sara leaned in and that little grin turned bigger. "It's like a James Bond movie or something." She waggled her brows.

A laugh tried to bubble through her, but Mecca tamped it down.

"But why are *you* helping them?" Sara asked.

Mecca took her gaze to where Will still hovered over Jorge. "I don't know." Jenny sat on the arm of the sofa, watching as Will did whatever medic-y stuff he was doing. "They were easier to hate before I found out that my best friend is one of them."

"I'll bet that's true."

"Oh, thank God!" Zoey said as Jorge struggled to sit up. Her green eyes met Mecca's. "Get him some water!"

Mecca didn't react, so Sara turned away to fulfill the request.

Oliver moved from where he'd been standing against the wall. "No. Wait." Mecca had forgotten he was even there.

"What?" Jenny said.

"Water isn't a good idea." Oliver stood beside the bed, looking down at Jorge. "He fed at the safe house."

"Yes," Zoey said. "He was weak. So?"

Oliver sighed, his shoulders rolling forward.

Zoey jumped to her feet. "Why?"

"He's been poisoned."

To say Zoey freaked out would be putting it very, very mildly. Quick as a flash, she had Oliver by the throat and backed against the wall. Just as fast, Jenny came behind them and grabbed Zoey's arm.

"Zoey!" Jorge's voice came out as a rattle.

"Let go!" Jenny yelled.

"He poisoned Jorge!" Zoey snarled. "I'm going to kill him."

Oliver gasped and clawed at Zoey's hand. She'd lifted him so that his feet dangled just shy of the floor.

"That's not going to help!" Jenny said, still trying to break Zoey's grip.

A part of Mecca that had remained disconnected from everything found this fascinating. Even with Jenny's extra strength, Zoey was stronger. And Zoey was tiny. What did that mean?

"He can't help us save Jorge if he's dead." Jenny finally jerked Zoey's hand from Oliver's neck, and he crumpled in a heap before them, gasping and clutching his throat.

Zoey stared at Jenny, stone-cold murder in her eyes.

Mecca dashed from the kitchen and was by Jenny's side fast enough to hear Zoey's quiet words.

"Don't you ever touch me again."

Jenny did not flinch from Zoey's gaze. "I will stop you if you're about to do something stupid. And if that requires touching you, then I will touch you."

"You are not the one in charge."

"So you want to kill the only person who knows anything about the poison that's killing Jorge? You're an idiot." Jenny took a step back and waved her hand at Oliver. "But be my guest. Kill him. And we'll all watch Jorge die because you can't control your damn self."

Zoey's eyes narrowed and moved between Jenny and Mecca and back again. She was so short that she had to look up at them. She scowled and turned away.

Jenny grinned at Mecca and squeezed her forearm. "Thanks."

"I didn't do anything."

"You were here."

A tightness in Mecca's chest made her turn away. Why was she feeling guilty? "It's no big deal."

"It is," Jenny said from behind her. "And it's something we need to talk about later."

"Yeah." Mecca moved away as she heard Jenny helping Oliver to his feet.

Zoey had already gone back to Jorge's side. He'd slumped on a pillow that Will had propped him up with. Mecca had to hand it to Will. He hadn't let the drama impact him at all. She supposed that was a skill learned by living with Visci for decades.

Chapter Twenty-Nine: Jenny

As everyone settled back down, Jenny, her heart still thudding in her chest, said, "How do you know he was poisoned because he fed? Maybe they stuck him with a needle."

Oliver kept wary eyes on Zoey and shook his head. "No. They don't have it there in that capacity. It's only in the lab."

"Then how…?"

Mecca gave a small sound of surprise. When they all looked at her, she sighed. "The humans. They're the delivery system."

They stared. Jenny couldn't believe that would be true. But Oliver nodded.

"Yes. Doctor Blume had all the human guards injected with the virus. It doesn't work on us. But it will transmit to you"—he waved a finger around most of the room—"if you draw blood from us."

"They infected you too?" Jenny asked.

He nodded, looking abashed.

Jenny considered what would have happened if she'd fed from him. Not that she would do that, ever. But if she had… She'd be on the sofa bed right beside Jorge. "How is he?" she asked Zoey.

She gave a shrug. "I'm not sure. I don't know what's wrong with him. If your little lap dog had some of the virus with him, I could probably figure it out."

She didn't look over and her voice remained level, but Oliver blanched. Jenny didn't figure she blamed him after what'd happened.

"*Do* you have some with you?" she asked him.

"No. I told you. They only have it at the lab."

Now Zoey stalked over. "Then you should go to the lab."

Oliver backed away, though Zoey didn't really make moves toward him. "I—I could." His furtive glance swung to Jenny for a moment. "But there might be something better. We have some antidotes of earlier versions."

That animated Zoey. She closed the few feet between them in a second. "That means you're definitely going back."

Oliver cringed. "But I don't know if any of them will work on this version of the virus."

Jenny stepped between them, and she swore she heard Zoey growl at her. Jenny put a hand up. "Chill out for a second. Oliver, you can get your hands on these antidotes?"

"Yes. I could probably get a couple vials out. But like I said—"

"Just do it," Zoey snapped before turning and stomping back to Jorge.

"Oh cool. Are we breaking into a lab?" Sara chimed in from the kitchen. Jenny had forgotten she was there. She was such a strange bird.

"Breaking into a lab?" Mecca asked. "No. No, we're not." She had that expression on her face that meant she was not fucking around.

"I don't think we need to break in," Will added. "Oliver should be able to get in on his own, yeah?" He'd turned his gaze to Oliver expectantly.

The other man gave a small nod. "Yes."

Zoey pulled a blanket up to Jorge's chin and said, "How do we know he won't go in and run to this Blume guy?"

Would he? Jenny wasn't sure. She didn't feel any different. How would she know if the blood worked?

"I won't," Oliver said, quickly. "I don't want to."

Zoey's eyes narrowed dangerously. "I don't trust you."

"Oh my God," Mecca said, her voice exhausted. "Just stop already, would you? Yes, yes, you want to kill him. Yes, yes, he's terrified. You're a badass. We all fear you. There. Happy?"

Zoey trembled for a moment, and Jenny didn't think it was fear. Jenny thought Zoey was barely holding it together. When the short Visci woman began walking, slowly, around the sofa, Jenny made to intercept her before she got to Mecca. Zoey held up one hand to her and moved past.

She got very close to Mecca and said, softly, her tone calm and level, "My best friend is lying there on that couch, dying. So if it makes you happy to be snarky, if it makes *you* feel like a badass, then go ahead. Do it. But I don't have time for you. *He* doesn't have time for you. Now either add something useful or shut the fuck up."

She turned on her heel and stalked back to Jorge.

Jenny and Mecca both stood there looking at each other. Jenny had never seen Zoey that laser-focused, that serious, that raw. It was unnerving.

"Sorry," Mecca said, finally.

Will stepped in. "Okay. So Oliver, you're going to the lab. I can drive you."

"No," Jenny said. "I'll drive him." When both Will and Mecca began to speak, she raised her own hand. "I'm responsible for him. I am driving him."

The other two closed their mouths and nodded.

"So, if you're going anyway, Oliver," Sara said, turning to him, "I've got something I'd like you to take with you."

Now everyone looked at her. She gave a grin and a little wave.

"Yeah, so it'd be useful to get into their network. I'll need to run home real quick, but I can give Oliver a flash drive with a program that'll let me basically remote desktop into his machine at the lab."

That couldn't be a good idea. It might get him killed. Jenny started to protest when Zoey said, "Yes. Having the data on the poison or virus or whatever it is would help in figuring out how to counteract it, if the antidotes don't work."

Jenny could almost feel Oliver's alarm. "If he gets caught, they could kill him. And then Jorge would die too."

"It won't be anything big. It'll look totally normal on your machine." Sara was talking directly to Oliver. "I won't get you killed. Promise."

He didn't look convinced, and he ran his gaze to Jenny, as if looking for something. Approval? An order? She had no idea.

"If you don't want to do that, you don't have to."

"Yes—" Zoey began.

"No," Jenny said, flatly. "He has to get the antidote. He doesn't have to do this."

"The antidotes may not work," Oliver whispered. "I really don't know if they will or not." He looked to Sara. "I'll take your flash drive. But it's not likely you'll get anything off the computer. They're labeled with batch numbers. There isn't any information on what's actually in the serums. We only test it. He develops it."

"This Doctor Blume?" Zoey asked from the sofa bed.

"Yes. I've seen nothing on my system that would identify the ingredients. I assume he keeps all of that in his office. He probably has a lab back there. Otherwise, he'd have to do all his experimenting and creation offsite. But he's *always* there. So that's doubtful."

Zoey watched him as she listened, and she nodded. Her face looked more passive than it had all evening.

Jenny didn't like any if this at all. She didn't want Oliver put in such danger. It was already risky, him getting the antidotes.

"If you're going," Mecca said to Jenny, "I'm going with you."

"I'm only driving. I'm not going in." There was no reason she needed anyone else risking the trip.

"I don't care. I don't want you there on your own. No one else can kill one of these thi—people without a bunch of fighting and blood. So I'm going with you."

Silence descended on the room. Mecca's brow crinkled as all attention went to her.

"What? You know what I mean. It's not like I'm a murderer or something."

Jenny didn't miss the glance she exchanged with Will, and she wondered what that was about. But she said, "No one thinks you are. If it will make you feel better to ride with us, then you can come. Sara, you said you needed to get something from home?"

"Yeah, but I need a ride, obvs. Don't have my own wheels here, plus..." She waggled her slinged arm a little bit.

She must have some great drugs onboard to be so cheerful.

"I'll take you," Will said. He gave Mecca another pointed expression as he grabbed his bomber jacket. Jenny would have to ask about that too. Will draped the jacket over Sara's thin shoulders and escorted her out.

--->>><<<---

Jenny sat in the car with Oliver driving—he knew the way, so Jenny though that would be easiest—and Mecca in the back seat. He'd said the lab wasn't far, and Jenny thought they'd ride in silence.

So she was surprised when he said, "What do you plan to do with me?"

"Huh? Do with you?"

"Yes. Once this is done. What will you do with me?"

"I didn't plan on doing anything with you." She totally didn't understand this line of questioning. What was she supposed to do with him?

"I'm bound to you now. I'm your anculus."

"Umm. I was planning on just, y'know, letting you go live your life." She looked to Mecca for help.

Her best friend shrugged and mouthed, "I have no idea."

"I don't really have a life."

That hung in the air for a while.

Did Visci usually dictate what their people did?

What was she supposed to say?

"All right," he said, before lapsing into silence. It felt uncomfortable, but Jenny didn't know what to do to fix it. So she did nothing. And she had no idea whether that was right or wrong.

Oliver had been right about the lab being close by. They'd only been driving another five or six minutes when he pulled into the parking lot of a low, squat, but modern-looking building. The sign in the driveway said "EpiGen Laboratories - Deliveries in back."

Oliver drove to the back.

"Employee door is here." There were half a dozen cars in this part of the lot. He reversed into a space that allowed them to face the loading bay, as well as the employee entrance.

"They won't think it's weird that you're coming in at this hour?" Mecca asked. Jenny wondered that same thing.

"No. I'm in and out at all different times. It'll be fine." He leaned past Jenny and opened the glove box. Inside, she saw his ID badge with his photo. He grabbed it and slammed the box closed again. "I'll be back in a few minutes."

And before she could say anything else, he was out the door.

They watched him sprint across the lot and swipe his ID at the entrance lock. Then he was gone.

Jenny was actually glad for the alone time with Mecca. She turned in her seat and looked at her best friend. "Why did Will stare at you when you said you weren't a murderer?"

Mecca's eyes went wide. "Wh—what do you mean?"

"He looked at you... His face... There was something between you, something he was saying without saying anything."

Mecca snorted. "Okay, whatever."

"I'm not kidding around, Mecca. What the hell is going on?"

Mecca stared at her, anger flashing across her expression and disappearing. She frowned and shook her head. "I don't know. I can't—I haven't—" She swore. "It all seemed so simple. And it's just not anymore."

"Yeah. But we both had secrets, and we can get through this together."

Mecca shook her head again. "You don't get it."

What was she talking about? "Okay, so tell me."

Mecca chewed on her lower lip for a moment and stared out the windshield. Finally, she said, "Did my dad say what they wanted me for? Why Emilia kidnapped me in the first place?"

"No. Do you know why?"

"Yes. She told me."

"Okay?"

"She found out about my Gift. I don't think she understood it. But she knew it could kill them. And she wanted me to…work for her."

Jenny scrunched her nose. "Work for her?"

"Yes." Very pointed.

Jenny felt like she was missing something. "What do you mean?"

Mecca sighed. "She wanted me to kill other Visci for her."

"What?" Jenny would never have even thought of that. But her mom's words about how Visci maneuvered and manipulated came back to her. Maybe they'd also kill. She wasn't sure it would surprise her.

"Yeah. Her whole reason for kidnapping me was to get me to kill for her."

"That is so crazy."

They sat in silence for a moment. Then Mecca continued. "When I… When I got away, it felt so easy to hate them all. They were horrible. Emilia, Claude, all of them. They had Will in captivity. Stole me off the street. Who knew what else they'd done? Hating them was so easy."

It clicked into place. "And then me."

Mecca met her gaze, her eyes pained and sad. "And then you."

It all made sense now. Mecca's reaction to her secret.

"Now I'm not sure what to do." She fiddled with the edge of her jacket. "I swore I'd kill all of them. But now…" She let out a small frustrated sound.

Jenny wished she could fix it. She couldn't, because she was a Visci and that would never change. Could never change. "You don't have to kill anyone, you know."

Mecca raised her eyes again, and they shimmered with tears, though none fell. Her best friend blinked quickly to clear them. "What do I do if I don't kill them, though? I mean, how can I live in a world where I know they exist?"

Jenny tried not to take that personally. It wasn't meant for her. "How do you live in a world where you know serial killers exist? Or rapists? Or people who pirate ebooks, for that matter?" She gave a smile and Mecca responded with a barking laugh. "You just do."

"I guess."

Jenny reached back and put her hand on Mecca's forearm. "It's not your job to save the world."

Mecca wrinkled her nose and frowned. Jenny wasn't sure what that meant.

"I'm not trying to save the world," she said. It seemed like there was more, but it didn't come.

And then Oliver opened the door and ducked into the driver's seat. He held out a hand. On his palm lay two syringe tubes, no needles, marked with identification numbers. "These are the only two I was able to get. They're the batches we still have antidotes to."

Jenny grabbed them from him. "You didn't have any problems, did you?"

He started the car. "Not really. Doctor Blume was there, but I avoided him."

"And the computer?" Mecca asked from the back seat.

"Yep. No problems there. It was as easy as she said it would be."

"Great," Jenny said. "Let's go." She looked to see if Mecca was okay, but her friend had settled back in her seat and was looking out the window.

Chapter Thirty: Jenny

When they returned to the apartment, they found Zoey still tending to Jorge, who was awake, but not looking well at all. His normally light brown skin had gone pale. When he looked at her with dull eyes, she had to look away.

Jenny hoped and prayed the liquid in one of the syringes would work. Sara sat at the kitchen island with a laptop open in front of her, an expression of intense concentration on her face as she occasionally typed on the keys.

Jenny didn't see Will right away. He'd settled in an old brown armchair that had been pushed into a corner of the living room. His gaze jerked up as they entered. He looked directly at Mecca.

"You're all right?"

"Yes. Nothing happened. We just sat in the car."

He nodded, and the relief was plain on his face. Jenny didn't understand their relationship. She didn't know who he was to Mecca, and she really didn't know who Mecca was to him.

"You got it?" Zoey asked, coming toward Oliver.

"They're here," Jenny said, holding out the two plastic tubes.

Zoey snatched them from her and disappeared behind one of the bedroom doors. Jenny glanced around the room at the puzzled faces—except Sara, who was still nosed in her computer—and followed Zoey.

After stepping through the door, she paused. Now she got why the living room was a bedroom. Zoey had converted this space into a small lab. Tables lined three walls, two with equipment Jenny wouldn't have been able to identify if her life depended on it. The third housed two large monitors with a laptop between them. All the screens were dark.

It reminded her of something out of those CSI shows, only nothing gleamed in the light. The equipment looked old, tired, but it was all still clearly functional. Jenny couldn't imagine Zoey keeping anything around that didn't work.

Zoey's gaze didn't move from her task: squeezing a tiny amount from each syringe into separate small vials. Without looking up, she said, "You shouldn't be in here."

"Wow, Zoey. What the hell is all this for?"

"None of your business. Go back out there."

Jenny ignored her, approaching one of the work tables. A very fancy microscope—much more involved than any she'd used in science classes—took up a good portion of the first tabletop. As she ran a fingertip along the edge of the platform, Zoey looked up.

"I said get *out*."

"Not til you tell me what you're doing in here."

Zoey sighed dramatically. "I'm taking samples from each of these. I want to reverse engineer them. Anything common between them could lead me to whatever compound they're using to create this…whatever it is."

"Cool. But I really meant all of this." She waved a hand at the equipment.

"I already told you that," Zoey said, going back to labeling the vials. "None of your business."

Jenny couldn't imagine what Zoey would be cooking that required her to turn her bedroom into something that looked like it belonged in some research facility in Switzerland. She wondered how much more about Zoey was this surprising.

And then she wondered whether Zoey had been telling the truth about there not being a civil war. Suspicion curled its way into her mind.

"Does Jorge know you have all this?" she asked.

Zoey paused again, looking at her as if Jenny was the stupidest person she'd ever seen. "Seriously? You think he could live here, with me sleeping in the living room, and not know what I have in here?" She rolled her eyes and shook her head, which made Jenny feel like the stupidest person she'd ever seen.

"Yeah, okay. What about Helen?"

"Would you get out already?" She opened a dorm-sized refrigerator that Jenny hadn't seen underneath the computer table and dropped the vials into a small plastic box inside. Then she hustled Jenny out, following close, and slammed the door behind them.

They both went back to where Jorge lay. Jenny hadn't noticed Zoey grab needles, but she obviously had, since she began attaching one to the syringes. Zoey looked at Oliver. "These are dated. I assume the most recent is the last iteration of the virus?"

He nodded. "They may not—"

"I know. You said." She slid the needle into Jorge's arm and pushed the plunger faster than Jenny would have expected.

"You didn't clean his arm before you did that," Mecca said.

Zoey gave her what Jenny was starting to think of has her Patented "You're an Idiot" Look.

"She doesn't have to," Will said quietly from his chair. "Germs don't affect them, particularly. Getting the antidote into his vein before his skin heals is more important."

Jenny hadn't thought of that, though she should have, after her experience with the knife earlier.

Zoey yanked the needle from his arm. He gave her a weak smile.

"It's going to be fine," Jorge said, his voice breathy.

Zoey's face was an unreadable mask, but she nodded. "Yeah." After a long moment, she looked at Oliver. "How long will this take?"

"It should be noticeable quickly, though he'll probably still feel bad for a while."

They waited, watching him. The only sound in the room was the occasional clack of Sara's keyboard. Jenny didn't think Sara had any idea what was happening on this side of the room.

Five minutes ticked by. Zoey asked, "Is it any better?"

Jorge shrugged. "I can't tell. Let me try to stand up."

"Are you sure?"

"Yeah. I'm really weak and a little nauseous. But I've been feeling that way since I woke up. Here, help me." He'd pulled back the light blanket that covered his legs and torso, and now he held an arm out to Zoey. She steadied him as he used her to get to his feet.

Everyone watched as he swayed. It looked as if he was going to take a step, but then he shook his head and fell back onto the thin mattress.

"No. That's not working." A thin, pink-cast sweat had erupted on his forehead.

Jenny tried not to let his reaction crush her hope. But when she glanced at Oliver, his face did it. He met her gaze and gave a tiny frown. Jenny moved to where he stood not far from Will and Mecca, who also both watched silently.

"If he isn't feeling any change at all, it's not working," he whispered.

"I can hear you," Zoey said.

Oliver sighed. "Well, then you heard me."

"I'm going to try the second one, okay?" Zoey moved her attention to Jorge who gave her a nod.

"Will that be safe?" Jenny asked Oliver.

He didn't respond immediately, only looked at her. He said, "It will be safer than dying."

Jenny closed her eyes and sighed. Dread set up camp in her belly, like a knot of curdled milk. What would happen if he died?

Zoey must have heard their conversation this time too, but she didn't respond. Instead, she'd busied herself in getting the next injection into Jorge, who sat without moving right where he'd dropped.

Eyes closed, he didn't make any sound when the needle jabbed into his arm and Zoey smashed the plunger. She pulled it out just as quickly and looked at Jorge with an expectant gaze. They all did, really. Well, except Sara, who was still occupied with her computer.

Jorge didn't do anything. He sat there, sweating blood, and remained silent.

After a bit, Jenny sighed and looked away. It wasn't working. It wasn't going to work. Jorge would die. Rage and grief welled in her. She balled her hands into fists. How had this fucking happened?

"Umm...guys?" Sara looked up from her computer. "This may not be the best time, but there's a problem."

Oliver rushed over. "Did they find you in the system?"

She held up a hand to slow him. "No, no. I told you. They won't know I'm there. The problem is that there is no information about the poison or the antidotes anywhere that I can find. Everything seems to be done by identifying number, but what the numbers identify isn't here."

"They're probably on Doctor Blume's computer," he said.

"Yep, and that was my next point. There's a firewalled section of the system."

"I thought the whole thing was firewalled?" Mecca asked.

"It is, but…" Sara pursed her lips and began again. "Imagine you're walking down a hall. There's a door at the end, but when you open it, it's bricked over. So you're positive there's a room or something back there, because there's a passageway to it. But you can't get into the room at all. That's what I'm seeing, basically. I can see a path, but I can't get to the room."

"Can't you break into it?" Mecca asked, as if she entirely expected Sara to be able to do anything.

Sara stared at the computer screen for a moment and shook her head. "I don't think so. I mean, maybe, if I had a couple weeks and some fantastic, expensive software. But like this? No. And, I'll admit, that's kinda weird for me."

"So what does that mean?" Jenny asked, glancing at Jorge and Zoey. She'd eased him back to lying down. He didn't look any better.

Sara shrugged. "I mean, if I could get to this machine, I'm sure I could find something. There's a reason it's walled off."

Oliver had stayed silent the entire time, and Jenny realized he'd slowly backed up so he was flush with the wall, as if he were trying to meld into it. She turned to him directly. "You knew this."

"I told you we didn't have anything specific in our files. I told you that." His voice had gone high-pitched.

Did he think she would hurt him over this?

Will stood, finally, from the recliner. "Oliver, can you get us into his office?"

Oliver shook his head, looking adamant. And terrified. "Only Doctor Blume has access. There's an eye scanner and a keycard. No way I can get past that." He put this final bit in a whisper. "He'd kill me."

Zoey said, "You're dead, anyway."

They swung their gazes to her, and she glanced up, as if this were the most normal thing to say. "If Jorge dies, I'm killing you," she said, quietly, calmly.

"No," Jorge croaked, "you're not. He hasn't done anything wrong, and he's tried to help. It's not his fault none of this works."

Zoey's anger was almost tangible in the air, like a swarm of bees. But she said nothing against him.

"If I die, I die. But you need to stop this. Whatever it is. I'm not sure whether it's this war people are talking about or something else, like we thought. But if some humans are carriers and infected"—Jenny hadn't realized that he'd been awake when they were talking about that—"then you guys have to figure all that out because it could become an epidemic." He looked at Zoey, in particular. "You need to work on that." He nodded at her and waited until she returned the nod. "And," he said, looking at Jenny, "you guys need to find Helen."

Helen. Jenny had almost forgotten. She cringed and a wave of desperation came over her. How would they find Helen? Was she in the lab? Somewhere else? She didn't know.

"So fix the poison and find Helen. That's your job right now, and that's all. Anything else can wait." Jorge looked again to Zoey and rested his hand on hers. "And no killing people."

She gave him a small growl of frustration but nodded, turning her hand over and squeezing his. He smiled at her.

"Soooo," Sara said, drawing out the word, "*now* are we breaking into a lab?"

--➤➤◄◄--

Jenny sighed. They'd spent a good hour trying to hash out what to do. Zoey wanted to go herself. Jenny figured it might give her an excuse to kill people without violating her promise to Jorge.

Jenny suggested going in as a group. Safety in numbers and all that. But Oliver nixed that idea right away. He said there was no way he could get more than one or two inside without security noticing. No matter the scenario Jenny put forth, Oliver said it was impossible.

Will was vehemently, violently opposed to everything. Sara had gotten shot on their last expedition and that had been with them being very lucky. He didn't think they had any idea what they were going into nor how many Visci they'd find. Would they be armed? Would they shoot to kill? Would they bother asking questions if the little raiding party was captured? What was the exit strategy?

In the end, they decided that she, Oliver, and Mecca would go into the lab, with Will driving them. Sara would be their support, but stay here at the apartment, on her laptop. She could play with the security system and help them get through most issues that way.

"I don't know how we're going to get into his office," Ollie said abruptly. "There is an eye scanner and a swipe card."

"No keypad?" Sara asked.

Ollie shook his head.

"Crap."

"Now you tell us?" Zoey snapped.

"That makes it harder?" Jenny asked. It made sense, but she didn't know anything about hacking into security systems. She sort of wondered how Sara did.

"Yeah," Sara replied, rooting through the bag she'd brought back from her apartment. "I'm not sure how to do this without tripping the alarm. Biometrics can be hard to fiddle with. Well, anything aside from fingerprint scanners. Those are easy."

They all watched her as she pulled out a small, black gadget. It wasn't any bigger than a stack of four or five quarters. One end was flat, and the other had a small wire sticking up about a centimeter.

"Here we go!" Sara said with that grin. "Okay, so I don't know if this will work. It's possible it will not-work spectacularly. But still might be worth a try." She looked at them expectantly.

Jenny was glad everyone had looks in their faces that matched her cluelessness.

"What is it?" Mecca asked.

"It's…" She squinted and wrinkled up her nose for a second. "I'm not really sure how to explain properly. It's supposed to intercept, maybe jam, electronic signals sent among microchips and other tiny parts. But it's…" She waggled her hand back and forth. "Let's just say it's still in development."

"It's a bug?" Will asked.

Sara looked affronted. "I guess if you want to be simple."

He smiled and spread his hands. "I'm a simple man."

She smirked good-naturedly and continued. "Like I said, it may not work—probably *won't* work. But I guess it's better than nothing."

Jenny still didn't understand how the little black disk was useful. "What do we do?"

"Oh! Sorry." She turned to her laptop, tapped some keys, and pressed her finger against the disk. A tiny blue LED lit and flashed. She gave the screen a nod and then turned her attention back to them. "So you put it on the eye scanner. Not on the lens, but on the backside or top or whatever the scanner's encased in. This is magnetized, so if the case is metal, you can just slap it on there. But if the case is plastic, you'll need to hold the little guy, because it won't stay."

She moved her non-slinged hand to mimic what she said.

"I'll be on the other end of your phone, trying to get it to open up." She paused and swept her gaze across the group. "I'd explain that part but… You probably don't want me to, right?"

Mecca raised her hands. "No. Please don't."

Jenny snorted. "Where do you get these things?"

"If I told you that…" Sara winked.

Jenny shook her head, amused. "All right. What if that doesn't work?"

"Cut a hole in the wall?" This came from Oliver, who'd been very quiet during the entire conversation.

This got Will's attention. "Is that an option?"

"It could be, as a last resort. There's a supply closet beside his office. Mostly paper, ink toner, that sort of thing. If we had to, we could cut a hole in the drywall."

"That seems a lot more straightforward than…" Will waved a hand at Sara. "No offense."

"Pfft. None taken," Sara said, though she made a face at him and laughed.

"Can we get on with things?" Zoey snapped. "I'd really like to get a better sample to work with than antidotes that don't work."

Chapter Thirty-One: Mecca

Mecca climbed into the back seat of Zoey's car, and Will followed. Ollie and Jenny were already in the front seat, Ollie making the short drive again. They began talking about the plan.

"This is not a good idea," Will whispered to her. "Why are you so gung-ho about doing this? Only two days ago, you wanted to slaughter any Visci you could find." His eyebrows crinkled together as he stared at her with hard eyes.

"I'm not being gung-ho. But Jenny's going to do this either way." Her voice had taken on a determined quality that she hadn't recognized in herself in a long time. "And I will not let her get killed."

The hardness in his eyes slipped away, and he leaned back a tad. His face, expressionless for that moment, shifted into one that included something of a grin quirking up one side of his mouth. "But she's Visci."

She pursed her lips and then said, "I know."

"So not all Visci are bad?"

"Jenny isn't bad."

He said nothing, but he was trying to get her to admit that not all Visci needed to die. She was coming to terms with that. But she wasn't sure she was ready to say it out loud yet. Luckily, Jenny came to her rescue and she didn't have to.

"You guys know I can hear you, right?"

"We do now," Mecca said. She leaned back in the seat, the gun from the safe house tucked into her jacket pocket, pressing against her hip.

———»«———

They pulled into the back of the lab building, just like earlier. There were fewer cars this time—only three. As Oliver cut the engine, he said, "Doctor Blume is here."

Mecca let out a breath. "That will make this more difficult."

He nodded.

"You're staying in the car, remember?" Mecca said, when Will moved to follow them across the parking lot.

"No, I'm not."

"Yes, you are." She put a hand on his chest before she realized she was going to do it. *Never mind.* "We agreed that you'd stay in the car in case we need to get out fast. That is the only reason you're here."

He glared at her.

She leaned in, lowering her voice. "Please, Will. I can't be worried about you in there too."

His glare turned into a frown and he grumbled, "Fine."

"Thank you." She meant it. She turned away, fitting her Bluetooth bud in her ear and found Jenny and Ollie staring at her. "What?" She didn't give them a chance to respond before she rang up a group voice chat with them, Will, and Sara. "Can you hear me?"

"Got you, loud and clear," Sara said on the other end. "If you're ready, I'll loop the camera on the back door."

Jenny and Oliver fiddled with their earbuds, and Mecca didn't even look to see if Will was fixing his. She really wanted him with her, but she couldn't take the chance. She couldn't watch over him along with Jenny and Oliver. Straightening her back, she said, "Do it."

The three of them jogged across the small lot and up the stairs. Oliver swiped them in with his badge.

Here we go.

Chapter Thirty-Two: Jenny

They came in on a hallway that reminded Jenny of her high school. All institutional beige with pale blue accents. A time keeper terminal was stationed near to the entrance, beside a closed door with a sign that said "Break Room" on it. It was one of those doors you only find in institutional buildings. Metal, painted to match the walls, with a thin vertical window near the handle, glass reinforced with crossed metal filaments. In case they were trapped inside during the zombie apocalypse, no doubt.

Oliver led them down the hall and turned right, then left.

"I'm going to see if I can get you into the closet beside his office," he whispered. "Then I'll find out where he is. If he's inside, I'm not sure what we'll do."

That hadn't even occurred to her. They couldn't very well cut a hole in the wall beside his desk when he was sitting at it. Not subtle at all.

Ten seconds later, he was shoving them through the door of a medium-sized supply closet. One wall had stacks of shelving occupied by a few cases of printer paper, lots of office supplies, and random cardboard boxes. Jenny tapped the flashlight on her phone as the door shut them in darkness.

"Have you got the thingy?" she asked Mecca.

Her best friend fished into her jeans pocket and pulled out Sara's little black disk. Jenny took it and cracked the door open enough to put her eyeball against it and see out.

"Did you see the office door?" she whispered.

"No." Mecca crowded in behind her.

"It's just there." She pointed inside the closet at the wall on the left side of the door. "That's his office, on the other side." She leaned away, letting Mecca see. "You can barely make out the scanner thing at this angle, but it's right there." She crunched her finger in a hooking gesture.

"Yeah, I can see the edge. Oh, hey, Oliver's coming." Mecca pulled back and opened the door.

Oliver motioned them out. "He's in the main lab. I'll go down there and keep an eye on him. If he heads this way, I'll let you know."

They both nodded. The danger of the situation struck home. Jenny felt like throwing up. If they got caught...

Oliver rushed back along the hall, leaving them in silence. Jenny shoved her phone in her pocket after switching off the light. There was nothing to be done but move forward. "Keep an eye out," she whispered.

She moved to the electronic thing in the wall. It looked sort of like a camera eye with a dog's shame collar around it.

"Do I just put it on the outside—"

"Yes," came Sara's voice. "Just slap it on the metal."

"It's plastic."

"Didn't we talk about this? Put it on the side and hold it. Make sure the light is on."

"It is." Jenny held the little thing to the side of the scanner. The blue light blinked. "Is it—"

"It's fine. Well, it's not fine, because it's not doing what I think it should be doing. But you're holding it fine." Keys clacked on the line.

"What do you mean?" Mecca whispered.

"Nothing. It's fine. We're all fine. So weird. But fine."

"Sara." Mecca's tone had gone dark.

"Shh," Sara said.

"Is it working or not?" Jenny asked, glancing down the hall. She thought she could feel her blood pulsing behind her eyes.

"Not. Definitely not." Sara's voice had the same light, breezy tone it always did.

Mecca said, "Sar—"

"He's coming!" Oliver whispered, frantic. "I looked up, and he was gone, and he's in the hall now. Hide!"

Jenny looked at Mecca, who had the same startled look on her face that she must have had. She palmed the disk and they scrambled to get back into the closet.

"The signal's gone," Sara said. "Are you guys okay?"

"Sh," Mecca said in a quiet, clipped tone.

Jenny cracked the door eyeball-width again and peered out.

A short, thin man in a white lab coat came stalking from the direction Oliver had gone. Stalking was the only way to describe it. If there had been prey ten feet down that hall, this man would have walked just this way to capture it.

As he neared the door, Oliver's voice came ringing out, breathless. "Doctor Blume! Doctor Blume!"

The man, clearly irritated at being startled, turned. Oliver came racing up, looking all around. When he didn't see Jenny and Mecca, he let out a strained breath.

"What is it?" The doctor had a distinctly German accent. He reminded Jenny of some old comedy show her mom used to watch that was set in a World War Two prisoner of war camp. Not something Jenny herself would write a comedy about, but who understood the older generation?

"I—I'm sorry," Oliver said, slowly.

Please, please let him have thought of a story before he engaged the crazy scientist.

He hadn't.

"Well, I was wondering if…"

When Oliver didn't finish, Blume scoffed at him, his angled features shifting from irritation to anger. "What *is* it, Mr. Armitage? Do you need more to do?" He leaned in toward Oliver. "Or maybe less?"

"I—I'm sorry," Oliver repeated.

The man huffed, swiped his key card, and leaned in to the scanner. Oliver looked over and made eye contact. Every muscle on his face froze into a panicked mask.

Mecca gave Jenny a little push away from the door. "Come on."

"What are you doing?"

"There's only one way we're getting into that office."

Mecca blew past her and into the hall. Jenny didn't know what to do but follow. As the man opened the office door, she barreled into him and bullied him through. Oliver's shocked look matched Jenny's own feelings, but they were committed now, so she barreled in right behind.

"Close the door," Mecca said to Oliver as he came through.

"What is going on?" the man demanded in a voice that indicated he always got the answers he was looking for.

Mecca flashed a gun at him and said, "Sit down," waving it at a chair in front of his desk.

Jenny barely held in her gasp. Where had she gotten the gun?

Then she remembered. Bringing Oliver and Jorge back from the halfway house. Mecca had taken one of the thug's guns and held it on Oliver in the car. Jenny hadn't even thought about it since. And she didn't realize Mecca had brought it here. "What are you doing?" she whispered through gritted teeth.

"Shh."

So much shushing going on. Jenny tried not to let her panic overtake her.

The man, though, certainly wasn't panicking. He simply stood there, staring at them with a smirk on his face.

"Sit," Mecca repeated.

"I shall not," he said. "You are in more trouble than you realize."

"No, you are," she said. "Oliver, get his laptop."

Jenny hadn't noticed it when they'd entered, but there was indeed a laptop on the large, oaken desk.

The doctor wasn't any taller than Jenny, but rail thin and with very sharp, aquiline features. His gaze swung to Oliver, who drifted forward to comply. "Stop."

Oliver's movement ground to a halt.

Jenny said, "Get the laptop, Oliver," her voice stern.

His eyes, looking terrified, darted from the doctor to her.

She tried to convey calmness and gave him a nod. "It's okay. The laptop."

He blinked several times, as if he were clearing something out of his eyes. *Come on, Oliver.* Finally, he returned her nod and moved more decisively toward the desk. Blume stared at her, and she got the distinct impression he was studying her, measuring her as surely as if he'd held her in his hands and turned her over and over.

"Well, this is unexpected," he said, more than a bit of surprise in his voice.

Jenny straightened her back and looked him in the eye. "My friend told you to sit."

He snorted. "Yes, indeed, she did."

Oliver had gathered up the laptop, and Jenny handed him the small pack they'd brought. He slid it in and hoisted the pack onto his back.

Jenny had taken her attention away from Mecca and Blume but turned back when a sudden scuffle began. Blume grappled with Mecca, his hands over hers, which held the gun.

Jenny jumped toward them, knowing that Blume would be so much stronger. And she was right. He jerked the gun, and it popped from Mecca's grip.

But her other hand dropped onto the man's wrist.

A look of confusion slid through his eyes as Mecca abandoned the gun and grabbed his wrist with the other hand too. Her face had become a mask of fierce determination and anger. Rage, even.

At the halfway house, Jenny hadn't been able to watch the man above her as Mecca did her thing. She'd been busy trying not to die.

But now…

Even in London, she hadn't actually *seen* Noor kill the man.

It went quickly, the business of death. Blume's skin pulled tightly over his body. The gun clattered to the floor as he reached for Mecca's arm, trying to break her grip on him. But his strength—that Visci strength—seemed to be gone now, because he couldn't even get a handle on her, let alone pull away.

His cold, brown eyes widened as every one of his years took hold on his body.

And he must have been old.

He withered to a frail, skeletal thing. It reminded her of Holocaust photos. With one final wheeze, he toppled to the floor, his white coat billowing around him.

Only then did Mecca release him. She staggered back, unsteady.

Jenny rushed over. "Are you okay?" She pulled Mecca tight, supporting her.

Mecca nodded. "Yeah. Yeah. I'm fine. It's a big rush of energy. Just...huge." She turned away, bent, and vomited on the floor.

Okay, that was unexpected.

Mecca sucked in big gasps of air.

"Get some water!" Jenny said to Oliver.

He looked like a frightened puppy now, making half steps right and left. "Where?"

"I don't know! You're the one who works here!"

"If I go out—"

"I'm okay," Mecca said, straightening. She held up a hand. "I'm okay."

"Are you sure?"

Another nod. "Yeah. It just needs to...settle."

Oliver stood, staring at them both with horror.

Mecca finally noticed him. "What? You saw this happen before."

"I..." He didn't finish.

"Mec, you sure you're okay?"

"Yeah."

Sara, who'd been quiet this whole time, said, "Would someone please tell me what the hells is going on?"

"Umm..." Jenny looked at the husk on the floor. "We kinda have a problem."

--➤➤◄◄--

After Jenny relayed what happened, Sara let out a string of expletives that Jenny hadn't expected out of her. She finished it up with, "Did I hear you say that you got his laptop?"

"Yes," Oliver said. He'd recovered his wits a bit in the story's telling.

"Oh good. That will help. You guys should come back now."

"It's not that easy, Sara," Mecca said.

"No," Jenny added. The whole time she'd been talking to Sara, she'd been pondering how much more difficult their situation was now.

"Oh, yeah," Sara said. "You've got a body."

If that husk could be called a body, Jenny thought.

They brainstormed what to do and Sara finally suggested, "You could burn the place down."

Oliver's brow wrinkled. "There are people here."

"Right. So pull the fire alarm right before you start it. People will evacuate."

"And those in the rooms?" he asked, clearly thinking this was a stupid plan.

"What rooms?" Mecca asked.

"I told you they'd bring people back here for testing. Where do you think they stayed?"

"You make it sound like an elective procedure at a plastic surgeon's office," Mecca said under her breath.

Jenny held out a hand. They didn't have time for this. "Okay, so can we get them out too?"

"We could," he said, "with time. I can go into the system and see how many people we have, but I'll need to go to my office."

"Well we can't all go," Mecca said. "The fire needs to start here." She motioned to Blume's body. "To cover that."

Jenny began looking around the room to see if there was anything to start a fire with. It looked like an ordinary, if somewhat posh, office.

Except there was a door behind the desk.

"Where does that go to?"

"I've been here as long as you have," Mecca said. But she walked over to the door.

"I was asking Oliver."

"I don't know," he said. "His lab, probably. I told you he needs to have his own lab to mix the compounds and do initial testing on them."

"There's a card reader," Mecca said. "Get his card from his jacket."

Oliver took a step back, an expression of disgust on his face. "You get his card from his jacket."

Mecca turned around. "You know she can make you do it."

Jenny glared at her friend. "I'll get the damn card."

Mecca seemed nonplussed and only shrugged.

Jenny approached the withered corpse and crouched beside it. Dusty dryness settled in her nose. She tried very, very hard not to sneeze.

God, how gross would that be? Sneezing a dude? Eww.

She shook the thought from her head and began rifling through the coat pockets. It only took a moment for her to find the white plastic keycard attached to a short lanyard. She grabbed it and stood.

The door Mecca stood beside was a nondescript brown wood, much like the door to the office itself. No eye scanner, though.

Jenny swiped the card, and the lock gave a heavy click. Mecca nodded and turned the handle.

The room beyond seemed a lot like Zoey's room at the apartment, only larger and *much* more expensive. She didn't know what any of it was for, specifically. She pulled out her phone and took a few photos. When Mecca gave her a look, she said, "In case Zoey might be able to get some answers from what type of equipment is here."

"Ah." Mecca wandered off, looking at things, just as Jenny did.

"Oliver," Jenny called.

He appeared at the door, looking uncertain.

"Does anything in here seem important? I mean, something we should take with us that would give Zoey an idea of where to start?"

"I'll check," he said.

She was glad of that. He'd recognize something useful way before either of them would.

After several moments of searching, neither she nor Mecca came away with anything, but Oliver had found a small notebook. None of them recognized the scrawled words inside, but Jenny pocketed it anyway, just in case.

"Okay," Mecca said to Oliver, "what in here can we use to set a fire?"

--->>><<<--

Jenny hadn't planned on being an arsonist tonight. Or, really, ever. But here they were.

They'd decided to start the fire in the lab, with accelerant in the office to make sure the body was covered.

"I'm ready," Oliver said.

They'd put him in charge of finding things in the lab that might be flammable. He'd assembled two rows of different bottles and containers, each with some chemical he named off in turn. He added why they were flammable.

"Oliver," Jenny said, "if we pull the fire alarm, will they evacuate the Visci that are being tested now?"

"I have no idea."

"You never got instructions about that sort of thing?" Mecca asked.

"No," he said.

"Well that seems ill-advised."

"We should do a pass through all the halls where the rooms are," Jenny said.

Another voice came on the line. Will's. "You guys need to get out of there once the fire starts. Don't worry about the other rooms."

"I agree," Mecca said.

She would. Wanting to kill every Visci and all.

Jenny shook her head. "No."

"Fine. But we need to set the fire first."

"You risk not getting out in time," Will said, not liking this plan.

"It'll be okay. If we run through the halls, Oliver can tell us which rooms hold people. We'll open them, make sure to get the people out, and then we'll go ourselves."

"How do none of you hear what a horrible plan this is?" Will asked. "You're going to get yourselves killed. I'm coming in."

"No!" Mecca said at once. "Stay there. Bring the car around to the front though. If we go to the other end of the building, that is where we're going to come out, right?" She looked at Oliver.

He nodded, but said nothing.

Jenny pulled him aside and only half-listened to Mecca and Will arguing.

"Are you sure we can get the kidnapped people out?"

"Honestly? I don't know. Most will be sedated. We'll have to wheel their beds out."

Jenny hadn't considered that. Not at all. "Shit." She pulled the bud from her ear. The fighting was distracting her. "What if we wheel them all to the front? Is there a lobby? That way, emergency workers can get to them immediately."

Oliver looked dubious. "Are we going to leave before the fire department gets here?"

"We have to." The more Jenny thought about it, the worse it sounded. What if people died?

She shoved the bud back into her ear. "We can't do this," she said, raising her voice over everyone else talking. Apparently, Sara had jumped into the conversation.

"What?" Mecca said.

"People could die in this fire. We can't stay until the responders get here. Not if we don't want to get caught and asked a bunch of uncomfortable questions. So what do we do? Leave them on the lawn?"

"Why not?" Mecca asked. At first Jenny assumed she was joking, but a look at her face said that she was deadly serious.

"Because we can't. They're victims here."

Mecca scoffed.

"Stop it! You were kidnapped. So were they."

That shut her up for the moment. Jenny wasn't sure if they'd ever get past all this.

"Jenny," Oliver said, quietly.

He'd never said her name before. She looked at him.

"If they find his body here, not only will they realize the lab has been compromised, but if they know what she can do"—he nodded toward Mecca—"they will know it was her. She'll be in grave danger."

Jenny hadn't thought of that. Mecca's frown told her she hadn't either.

Will, also on the line, said, "That doesn't mean you have to burn the whole place down. It only means you need to get rid of the body."

The body.

A month ago, Jenny never would have fathomed being in a position to where that statement could ever be a part of her life.

Blume's corpse—a shell really—still lay on the floor in front of the desk. Could they get it out?

"What about a gurney?" she asked Oliver. "Could you get one in here? Maybe we could wheel him out the back. That's how you bring people in, right? The loading bay?"

He nodded. "That might work."

"Then he's just disappeared." She glanced at Mecca. "Not dead."

Mecca pursed her lips and gave a tight nod.

"Let me see what I can do." Oliver moved to the door, cracked it to peek out, and slipped into the hall.

"So we wheel him out," Mecca said, "and into the car. Then what?"

Jenny sighed. "Can we get through one ridiculous problem at a time?"

"I'll bring the car up to the employee door," Will said. The engine turned over in the background.

"Hey," Oliver said. "You're here late."

Jenny looked at Mecca, her confusion mirrored in Mecca's face.

Someone spoke to Oliver.

"Oh? An appointment this late? Um. I don't—I don't think he's here."

Someone was coming. That's what was happening. Could they get into the office without Blume? Jenny had no idea.

Mecca must have had the same notion because she said, "Help me," as she went to Blume's body.

It turned out that she didn't need Jenny's help pulling the body behind the desk and into the lab.

"Oh, well yes, I guess his car is here. But I haven't seen him. Are you sure you want—"

Jenny set a lamp straight that had been knocked over in the struggle for the gun, just as Oliver's voice came from both the earbud and outside the door.

"I don't think he'd want you in…" And then the door began to open.

Chapter Thirty-Three: Mecca

"Shit!" Mecca whispered, holding the lab door and waving Jenny to her. If someone found them... "Hurry!"

Jenny blurred around the desk and in beside her. Mecca blinked, trying to get her eyes to make sense of Jenny's speed. Jenny eased the lab door closed as a deep voice with an exotic accent responded to Oliver.

"Our employer requested that I meet with Doctor Blume. It seems strange that his automobile is outside, but I cannot find him anywhere in the building."

"Yeah," Oliver said, his voice reflecting his nerves.

"Come on, Oliver," Jenny whispered. "Keep it together."

"What about the lab there?" the man said.

I know that voice.

"Umm. It only takes a key card, I think." Then a pause before he quickly added, "I've never been in there."

"Shit," Mecca said again. There wasn't anywhere to hide in the lab.

Or to hide the body.

Jenny grabbed the thing anyway, and Mecca wanted to retch as she realized dust—Visci dust—was flaking off and leaving a light trail on the floor and a haze in the air. She dragged her gaze away from it and instead looked for places that might hide two human-sized women.

Jenny shoved the body beneath one of the huge metal tables that stood against the wall. She crammed it as far back as she could reach. Then she looked at Mecca with wild eyes that asked where they were supposed to go.

A sharp rap came on the door. They both stared at it, as if it would come off its jamb with the force behind the knock.

"Doctor Blume!" called the man.

That voice.

A click and a buzz came from the other side. And then again.

"My card is not working," the stranger said.

"Well, you know, Doctor Blume is pretty weird about other people being in his la—space."

One more click and buzz, and the man said, "What is your function here?"

Mecca closed her eyes. Dread settled at the base of her spine. She'd figured out the voice.

Salas. Claude's man.

Jenny came to her side and grabbed her hand, listening. Mecca's stomach sank to her feet.

Of course Claude is behind all this. Because of course *he is.*

Oliver, clearly taken off guard at the man's question, stammered his reply. "I run the lab. Out there. The lab out there."

Mecca hung her head and tightened her grip on Jenny's hand. Oliver was going to get them killed.

"Very well. Tell Doctor Blume that I was here."

"Y-yes, sir."

Jenny blew out a breath, and tension unwound from Mecca's muscles.

Oliver began to say something but then the sounds of a struggle came through their earbuds. Jenny's eyes widened, surprise etched in every feature.

What had happened?

"Do you think I cannot tell when you are lying?" Salas said, in a low, deadly tone. He must have been very close to Oliver's head for them to hear him so intimately.

Oliver gasped and choked. Then came the clatter of the Bluetooth earbud skittering across the floor.

"Shit," Mecca whispered. "Come on."

Without a plan, she unlatched the door and opened it enough to see out. Salas, tall and broad-shouldered, had his back to them. Mecca flung the door wide.

He held Oliver by his neck, suspended against the wall with a single hand and punched him hard with his other. He landed three hits in super-fast succession and didn't seem as if he was going to stop.

Oliver grunted and cried out.

Mecca bolted, shifting her sight just before slamming into Salas's back.

"Ooof!" came Salas's voice. He released his hold on Oliver, who crumpled to the floor.

Salas's Cavern, Mecca suspected, would be the hollowed out grey and dim place, much like Claude's.

But surprise cut her short. The golden glow of a human's soul met her vision. What did that mean?

But there was nothing for it, because he was turning now, looking at her. His astonishment showed in his eyes for only a second before caution—and action—took over.

He slammed the back of his hand against her jaw and sent her flying away. Everything slowed as spikes of pain hammered her face where he hit. She landed on her bad leg and that pain flashed electric through her entire body. She swallowed her scream into a yelp and pulled in a breath.

Jenny flashed past her, a blur again, and tackled Salas. He'd barely registered her coming before she was on him. He pushed her away, but she kept on.

The room swam and waved. Mecca ran a hand over her face and took another deep breath.

A part of her brain registered the silence over where Oliver sat crumpled against the wall, but she couldn't bring herself to look. She used the desk to pull herself onto her feet. She'd slammed against it on her way across the room, apparently. Her leg screamed at her, but she hobbled to where Jenny grappled with the tall, impossibly strong man.

Mecca's vision still showed his Cavern, and she noted the black tendrils woven through the golden light of his soul. It was like Will's and Oliver's, only more enmeshed. And much darker. So he was a human tied to…well, Claude, in all likelihood.

Jenny had never been much of a fighter, but it was clear that Salas was. Jenny's messy attacks never came close to doing him damage. She looked more like a boxer on her last legs than anything else.

Mecca thought all this as she staggered, limping, back to where they fought.

If she could only get a hand on him. Just one hand.

He wore a long-sleeved turtleneck and a light field jacket on top of brown Dockers. The only things exposed were his hands and face.

They would have to do.

As Salas flung Jenny off with a grunt, Mecca grabbed his hand. His eyes widened, and he jerked against her grip.

She sent her soul into his and began pulling. But his soul wouldn't come. Not the way it did with Visci.

But he felt it, because he yanked his hand away, his eyes wide with fear. She'd never seen that emotion on his face before. He backed toward the door. She moved with him. He broke into a run, pulled the door open, and dashed through.

Ignoring the very adamant protests from her leg, Mecca followed. She couldn't let him get away.

But he had long legs and some Visci blood, which meant he was fast. By the time she made it to the hall, he was already at the other end and his yell there brought two security guys in dark suits.

"Shit."

Mecca ducked back into the office. Jenny kneeled beside Oliver, looking panicked and trying to get him to wake up.

"Never mind," Mecca said. The desperation in her own voice scared her as much as it scared Jenny, judging from the expression on her face. "Get up. We have to go. Will, we're coming. Be ready. We're coming and fast."

"I'm at the door," he said. She was grateful that he didn't ask her what was happening.

Mecca went to grab one of Oliver's arms, but Jenny picked him up like a little kid and half-slung him over her shoulder. They couldn't worry about his injuries yet. They needed to get to safety first.

"The backpack," Jenny said, nodding at it.

Oliver had been wearing it earlier, and now it lay where he'd fallen. Mecca scooped it up and followed Jenny, who'd already made it out the door.

Jenny didn't even look back but made a beeline around the corner, heading for the door they'd entered.

"What's going on?" Sara said on the line.

"Later," Will snapped.

Mecca made the mistake of glancing along the hall before following Jenny.

Three giant men, dark suits stuffed with thick chests and huge arms, barreled down the long hall toward them.

"Go! Go!" she yelled, running full tilt behind her best friend, whose speed was leaving her behind. "Shit shit shit."

Jenny pushed into the employee door, and they were outside, cold air slamming them both in the face.

Will stood beside the car, three doors open—the two in front and one back seat. "Come on! Get in!" He rushed to help Jenny.

"Just get ready to drive. I've got him." And a second later, she'd hurled Oliver's unconscious form into the back seat and climbed in after.

Mecca hadn't even gotten to the car when the building door crashed open.

She put on a burst of speed—thank God for track—and catapulted into the passenger side. "Go!" She jerked her door shut as gunfire erupted around them. Everyone in the car ducked.

Will slammed the car into Drive and smashed the gas pedal, sending them leaping forward.

Mecca raised her head enough to peek out the side window as they careened toward the exit driveway. Three of the guys in dark suits lined the raised walk at the employee door, guns held in front of them. Salas stood in the doorway, watching.

The gunfire stopped as the car reached the parking lot exit, but Will didn't slow, taking the turn so fast Mecca jarred her shoulder on the window.

He didn't ease off the gas pedal until he got to the main road and had to meld with the late-night traffic around Emory.

"Everyone okay?" He peered at her.

She nodded. The energy rush from killing Blume still sang through her. Between that and the adrenaline, she wasn't sure she wouldn't have a coronary right here.

"I am," Jenny said from the back. "But Oliver won't wake up."

Mecca looked back. His face had gone ashen, and his body lay limp against Jenny. Her best friend looked like a small child: scared and wanting someone to fix it.

"Does he have a pulse?" Will asked, his voice steady and calm.

Jenny pressed two fingers against his neck. It took a moment of moving around, but she said, "Yes. It's faint."

"What happened to him?"

"A man held him by the neck, choking him, and punched him in the stomach. A lot."

"It was Salas," Mecca whispered to Will.

He cut his eyes at her, and she knew he understood what she meant.

Although now Mecca knew that Salas wasn't Visci, they both understood that he wasn't "merely" human, either. His punches hit much harder than a normal human's.

Just as Will's would.

Mecca supposed it was a benefit of the Visci blood.

"He can't die," Jenny said, her voice forlorn, as she cradled Oliver's head in her lap. "I promised I'd keep him safe." When she met Mecca's eyes, desperation lived there.

Leaning the seat all the way back, Mecca said, "Let me try something." She scooted up as far as possible, so she could reach Oliver.

"What are you going to do?" Jenny asked.

I don't really know, Mecca thought. She'd seen her dad try to save Jenny's father, when his life was leaking out over his office floor. It had been bloody and awful. Her dad hadn't known she was in the doorway or that she's shifted her vision to see the Cavern.

Both Caverns.

Jim Barron's *and* her dad's.

The memory assaulted her, but she let it come. She needed to see, to recreate what her dad had tried to do.

She couldn't save Jenny's dad, but maybe she could save Oliver.

Oliver's face was swollen. Bruises started to form on his cheek and just over his right eye. Had Salas punched him before they'd gotten into the room? He must have.

She didn't know if there was more damage to his head or to his gut, but she was able to reach his belly more easily.

"Mecca?"

She'd forgotten Jenny had asked her a question.

"I'm going to try to help him. I don't know if it will work, because I don't exactly know how to do it. But I think it can be done."

I hope it can be done.

From the corner of her eye, she caught Will dividing his attention between the road and her. She ignored him. If he wrecked the car… Well, they'd deal with that if it happened.

She took a breath and tried to relax. The adrenaline still pumped through her and she had that jittery sensation she always got when the chemical dumped into her bloodstream.

She shifted her vision.

Oliver's Cavern superimposed itself over his broken form. As before, it held the warm golden light of a human's soul. And the grey-ish-green tendrils that snaked their way through the light were there too. But the difference from when she viewed his Cavern in Jenny's basement and her view now was radical.

Where before, the light seemed almost like a golden cloud with its radiance suffusing the entire space, now the light—muted—covered the ground in a fog. The top half of the Cavern had dimmed and looked murky.

The tendrils still wove through everything, but now they pulsed and moved, as if looking for more of the light to feed from. It reminded her of the trash compactor scene in *Star Wars*.

It also reminded her of Jim Barron's death. His Cavern had looked much the same, but without the grey parts that Mecca now associated with Visci hold.

How could she fix this?

"Lift his shirt."

Jenny obeyed without hesitation.

Oliver's torso was colored pinkish, with splotches of dark red. A deep purple layered beneath the red.

She set her hand gently on his skin. Warmth heated her palm.

Taking another breath, she focused solely on the Cavern. If she could use her soul to take a stolen human soul from a Visci—killing him—then it made some kind of sense that she should be able to push her soul into Oliver's to…keep his from draining away?

She didn't know, but she had to try. Jenny wouldn't forgive herself if Oliver died. Mecca couldn't let that happen.

The gold color of the human soul was universal, but many people had tinges of other colors around the edges. Mecca didn't know if the colors meant anything. Her own edging was a bright blue, as was her dad's, her Uncle Ken's and her Gramps's.

Oliver's was only golden. Had it been edged in a color earlier? She didn't remember.

She tried to concentrate only on what she was doing right now.

Trying not to let her fear and panic color her mind, Mecca concentrated on gathering up a column of her own soul.

Letting her eyes drift closed for a moment, she thought of her own soul, about molding a piece of her soul into a hand, an arm. Something that could extend away from her and toward Oliver. The low thrumming beat that had been in her veins ever since Blume's death began to echo outward.

When she opened her eyes again, a long column of gold wove itself into Oliver's Cavern. It slid into the fog of Oliver's soul and wound circles around the ebbing light. The difference in the vibrancy of the colors was stark. Her own bright; his dim, dull.

She wasn't directing it exactly. She'd pushed a bit of her soul into his, but once the light of her essence was there, it seemed to work on its own. Mecca had become a spectator.

Within a few moments, the distinct edges of her soul were no longer visible. The blue had melded into the rest and taken on the same golden hue. It entwined and become one with Oliver's. The fog-like parts became denser, brighter.

"I think it's working," Jenny whispered.

Mecca focused back on the real world. The red patches on his face had melted away. They didn't even look pink. On his torso, the purple marks were still visible, but they were red now and fading too.

Mecca's thoughts had halted altogether. She couldn't even fathom quite what was happening. She shifted again to the Cavern.

Oliver's soul—the piece of hers seemed to have melded with his now—had risen from the floor to almost fill the entire space. It was very near to looking normal now. Its color had leveled out and become more uniform.

How could this have *possibly* worked?

For the first time in her life, she regretted not letting her father teach her more about her Gift.

"Jenny?" Oliver's voice broke through her thoughts, and she snapped her vision to the here and now, letting the Cavern scene close altogether.

"I'm here!" Jenny said, her voice filled with relief and awe. "You're okay. You're going to be okay."

Mecca let out a breath and slumped down in the seat.

Now that the crisis had passed—*it worked!*—weariness invaded her bones. She closed her eyes. Muscles that had been tense and tight felt sore, as if she'd run all-out crazy to place in a track meet. The adrenaline, the rush from Blume's death, all that was gone, leaving her with a bone-numbing exhaustion.

All she wanted to do was sleep for a week.

"Guys." Sara's voice came across as quiet, subdued. And that wasn't like Sara.

It brought Mecca's awareness back, and she opened her eyes. That feeling, like dread, that creeps up and makes it seem as if the floor will drop out from under you at any moment crept over her.

"What's wrong?" Will asked.

"Jorge. He's…"

Will took the next corner at a snail's pace. "He's what?"

Even in the gloom, Mecca saw Jenny's pained expression. It was as if they both knew what Sara was about to say—the only thing she *would* say in that tone. And neither of them wanted to hear it.

"He's gone," Sara said, hushed.

"What?" Jenny's voice, high-pitched and on the verge of frantic, matched the look on her face.

Mecca laid a hand on her best friend's wrist.

"He just…" Sara's voice cracked. "He's gone."

Chapter Thirty-Four: Jenny

"Hey," Sara said quietly, as she let them into the apartment.

The happiness and elation Jenny had felt after Mecca had healed Oliver was long gone. Her own mood matched Sara's somberness.

And then she saw Jorge. Or rather, the blanket on the sofa bed that covered him. Tears pricked at her eyes.

They'd let him down. He'd needed them to be there, to get the thing done, and they'd failed.

"Here," Mecca said to Sara. "We managed to get his laptop out. It fell on the floor once or twice, but hopefully it's not damaged. Maybe you can get something off it about the poison."

"What's the point?" Jenny said, not turning to look at them. "He's dead."

Mecca's hand rested on the back of her shoulder. "I'm sorry." They stood in silence for a moment before she continued. "But there is at least one infected human out there. Maybe more. We can't be sure."

The irony of Mecca's words wasn't lost on Jenny. Mecca, who'd vowed to kill every last Visci, was now wanting Sara to find something they could use to figure out a cure for a poison that would kill any Hybrid— more than half the Visci.

I guess mass execution doesn't have the right flavor.

Guilt stabbed at her. She didn't want to think of Mecca that way.

"Where's Zoey?" she asked.

"She's in that room. Her room, I guess," Sara said as she set the laptop on the kitchen island beside her own. "She's been there ever since…"

Jenny turned around to face Mecca. "I'll talk to her. It's probably better if you stayed in here."

Mecca nodded.

Jenny moved to the other door—the one that was not the bathroom or a bedroom, but instead was inexplicably a lab. She knocked.

There was no answer.

"Zoey?"

Still nothing.

She felt someone behind her.

Oliver.

"I have something," he said.

"What?"

"I want to show Zoey."

She searched his face, but he seemed sincere. She turned back to the door. "Zoey, I'm coming in."

She turned the handle, half expecting it to be locked. It moved smoothly.

She opened the door onto Zoey's little lab. It looked very much like Blume's, only much smaller and not as…expensive-looking. Instead of shiny metal tables, Zoey's equipment was organized on white plastic pop-up tables, the centers reinforced with wooden saw horses. DIY lab, apparently.

Zoey was hunched over a microscope, a laptop open on the table beside her. "What?" she asked, without looking up.

Jenny stepped into the room, leaving the door open for Oliver to follow. "I wanted to see how you're doing."

"Busy."

"I see that." Clearly, Zoey was one of those who threw themselves into anything to distract them from their feelings. Jenny could relate. "You're looking at the antidote?"

"That didn't work? Yeah. And after, I'll tackle the other one that didn't work."

As Oliver stepped forward, he met Jenny's gaze, looking for support. It wasn't surprising that Zoey intimidated him. After all, she'd almost killed him.

"I have something that might help," he said, his voice soft.

Zoey swung her head around and glared at him. "Help? Like these helped?" She waved a hand at her microscope.

"I said that I didn't know whether they'd —"

"And they didn't. Help." She turned back to her work.

"This might." He took a few tentative steps and stretched a hand forward, as if he didn't want to get any closer than he had to. He laid three vials on the table beside her and then backtracked to Jenny's side.

He was definitely brave, Oliver.

Scowling, Zoey glanced at the vials, but she straightened up and turned around to see them both properly. "What are these?"

"The most recent batch of the poison that was in the main lab," he said. "It's possible that's what was put into the guards."

She lifted a vial between her fingers and stared at it, turning it back and forth. "If this is tainted, I'll know."

"I only want to help," he said. He looked at Jenny again, and she gave him a nod. She hadn't known he'd pocketed the vials. He hadn't said a word. Oliver took her nod as an excuse to leave, backing out of the room quickly, but without turning his back on them.

"So no headway?" Jenny asked.

Zoey's attention moved from the vials to her. "Does it look like I've made headway?"

"Honestly, I'm not sure I'd recognize what that would look like."

Zoey snorted. "No, I haven't."

"I hope those help. There's also Blume's laptop. Sara is working her magic on it right now."

Putting her back to Jenny, Zoey grabbed a couple latex gloves and pulled them on, before setting about creating new, smaller vials from the first one Oliver had left. "Tell her to give me a heads-up when she gets into it."

"Are you okay? About Jorge, I mean."

"That's a stupid question."

Jenny had expected Zoey to rant and rail. So her quiet, nonchalant response was a surprise. "I guess it is."

"After she breaks into the laptop, get Sara on trying to find Helen."

Helen.

In the evening's chaos and the wake of Jorge's death, Jenny had forgotten about Helen. She kept doing that.

"I will," she said. "I'm not sure what she can do, though."

"She's magic with computers. I'm sure she can do something."

Jenny nodded, thinking Zoey was probably right, though surprised she'd compliment anyone. After a moment, Jenny asked, "Why do you have this? I mean, who turns their bedroom into a lab?"

"Obviously, I do."

"Yes. But why?" It seemed weirdly convenient that Zoey happened to have a full lab in her apartment.

"It's not your business, is it?"

And Jenny supposed it wasn't. As she turned to leave, though, Zoey spoke again.

"I'm a grad student in bio-chem."

Jenny paused and half-turned. "Do all bio-chem grad students build their own labs?"

Zoey shrugged. "No idea. Now let me work."

Jenny did as she was asked and went back into the apartment proper. Sara sat hunched over at the kitchen island with both her laptop and Blume's in front of her. A small black box with wires running to both machines, like an umbilical cord.

Mecca stood next to Sara, observing, with Will beside her. Oliver sat in the recliner in the corner of the living room.

Avoiding going anywhere near the sofa bed, Jenny headed to the kitchen. "Mec, can I talk to you for a second?"

"Sure."

Leading her into the bathroom, Jenny took a deep breath and put her thoughts together. After closing the door, she said, "I wanted to thank you for saving Oliver. I'm sure he would have died if you hadn't helped him."

Mecca shifted from foot to foot, distinctly uncomfortable. "No problem."

"How did you do it?" This is what Jenny had been wanting to know since it happened. How had she done it? Why hadn't she tried to do it with Jorge? Was it because he was Visci?

Why hadn't she done it with Jenny's dad?

"I—I don't know, exactly. I just pushed my energy into him. But I had no idea if it would work or not. I've never done anything like that before. I don't even have any idea how it worked."

The bathroom, small and tight, made them stand very close together. Jenny had never been uncomfortable with her best friend, but things were a little different now, weren't they?

"Why didn't you try it with Jorge?"

A startled expression passed across Mecca's face, but only for a moment. "Honestly, I didn't think of it."

"Is that because he's—" She stopped herself. "Was… Is that because he was Visci?"

"What? No." Mecca seemed genuinely surprised. "I would have tried it with him if I had thought of it."

"But you want to kill Visci."

For the first time with this topic, Mecca looked almost sheepish. "Yes, I did. But he was your friend. And if I could have helped him, I would have."

Jenny considered this, and she hoped it was true.

Mecca searched her eyes. Jenny didn't know what she was looking for.

"I didn't have to help Oliver," Mecca said.

"No. I guess you didn't."

She wanted to ask the question about her dad. Wanted to ask very badly. But she was afraid of the answer. What if the answer was "no, I didn't try"?

Mecca leaned against the counter. "I need to tell you something."

Her voice was so serious, so grave, that Jenny pushed aside thoughts of her dad and focused on her best friend.

"The man who came into the office. The one who hurt Oliver. I know him. Sort of."

"What do you mean 'sort of'?"

"I think Claude is behind the lab."

How had she made that connection? "I don't follow."

"The guy in the office. He's Claude's. There would be no reason for him to be there unless this was Claude's operation."

If the guy who beat up Oliver really worked for Claude, then Mecca was right. "And there's no chance that he's doing this on his own? The dude in the office?"

"I doubt it. I got the idea that he doesn't fart without Claude's permission."

"How do you even know him? The guy?"

Mecca's brow creased. "Because he helped me escape Emilia."

If Jenny felt she wasn't following before, now she wasn't following for sure. It must have shown on her face.

"Claude was one of the people who watched me while Emilia had me chained to the bed. When I got free and was trying to find my way out, I ran into a room. Claude and this guy were there. Claude told me how to get out of the house and off the property."

"Why would he do that?"

Mecca shook her head and shrugged. "But when I got to the back gate, Salas came and lured the guard away so I could get out."

None of that made any sense. Jenny was sure it was true, but why?

"Those scenes play over and over in my head," Mecca said. "And the only thing I can think of is that Claude was working on his own plan. I mean, that's got to be the answer, right?"

Mecca was really asking, her tone almost imploring.

"I guess," Jenny said. "I can't figure out another reason. I mean, he told my mom he took care of Emilia, so—"

"Wait, what?"

Jenny didn't understand what part of that was confusing. "Yeah, he didn't say he'd killed her, really, but he said he took care of her."

Mecca scoffed and shook her head. "Of course he did."

"What do you mean?" Jenny was getting tired of feeling confused.

"*I* killed Emilia," Mecca said, flatly. "He didn't 'take care' of her. I killed her."

Not breathing for a moment, not even blinking, Jenny stared at Mecca. "You killed her?"

"Yes. In the woods at the back of the property. I went back—which was so stupid—and she was there. We fought. I won. Claude was there too. He...sort of helped me, even then." She shook her head again. "I don't get his angle."

"I don't either." Jenny knew *nothing*. But it was something to say. "That's why you ran after him. Because you didn't want him going back to Claude."

Mecca nodded. "We're fucked once Claude finds out. I'm not sure what he'll do."

"This guy, is he Visci?"

"No. He's like Oliver. Attached. Only I expect he's been attached for a lot longer, because the grey was everywhere. It was almost black."

"The grey?"

Nodding, she said, "When I look at someone's Cavern—that's where their soul lives—people who are attached to Visci have these grey snakes going through their soul, holding it down. And he had a *lot* of grey snakes."

Jenny thought on this for a minute. How incredible was this thing Mecca could do? She wanted to ask a million questions, wanted to find out how her soul looked. But before she could speak, Mecca raised a hand, as if she recognized what was in Jenny's head.

"We need to figure out what to do about Claude."

Jenny put her curiosity on pause, though it was not easy. "Maybe we should go to my mom. Get the Council involved."

"I don't know. Have they ever done anything good?"

A very stark question. Jenny had no idea whether or not they had. But this was way bigger than Jenny, Mecca, all of them. "I don't think it would be a bad thing to talk to Mom. She's known Claude all her life. She might have an idea what to do."

"Are you sure she's not on his side?"

Mecca's tone didn't hold accusation, but Jenny couldn't believe she would even ask.

"What the hell, Mecca?"

Raising her hands, palms out, Mecca shook her head. "No, no. I'm sorry. I didn't mean it like that. I only meant that if they've been friends for a long time. It's possible she hasn't seen this side of him."

"I don't think they're friends."

"Okay. Okay."

Jenny ran her hands over her face. God, this sucked so bad. "So do we tell them about Salas?" She tilted her head toward the door to the apartment.

"I'm not sure." Mecca's dark eyes looked at her for a long time. "Do we care anymore?"

"What?"

"What if we just let Claude do whatever he's going to do?"

The thought horrified her. "We can't."

"Why not?" She wasn't being argumentative. Jenny understood when Mecca wanted to pick a fight. She didn't sound like that now. And that surprised her a little, considering they were talking about Visci.

"Mec, he wants to poison Hybrids." She poked herself in the chest. "*I'm* a Hybrid."

Mecca leaned away, thinking this through. Then she nodded. "Okay. Okay. You're right. We should keep going."

"Besides, we've still got to find Helen."

"Helen?"

"Yes, my friend—other friend—who's missing? We talked about it back at Sara's?"

"Oh shit, yes. I forgot." She tilted her head. "Do you realize that you are having something of an epidemic of friends being kidnapped? What is it about you?" She cracked a smile at the last moment.

Even though it was a joke, there was truth to it. "That's weird, isn't it?"

"So weird." She paused. "I'm sorry about Jorge. I really am."

"Thanks," Jenny said, trying very hard not to feel anything. So much death.

"And I'm really glad we're all okay," Mecca said.

"Me too. And Oliver. Thank you again."

Mecca smiled. Jenny leaned forward and wrapped her in a hug. And when Mecca hugged her back, it was all she could do not to burst into tears. How much had she missed having her best friend in her life like this? It wasn't something she'd realized until quite this moment.

Mecca pulled back. "Let's go see if Sara can crack that laptop. And then we'll find your friend."

Epilogue: Four Days Later

The pews in St. Mark's were more crowded than Jenny would have thought. She didn't realize Jorge had such a large family. The first four rows on both sides of the aisle were crammed full of what she assumed to be his relatives. People ranging from ancient to infants. She wondered how many of them were Visci and how many human. Most human, she guessed.

An African American priest stood at the lectern and spoke about redemption and God.

In the second seat on the center aisle side of the ninth row, she realized she hadn't expected their whole little group to come. She thought it would only be her and Zoey, who sat beside her, on the aisle. But Mecca had come, so she had her best friend on her other side. Will was next to her. Oliver and Sara sat directly behind them.

That they all showed up had brought tears to Jenny's eyes when they first arrived. They didn't have to come. But they had. That meant something.

Cool fingers grasped her right hand gently. When she looked to her right, Mecca caught her gaze and gave her a supportive smile. With the difficulty between them lately, that smile, that grace, more than anything, helped her heart.

Zoey's hip, pressed against her own, vibrated. A normal sound. Usually a quiet sound. But here, now, in the church's silence, it was louder than Jenny ever could have expected. The people in the row in front of them turned around and gave them stink-eye as Zoey pulled the phone from her pocket.

Who leaves their phone on in a church? At a funeral, even? Jenny completely agreed with the stink-eye. But Zoey clearly didn't care.

Zoey swiped the phone to open it, and Jenny peered at her. But when Zoey's face when stark white, Jenny looked at the phone screen. It was a long text, and she only caught a few words before Zoey jumped to her feet. She rushed down the aisle and out.

The text said:

Unknown: Do NOT reply to this. It's Helen. I need hel…

The End

Did you like what you read? Please be sure to leave a review! Reviews are how authors get readers. The more good word of mouth about the book, the better it is for the author! So leave reviews for authors you love! ☺

Leave a review at your favorite bookseller!

https://books2read.com/Visci

Ready for the next Soul Cavern book?

Book 3 — Hybrid — is coming in May!

And there's going to be another installment of Ken's
adventures in London too.
Don't miss anything! Get the scoop on all the books!

Stay updated:

https://www.venessagiunta.com/sc-signup/

Acknowledgements

As always, I am incredibly grateful for the support I get from everyone around me. Some folks earn a special shout-out:

Much thanks to Mark Binicewicz for his knowledge of TASERs, guns, and overall badassery.

I'm indebted to Heather-Leigh Owens Nies, Mags Nightingale-Mellema, Stacy Christie, and Elegant Pamela for their input on the story in early form. They're great beta readers!

My proofreader, Melissa McArthur, came through for me in a bind, and I can't convey my gratitude enough for that.

Any and all errors are my own and not a reflection on the wonderful folks who've helped me along the way.

We've got another novelette and then the third novel of the series coming up. Stay tuned! ☺

Venessa G

PATREON

Back in the old, old days, artists were supported by wealthy patrons who took care of their living expenses so that the artist was free to create their art.

These days, though, not many of us are so wealthy as to support another person fully, but you can pledge a few dollars a month to help your favorite creatives focus on their art.

Patreon allows folks to toss in a few bucks per month to help their favorite creatives focus on their art.

My Patrons get peeks into the "backstage" of how my writing works. I also post character sketches and deleted scenes. Patrons get first look at cover reveals and excerpts from new books and get input on stories when I run into snags. Higher level Patrons even get physical books!

Become a Patron.
See you on the inside! ☺
https://www.patreon.com/VenessaG

The Soul Cavern Series

Jivaja

Blue-Edged Soul

Visci

Venessa Giunta

Venessa Giunta is a writer of weird things. She holds an MFA in Writing Popular Fiction from Seton Hill University and has worked on the editorial side of publishing for a decade. Her non-fiction essay "Demystifying What Editors Want" can be found in the book, Many Genres, One Craft. She is active in convention life, having held a number of organizational positions over the years and is currently Second to the Director of the Writers Track at Dragon Con, a SF/F fan convention with more than 80,000 attendees.

Venessa lives with her hubby in Atlanta, Georgia, and shares a home with three cats who all seem to think they rule the castle, but none of which pay the mortgage.

Follow her on Twitter @troilee or check out her website at https://www.venessagiunta.com, where you can find lots of good info for writers, especially.